Dangerous Craving

Nicolette Charlebois

CONTENTS

1. Chapter 1   1

2. Chapter 2   6

3. Chapter 3   13

4. Chapter 4   19

5. Chapter 5   26

6. Chapter 6   33

7. Chapter 7   42

8. Chapter 8   55

9. Chapter 9   64

10. Chapter 10   74

11. Chapter 11   83

12. Chapter 12   91

13. Chapter 13   104

14. Chapter 14   115

15. Chapter 15   123

16. Chapter 16   132

17.	Chapter 17	141
18.	Chapter 18	149
19.	Chapter 19	159
20.	Chapter 20	166
21.	Chapter 21	174
22.	Chapter 22	182
23.	Chapter 23	190
24.	Chapter 24	201
25.	Chapter 25	210
26.	Chapter 26	218
27.	Chapter 27	228
28.	Chapter 28	235
29.	Chapter 29	245
30.	Chapter 30	256
31.	Chapter 31	268
32.	Chapter 32	274
33.	Chapter 33	290
34.	Epilogue	295

CHAPTER 1

C AITLIN

For me, the sexiest place for a man to have tattoos were his hands. Especially the fingers.

Don't ask.

At the moment my mind was occupied by erotic thoughts and one of those scenes included a tattooed hand wrapping around my neck and a hunky body fucking me until I no longer knew my name.

Reason for all those thoughts? The fine specimen with tattoos and a drink in one hand looking at me from across the very occupied bar.

Fuck, he's hot.

I first noticed him when I felt eyes at the back of my head. You know...that feeling that someone is watching you and you can't help but glance around in search of the culprit. It led to my eyes landing on him.

He was beautiful. His face, a strikingly angelic handsome face with brown eyes, a chiselled jaw line and plump lips. By far the sexiest man I've ever seen and it had me shifting in my seat uncomfortably.

I had recently called off things with my regular fuck buddy who was a human blank canvas. As untouched as the day he was born. The complete opposite of the man currently looking at me like he wanted to eat me alive.

Blake's idea of kinky was aggressively rubbing my clit during sex and saying, 'Awe, you like that?'

He was hot, a typical frat boy - a bit childish at times - but in a cute way. I didn't want cute. He also had a big dick with the inability to use it correctly but bless him...he tried. Compatibility wasn't something that could be forced no matter how badly you wanted the person.

It just didn't work and I was beyond sexually frustrated.

Which is why I came to the bar - to get my mind off things and possibly drink my sorrows away. But instead I was placed under a scrutinizing gaze from the hottest goddamn man I've ever seen. His eyes were zeroed in on me and I pursed my lips in contemplation. Just come over here, for fucks sake.

Without thinking I gave the man a slight nod gesturing for him to come over. I immediately turned around in my seat suddenly scared to see his reaction.

The thought of him laughing at me and turning away had my face grimacing in embarrassment. What if he wasn't even looking at me?

Just act normal, you fucking idiot.

Honestly, if it was anyone else staring at me like that from across the room I would have told them to stop being creepy. But he was a hot and I was a biased bitch who wasn't ashamed to admit it.

I took a small sip of my whiskey and took a deep breath in. My elbows were rested on the counter as I swirled the brown liquid around in the glass. I wasn't a light weight - on the contrary actually if I had a full stomach.

I felt his presence before I heard him.

"Never had a woman call me over before." A deep and smouldering voice caused me to look up from my drink. I didn't expect the rich accent he had and it automatically made him ten times hotter. The stranger sat down on the empty stool next to me so close that I could smell the subtle cologne he wore.

When I tell you that he was inked, I mean inked from the back of his hand all the way to his neck. It disappeared underneath the white dress shirt.

He was more gorgeous up close.

"You were staring at me. You scared to make a move or what?" I asked with a raised eyebrow taking another sip of my drink. I sucked in a small cube of ice and swirled it around in my mouth enjoying the coolness.

"Scared?" He chuckled slightly showing off his perfect smile. "I was making sure you weren't waiting for a man since you are all alone." He said taking a sip of the clear liquid. I'm guessing vodka.

Feeling a little bit of courage I turned in my stool and let my bare knees touch the side of his thighs. "Oh, yeah? You care about stuff like that?" I asked tilting my head to the side curiously. He wasn't overly muscular and big and the way he moved told me his strength lied in the agility department.

He looked down at my knees and his eyes darkened while his hand visibly tightened around the glass. "No I don't. But you probably do."

"Bold of you to assume anything about me from ten feet away." I said playfully leaning one elbow on the counter and leaning forward. The strangers' eyes dropped to my cleavage before making eye contact with a small smirk.

"Ah," he nodded his head. "It's rare seeing a beautiful woman sitting alone."

If I had it my way I would strip naked on that very bar and have him fuck me into oblivion. My core tightened at the vivid image.

"Do you have someone in your life that will be upset that you're sitting here and complimenting me?" I asked. I had to make sure - the last time some random girl tried to fight me because her man flirted with me.

I would never understand why she attacked me and not the person supposed to be loyal to her.

He smirked and asked playfully, "Why? You can't fight?"

I looked at him amused. "Over a man? I'd rather eat glass."

"I respect that," He nodded his head and pursed his lips. "To answer your question, no there's not."

"Glad we're on the same page now." I said feeling a little more comfortable.

"What's your name, angel?" He asked and set his glass down to face his body towards me fully. His legs were long - I could see how firm they were through the pants he wore and I crossed one leg over the other to hide how affected I was.

"Definitely not angel. Caitlin." I took a sip of my drink, enjoying the slight burn it offered.

"Caitlin," He tested it on his tongue and unashamedly checked me out from my head to my feet cladded in strappy heels. "Such an innocent name."

I laughed. "Aw, I'm anything but. Are you going to tell me your name?"

He leaned forward brushing my long dark hair from my shoulder to behind me. I didn't know him from a bar of a soap but the lust in his eyes was evident. He licked his bottom lip, the action was almost enough to have me dropping to my knees.

"If I do, you have to promise to be mine for the night." He said so softly that I wasn't sure I heard him correctly.

"And if I don't?" I asked tracing my fingers up his thigh. I wasn't new to the whole one-night stand situation. I've had my fair share of it in the past and I desperately needed a release. Blake couldn't give that to me and I wasn't about to call him up just to be disappointed again.

"Then we have no business even having this conversation, right angel?" He was straightforward - just the way I liked it. He was a man who had an intention - no beating around the bush and it was a breath of fresh air.

I smirked. "I was yours the minute I laid my eyes on you. Name."

I am a twenty two year old woman acting like a horny teenager.

The strangers' lips tilted up in a small smile and he bit his lower lip, humour dancing around in his brown eyes. "Dominic."

I picked up my clutch and placed a few notes underneath the empty glass. I stood up, raising to the same height as him even though he was still sitting. He was watching me intently as I walked behind him and leaned forward until my lips were just barely grazing his ear.

"My place or yours, Dom?" I asked softly. He stared at me for a few more seconds and picked up his drink to take one last gulp.

Without warning he stood up and grabbed my waist placing a hard kiss on my lips. His mouth was cold and tasted of minty vodka - an odd combination but I found myself moaning into his mouth.

The kiss alone was enough to have my pussy quivering.

"Yours." Dominic responded against my lips. I nodded, still in a daze. He grabbed my hand and started leading me out of the bar.

I stopped myself from smiling. I missed it - I missed the excitement of fucking someone new and I was so damn ready.

CHAPTER 2

C AITLIN

"Dominic." I moaned against his mouth as we entered my apartment.

"My neighbour is an asshole, we have to be quiet." I muttered and kicked the door closed with my foot. He bit my bottom lip, tugging it between his teeth and then sucked on it gently. Wetness pooled on my lace thong.

The man knew how to kiss, definitely.

"Quiet? I don't do quiet, angel." He mumbled, trailing wet rough kisses down my neck and firmly gripping my ass in his large hands. I ran my fingers through his soft hair throwing my head back and giving him more access.

"Yeah? What do you do?" I asked breathlessly. Dominic grabbed my hand and placed it over his slacks, right on his very prominent and erect bulge. My eyes widened at the feeling of his thick and long dick through the material.

"Hard, rough." His voice deepened as he squeezed his hand over my own. "Loud."

That's exactly how I liked it.

"I want to hear you scream my name while I fuck you how you so badly want me to." He whispered and bit my earlobe sending a shiver down my spine. My eyes fluttered closed involuntarily. At that point, all I could think about was filling myself up with him.

His hand reached up, clasping around my neck and causing my eyes to shoot open. "Tell me how you want to be fucked, Caitlin." He taunted licking his bottom lip as his brown eyes darkened. There was a predatory lust on his features as he stared at me.

My rational brain switched off - allowing me to completely be controlled by the pure lust I felt.

I smiled when his hand tightened. "However you want."

He smirked, visibly pleased with my answer. "You got a little vixen inside of you, huh? But first, I want to taste what I'm dealing with."

Dominic pushed me against the wall of my living room and I stumbled backwards almost tripping over my own two feet.

He reached under my dress, wiggling my underwear over my thighs until it pooled around my heels.

"Your skin is so soft," he murmured grabbing the thick flesh on my bare ass. "And you smell so good, angel." He groaned and dropped down to his knees.

I gasped when he grabbed the back of my calf and pulled my leg up to rest over his shoulder. He wrapped an arm around me supporting my balance so I wouldn't fall over.

His eyes were now level with my bare pussy and he stared at it with parted lips, lingering a few seconds longer. Suddenly, I began to feel insecure when he didn't say anything and I tried removing my leg from his shoulder.

"Uh-uh, keep them open." He warned grabbing my thigh hard and placing it back in its prior position.

"So pretty," he said as his finger reached up to swirl my wetness around. "And so ready for me."

I moaned, barely able to think straight as he played with my clit sending waves of pleasure through me. I nearly lost it when his head ducked underneath my dress and his warm mouth enveloped me. My head fell back on to the wall as a whine emitted from my throat.

He bit the soft pebble gently, almost resulting in my knees buckling beneath me but I quickly steadied myself.

I was so heavily sexually attracted to him and how fucking good he looked as he ate me out like I was his last meal. There was just something about seeing a man on his knees as his tongue caressed my most intimate part unashamedly.

My legs began to shake embarrassingly and I groaned trying to push his head away. The pleasure was starting to override and my satisfaction was a hair width away.

"Behave." He ordered looking up at me daring me to make another move.

"I can't - it's too much." I breathed out almost gasping for air. I sound like a fucking virgin. Get it together, Caitlin.

It wasn't my first time receiving head but none of past experiences compared to how Dominic made me feel. His warm wet expert tongue almost had me cumming like a bitch in heat.

It felt like absolute bliss.

I grabbed the hem of my dress and pulled it over my head, moaning when my hot skin hit the cool wall. Dominic gave my clit one last kiss before standing up and pressing his lips against my own.

"Condom?" he asked looking at me through droopy sensual eyes.

"Room." I replied grabbing his hand and leading him to my bedroom. He trailed behind me, our footsteps heavy and rushed. I opened the door to my dimly lit room and turned around to face him. It was in times like these that I loved living alone.

He wrapped his arms around the back of my thighs and threw me down on the bed. My yelp got muffled by his mouth as I landed on my back, bouncing a couple of times.

"Left bedside drawer." I mumbled, moving my hands through his hair.

"My left or your left?" He asked as his skilled fingers worshiped my bra covered breasts. I almost rolled my eyes.

"Mine."

He reached over, rummaging through the irrelevant contents before grabbing a gold square.

"You are wearing too much clothes." I whined, tugging on his jacket. I wanted him stark naked - I wanted to see everything he had to offer because I knew it would be fucking magnificent.

Dominic removed his suit jacket and then slowly started unbuttoning his shirt. I licked my lips as his bare skin started to come to view.

My eyes scanned over his chest that had tattoos littered all over. My jaw dropped, it was better than I imagined - so smooth and tanned and hard and big. I almost cheered.

"You're a hard worker, aren't you?" I asked softly gently stroking his skin with my fingertips.

He chuckled. "I guess you could say that."

My hands trailed down his back, enjoying how amazing it felt. My body stiffened as I felt something hard and Dominic frowned at me before realisation dawned on him.

"Oh, right. I'm sorry-" He started but I shut him up with a hard kiss. I grabbed the gun from the hem of his pants and opened my right drawer, placing it next to my own. Dominic looked at me in surprise, not expecting me to react so calmly.

"It's okay. We all have to protect ourselves somehow." I assured, not bothering to ask any questions. I was sure he had his own reasons. The only thing on my mind at that moment was getting fucked.

"That's so fucking sexy." He breathed out.

I undid his belt, before moving to his button and then the zip. I needed to feel him - drown his dick in my pussy until we both reached our peak. It was a must.

He slid his pants and boxers off - letting his cock jump up, standing to full attention. It was massive and I almost changed my mind about the whole ordeal. Clear droplets of pre-cum leaked out the head and I licked my lips in anticipation.

Dominic ripped the wrapper open with his teeth before removing the condom and rolling it on. I turned around getting on all fours and arched my back giving him full access.

"Oh." He murmured sounding surprised. I wasn't a fan of missionary - it felt a bit too intimate.

I felt his tip at my entrance as he held onto one ass cheek. He moved it up and down spreading my juices around.

"Is there a reason why you're taking so fucking lo- ahhh!" he cut me off by shoving himself into me balls deep. I clenched my eyes shut and grit my teeth. Fuck, it stung.

He grabbed the back of my neck, turning my face around and squeezing hard. "Chill with the fucking attitude, angel." He growled glaring down at me, his hard accent coming through heavily.

I glared back even though I was absolutely enjoying every second of it.

"I'm going to move now, is that okay?" Dominic asked rolling his eyes and I dropped my head onto the bed with my ass still in the air.

"Yes."

Waves and waves of ecstasy swept through me when he started moving in and out. I couldn't help but moan into my bed sheets. My head was turned, pressing my cheek into the bed and my hair was moved out of my face by his free hand.

"Damn." He breathed out, digging his hands into my skin.

"Shit!" I cried out loud, not being able to contain myself as he continue to thrust into me, gradually speeding up in urgency. My inner muscles clenched around him and he groaned dropping his head onto my back.

I saw stars.

The sound of skin slapping against skin resonated throughout the room and my mewling filled the air. It felt so astonishingly good that I was barely able to form a coherent sentence. I closed my mouth with the palm of my hand to stop myself from scream-ing out in pure pleasure.

Dominic didn't like that.

He shoved my hand away from my face. "I said I want to hear you." His voice was so deep and so demanding that I felt obligated to obey.

"Dominic! Stop - no, wait. Don't stop. Fuck!" I screamed out as he continued to thrust into that toe-curling spot. My words surprised me, never in my life had I felt so out of control and at the brink of tears from all the pleasure flowing through me.

He laughed. He actually fucking laughed at me while still pounding into me.

It wasn't my fault that he had magic dick.

"You feel so fucking good." He croaked out and when I looked back at him he was watching himself move in and out of me.

My orgasm approached faster than I expected and with one last scream I collapsed onto the bed unable to hold myself up any longer. Dominic moved with me and continued to fill me up mercilessly while I laid flat on my stomach. He wasn't finished.

"Oh my God. Ugh!" I growled and fisted the sheets in both hands pressing my forehead against the bed.

"I'm not done with you." He snapped and I closed my eyes trying to breathe through my nose. He was relentless as he slapped my ass hard causing me to jerk. He left my skin throbbing with red hot heat as it stung.

"That feels so good." I whined. The feeling was beyond overwhelming but still astoundingly good regardless.

Eventually with one drawn out groan he emptied himself into the condom and I sighed in relief.

"Wow." I whispered in a daze still trying to come off my high. My lips tilted up into a smile.

I was right - Dominic was definitely a good fuck.

CHAPTER 3

CAITLIN

"Dominic?" I called after a few moments of silence.

"Mmm?" He hummed into the crook of my neck. I shifted beneath him, nearly suffocating underneath his weight. His body was warm as his bare skin laid flush against mine and he started mindlessly trailing his fingers down my side. It was odd.

"You're still inside me." I whispered and he groaned when I wiggled my ass.

My bare cheeks were against his pelvis and I felt him harden ever so slightly from his prior semi-erect state.

"I know. I love it here." He responded and started moving his hips rhythmically while laying kisses on my neck.

"You better stop before that condom breaks and you breed me." I joked and he laughed before pulling out completely.

I sighed at the now empty feeling and turned to lay on my back. I was exhausted and I barely did anything.

Dominic climbed off the bed and disposed of the used condom in the trash. A few seconds later he returned with tissues from my bathroom and silently separated my legs to wipe me clean.

I frowned as I watched him carefully - I never had a man clean me up after sex and it was weird to say the least.

"Thank you." I muttered, not knowing how to react. Dominic shrugged before wiping his dick and pulling up his boxers.

"Do you need anything?" He asked looking down at me as he stepped into his slacks. I watched his stomach muscles flex as he moved and I licked my lower lip before prying my eyes away from the sight.

"Just that t-shirt, please." I responded pointing to my white drawer where a large t-shirt was resting neatly folded. I sat up when he handed it to me and I offered him an appreciative smile before pulling it over my head.

My legs still felt tingly as I rubbed my thighs with the palms of my hands.

Dominic really fucked me up.

He bent down and gave me a rough kiss on the lips. "You were great, angel."

"You weren't too bad yourself." I said playfully and he frowned at me.

"That's all? Not too bad?" He asked, looking slightly offended.

"Yeah, I've had better." I continued to tease him, hiding my smirk. He scoffed at me before grabbing my ankles and pulling me so hard I landed on my back.

"Whoa! I was kid-"

"Shut the fuck up." He snapped at me and immediately buried his face between my legs. I yelped when his wet tongue began fucking my hole as his grip on my thighs tightened.

He moaned against me and my hands moved to hold onto his hair.

I was a gasping mess as I watched his back muscles tensing.

Pleasure surged through me and my body jerked when his thumb started circling my clit. I was so turned on.

"I was fucking...joking." I said breathlessly throwing my head back onto the bed.

He laid flat on his belly as he continued thrusting his tongue into me, circling my hole and moving his head side to side. I looked down at him and whined when I saw that he was looking directly at me.

"I'm a little offended so lay there and fucking take it." He growled glaring at me. I didn't know it was possible but that turned me on even more.

"Fuck." I moaned gripping the sheets and clenching my eyes shut. They shot open when Dominic flipped us around and he was underneath me still eating me out. My hands gripped the headboard so hard my knuckles turned white.

"Ride my face, angel." He whispered digging his hands into my ass so hard that I was sure it would leave bruises. I moved my hips, not caring that my cum was dripping all over his face and making a huge mess.

"Shit, shit, shit." I muttered throwing my head back and grabbed onto one of my breasts, moulding it in my hand.

"You like that, don't you? I can feel you throbbing." Dominic mumbled and closed his eyes. My core clenched so hard and my breath got heavier by the second.

I was being overstimulated and my pussy was practically begging me to tell Dominic to stop. I just couldn't. I loved every second of it.

"Yes I do!" I whimpered. He pulled his tongue out and sucked my clit into his mouth. I hissed at the intense feeling.

"Your pussy tastes so fucking good. I could eat you all day." He said as my body quivered with the impending orgasm. My legs shook underneath his grip and my mind went blank as my stomach tightened. I looked down at him as he mercilessly lapped me up and down.

"Dom... why..." I breathed out.

I must have really offended him.

"Why? I don't like being teased." He mumbled harshly and the vibrations caused a different feeling of pure desire to flow through me. My mind was blown - struggling to comprehend what the fuck was happening.

For the second time that night, I had one of the best, overpowering orgasms ever and all he used was his mouth.

Okay, now I'm completely and utterly fucked up.

My body collapsed on the bed besides him, my chest heaving as I struggled to catch my breath. My lower lips were swollen and my clit pulsated.

"I swear if you touch me again I'm going to kill you." I mumbled into my sheets clutching my stomach. Of course I didn't mean it, my mind was just foggy and I could hardly form comprehensible thoughts.

My body felt drained.

"Not so bad, huh?" Dominic laughed arrogantly and I felt him get off the bed. He picked up a tissue and wiped his face.

"Hahaha, shut the fuck up." I said in annoyance and turned to lay on my side in foetal position. I needed to recover as my eyes shut close on their own accord.

I could fall asleep right then.

"You-" He was cut off by the blaring of a ringtone. It wasn't mine. I opened my eyes to see Dominic rummaging through his suit jacket while sporting a scowl. He looked upset at the sudden interruption.

"What is it?" He spoke into the phone and my eyebrows shot up at the foreign language. I hadn't expected him to sound so...terrifyingly sexy.

"None of your business. What's so urgent?" Dominic mumbled as he looked down at me before turning his back to me. I sat up and rolled my neck trying to ease the built up tension. When I stood up, I fell right back down on the bed.

My legs no longer worked.

I groaned but snapped my mouth shut when Dominic turned to look at me with a cocked eyebrow. Asshole was fucking proud of himself.

"I'm on my way. Keep him alive for me." I had no idea what he said but it sounded like he was about to leave. It was a good thing because I desperately needed to shower.

He put the phone off and started dressing himself.

"I have to go. Thank you for this, you were amazing. Is there anything I can get for you before I leave?" Dominic asked buttoning his shirt and looking at me. I almost started pouting as the toned stomach got hidden.

"I'll just sit here and wait for my legs to work." I chuckled.

Dominic smiled, an actual genuine smile and for the first time I noticed the dimple on his cheek. It was beautiful.

"Right. Sorry about that." He muttered sheepishly and opened my drawer to collect his silver gun. It was a lot bigger than mine and it also felt a lot heavier. He tugged into the back of his pants.

"Don't worry about it, you were..." I trailed off speechless while shaking my head. I had no words.

"Don't forget to lock the door." Dominic said sternly and grabbed my cheeks with one hand to place a rough kiss on my lips. I could taste myself on him and I moaned against his mouth.

"See you again, angel." He said and before I could speak he was out of my room and the front door was slammed shut.

All I knew is that I definitely wouldn't mind seeing him again.

Chapter 4

D OMINIC

"See you again, angel." I greeted the beautiful woman with a quick kiss against her soft lips. It took everything in me not to wrap my hand around her neck to deepen it and have my way with her, again.

She gave me a tired smile, almost seductively and I groaned before rushing out of her room.

The little she-devil had me by the balls and she didn't even know it.

My dick was still hard from eating her out and I looked down. How the fuck am I supposed to hide this?

I clenched my jaw trying to adjust the bulge with the palm of my hand to make it less obvious. It didn't help that I could still taste her essence on the tip of my tongue, reminding me of what I had just experienced. It made blood rush down to my cock making me want to turn around and shove it inside of her warm wet pussy again.

My mood changed entirely as soon as I exited her secured apartment complex, the erection dying down immediately at the thought of why I had to leave.

"I'm sick of this shit. Always fucking interrupting me." I muttered to myself, probably looking like a mad man as I rushed to where my driver, Kuzma, awaited.

He shoved his phone into his pocket when he saw me approaching the Mercedes and I climbed into the back seat, taking a deep breath in. Kuzma cleared his throat and looked at me knowingly but with one glare from me he diverted his gaze to the road ahead.

"Not a word." I warned him. Nobody could know that I had left the bar to fuck a woman, it went against every rule I had made for myself.

However, when my eyes caught sight of her slender tanned back, and the curve from her waist all the way down to her ass as she sat on the stool, I just couldn't help myself. I just had to have a little taste.

She was the most breathtakingly stunning woman I had ever laid my eyes on. Thank fuck she wasn't shy because heaven knew how I couldn't stand shy girls.

"You got it, boss. Where are we headed?" Kuzma asked starting the car. I trusted that he wouldn't say anything, it was his head on a stick if he did so happen to speak out of turn and he knew that.

"Work. I have a guest waiting for me." I said leaning back into the seat and looking out the window.

"Guest? Ah, I see." He said with a nod of his head.

"A very special one."

Twenty minutes later we were driving through the mountains where our large mansion was situated on a hill overlooking the city. To avoid suspicion, from the outside it looked like a regular family home.

"You can stop here. Go home, Kuzma. I'll drive myself when I'm done." I told him before opening the door and stepping out. He looked at me in surprise, and almost relief undoubtedly happy to finally go home to his wife and kids. I always preferred driving alone.

"Thank you, Mr. Romanov." He said appreciatively but I waved him off. It was dark but I trailed through the incline pathway, greeted the guards with a nod and walked until I reached the front double doors. I looked at the time on my watch, 01:40. It was late but I preferred it that way.

"Took you long enough." My little brother, and also my right hand man greeted me sounding exasperatedly annoyed. If he wasn't blood I would have surely cut his tongue out for addressing me in that tone. I glared at him but he only smirked in response like the little brat he was.

"Watch it. I'm not above breaking a knee or two." I scowled walking past him and through the foyer. He followed next to me.

"You should watch it. You have 'I just got fucked' hair." Yurik reached his hand up to my head but I hit it away, my eyebrows furrowing.

"Be quiet." I said and soothed my hair down taking a deep breath in. Yurik was four years younger than me and if it was up to me he wouldn't be involved in any of the businesses I conducted but he was good. Almost too good. We were complete opposites, he had short silver hair and my mothers carefree attitude.

"Don't worry, your secret is safe with me. Might want to clean that cum on the side of your mouth, though." He said nonchalantly and my hand flew up to my lips. He only burst out in laughter, nearly toppling over by how he couldn't control himself. My glare hardened but I couldn't help but crack a small smile.

Yurik will be the death of me.

"Hah! Made you look." Yurik laughed, showing off his tongue piercing that I wanted to rip out. I gave him a slap on the head and his face contorted into an expression of pain.

"You are unbelievably annoying." I muttered walking into the downstairs bathroom to wash my hands and face. I needed to get Caitlin off me.

"You love me." He shouted when I closed the door in his face and I sighed.

"Unfortunately." I said under my breath and proceeded to freshen up. When I was done, Yurik was leaning against the opposite wall waiting for me. I prevented myself from rolling my eyes.

"I heard that. Your guest is waiting for you, Domo." He told me, pushing himself off the wall and walking alongside me. I clenched my eyes shut and exhaled in frustration.

Irritating little sibling who I'd kill and die for.

"How many times do I have to tell you to stop calling me that? For fucks sake."

"I like it." Yurik shrugged before digging into his pockets. He pulled out two switchblade knives, handmade and engraved with traditional Russian dialect.

"Which one do you think I should use? I like them both but I don't want to get both dirty, do you see my dilemma? I can't decide." He said holding up the knives eyelevel as we walked down the steps and into the basement. One of my men guarding the door stepped aside and I nodded at him in acknowledgement.

"Use the one in your dominant hand. It's obviously the one you like the most." I told him. We stepped into the dark room and I flicked on the light.

A grin formed on my face as I looked down at the man. He was bound to a chair, hands behind his back and a gag was placed in his mouth.

"Ah! Mr Wilson. It's so nice to finally meet you." I greeted chirpily. Isaac screamed into the gag, his eyes wide and terrified. His blue dress shirt was wet with sweat and the tie hung loosely. He was definitely roughed up by one of my men. I shrugged off my jacket and rolled up my sleeves.

"Yurik." I nodded my head while heading to the corner of the room where my gloves rested on a table. I put them on while he removed the cloth around Isaacs mouth. I could see how excited Yurik was as he held a sinister smirk on his face.

He was about to enjoy it just as much as me.

"Please - I-I don't know why I'm here. You must have the wrong person." Isaac pleaded shaking his head as he looked down to his lap. I grabbed a chair and placed it in front of him before sitting down.

"Your name is Isaac, right? Named after the prophet or no?"

"How do you know my name?" He asked and I smiled at him before looking up at Yurik. He instantly flipped the knife open.

"Wait. I-" Yurik grabbed Isaacs head and start leading the tip of the knife along his jawline, blood gushed out. His face scrunched up in agony and he screamed so loud I couldn't help but grimace. Aggravating.

"I'm the one asking the questions here. Is that understood?" I said leaning forward resting my elbows on the top of my thighs. I clasped my hands together as I tilted my head to the side, studying him. He knew damn well why he was here.

"Please. I have a family - I have a wife. They need me." He begged breathing heavily as he struggled against the binds but it was futile.

I removed the gun from my waistband and leaned back into the chair. "Your wife, Mr Wilson, is the reason why you're here."

"I don't know what you mean. Does she owe you money?" He asked shakily looking between me and Yurik before he stilled, realising his mistake.

"I'm sorry, I-" He was cut off by Yurik punching him so hard in the nose that it split open and red liquid spilled out, dripping down his face and onto his shirt. He screamed out, thrashing against the ropes.

"You better shut that fucking mouth." I said calmly standing up and towering over him. My fists were aching to reach out to snap his neck but his wife had given specific instructions to make him suffer. To make him regret ever holding her down and forcing himself on her all those times.

"Lola has paid me a lot of money for you to be here. Not that I'll accept it, you know. Killing a rapist is my favourite sport."

Isaac froze, his face turning into a look of pure horror.

"L-Lola? I don't understand. I've never- She's my wife! It's not possible!" He yelled out.

"Then why threaten to kill her if she ever said a word? Why threaten to kill her if she ever spoke to the cops? Why do all of that if you're apparently innocent? You're here because your wife wants you dead and gone without a trace, Isaac." I said and suddenly his whole demeanour changed. The façade he was wearing slipped off.

"That fucking dumb bitch. Who would've thought that she'd eventually grow some fucking balls." Issac laughed throwing his head and showing off his bloodied teeth. He laughed like it was funniest thing in the world and I raised an eyebrow at him.

"You should try it. Pussy is the best when-" I cocked my gun, the sound causing him to stop talking immediately. I pressed it against his knee and pulled the trigger without wasting a second.

The loud sound echoed through the room before he screamed and screamed until his voice cracked and tears were spilling down his cheeks. His head flopped down, the pain causing him to slip in and out of consciousness. Yurik chuckled from besides me.

"Just for that, I think I'll keep you alive for a few more days. I hope you enjoy your stay, Mr Wilson." I said turning my back to him and walking towards the door.

I had enough of his loud ass.

"I'll give you and my brother some alone time." I said before opening the door.

"I'm going to enjoy this so much, Domo." Yurik laughed rubbing his hands together and grinning. I gave him an unamused look because of the stupid nickname but I let it go.

"Please! I'm begging you. Whatever she's paying you - I'll triple it." Isaac croaked, a whimper escaping him.

"He said he's not taking the money, dumbass. Now hush before I stick my knife down your throat." Yurik growled grabbing Isaac by the hair and pulling his head back.

"Prolong it as much as possible." I instructed before leaving, the screams and cries muting as I shut the door behind me.

A text came through from an unknown number and I unlocked my phone.

'Thank you.'

CHAPTER 5

C AITLIN

A loud and rapid knock coming from my door nearly made me spill my glass of wine. I dragged the blanket off me and got up from the couch scowling at whoever was behind the wood.

"Caitlin, can you open the door please?" My brother's voice reached my ears. He sounded like he had been running and my frown deepened in confusion as I set the glass down on the small table.

"Caitlin!" He yelled out and continued banging like a maniac.

"I'm coming. For fucks sake." I mumbled. As soon as I unlocked it, I was pushed backwards and my brother's large body entered my apartment. He quickly shut the door behind him and locked it again, breathing heavily.

His black windbreaker was covered in dust and my eyes widened when they landed on the blue bruises on his neck when he removed his hood.

My heart dropped. Micah looked like he was running away from someone.

"Micah, what's going on?" I asked nervously and also in shock. He didn't answer me. Instead he turned around and pulled me in for a tight embrace surprising me.

"Thank you." He whispered and I slowly wrapped my arms around him, still feeling slightly confused. It was the first time seeing him in nearly two months and he looked different.

"Are you in trouble?" I questioned when he pulled away. He ignored me and walked straight to my kitchen, opening the fridge and pulling out a bottle of water.

"Micah, can you fucking speak? You're scaring me." I nearly shouted. My brother meant the world to me but it wasn't a rare thing for him to often get in trouble and bring said trouble home with him. It was one of the reasons why I learned how to protect myself and defend myself.

He turned to me, bloodshot brown eyes meeting mine. He looked utterly exhausted. "I need a car."

"What am I supposed to do about that?" I asked scrunching my eyebrows.

Micah walked up to me and grabbed my shoulders. "You don't understand. I need your car."

"Why do you-"

"And your gun." He interrupted, the grip he had on me tightened and I looked at him incredulously before shrugging off his hold. I took a step back.

"You're hiding from someone, aren't you?" I muttered slowly. "And you decided it would be a great idea to lead them right here, where your sister lives. Alone. I can't fucking believe you, Micah." I said, my voice lacing with disappointment. His eyes faltered, a solemn expression on his face.

He was three years older than me but most of the time I felt like the older sibling.

"I have nowhere else to go! You are the only one who will even think about helping me. I have no one else!" He yelled out and I couldn't help but close my eyes in frustration and partial sadness.

"Do you ever think about anyone but yourself? Just tell me what happened and we can try to sort it out but you're not taking my car or my gun." I told him shaking my head. I couldn't give him my things. When used it could very well be traced back to me and I wasn't about to risk that.

"It was worth the try." He muttered in defeat.

Micah sighed before sitting on the couch and my heart shattered in my chest. He looked so vulnerable, so helpless.

"I owe some people money. They-"

"How much?"

He stilled before looking up at me as I sat down next to him. "15K. These guys...they don't care about the amount. It's deeper than that."

I took an unsteady breath in. I was knee deep in student loans and there was no way I could afford that. On the other hand, I was terrified of losing my brother and I just wished he would stop getting himself in so much fucking trouble.

"I was supposed to finish a job, but I got jumped and the product was stolen. They gave me twenty four hours to get the money and if I didn't...I'll pay with my life. That was two days ago and I've been running ever since." He admitted while rubbing a hand over his face. I bit my lip to stop myself from hitting him.

"Drugs?"

"Cocaine." He stated with a nod and I threw my head back onto the couch. What a mess.

"Were they chasing you right now?" I asked and turned to stare at the locked door. I hope and prayed that nobody had followed him straight into my home. There was no negotiating with people like that.

"No, I just had to get out of the public eye. We're good. I just can't go home right now." He assured and I nodded my head, sighing in relief.

What kind of sister would I be to just kick him out when he looked like he needed me the most? Guilt gnawed at me as I thought of every possible scenario.

"I'm sorry, Caitlin. I really am. I don't know why I-" Micah's voice cracked and my face softened. I couldn't help but feel bad for him so I scooted closer and wrapped my arm around his shoulder. His head dropped and he took a deep a breath in.

"We'll figure something out." I said trying to convince him, although I had no idea where to even start.

"I shouldn't have come here. It was so inconsiderate." He announced suddenly and stood up. He started to pace around the living room while dragging his hands through his hair.

"Stop. I'll get you something to eat. You must be starving." My tone left no room for arguing and he sighed, stopping his movements.

"Thank you." His voice was a mere whisper. Micah sat down on the couch before dropping his head into his hands. My heart twisted at the sight but I got up and walked to the kitchen.

I didn't have much so Ramen it was.

A few minutes later I handed him the cup and fork. He offered me an appreciative smile and started digging into his meal.

"Micah..." I sighed after a moment of silence. "I still have moms ring. It won't be enough but-"

"No."

"But-"

"No."

My lips tightened into a straight line and I inhaled deeply to calm myself. Stubborn.

When he was done, he walked to the trashcan to dispose of the now empty cup. He froze, both our gazes snapping into the direction of the door and I stood up immediately.

There was slow and steady knocking emitting from it.

"Oh, fuck." Micah muttered with widened eyes. I grit my teeth and gave him a much deserving hard punch on the arm. His body jerked and he rubbed the sore area while glowering down at me. My fists balled up ready to punch him again.

"You fucking dumbass. I can't stand you." I whispered, the sympathy I felt vanishing quickly. It was replaced by pure anger.

"Ssh. Maybe they'll go away." He whispered back as we stood there staring at the door.

We listened carefully. Quickly the tone of the knocking changed and my mouth dropped - it sounded like someone had switched their fists for something made of...metal.

"That's a gun, isn't it?" Micah asks softly and I nodded in response. We were on the third fucking floor with zero fire escape. I softly padded to my room and grabbed my weapon from the drawer.

"Hello? Anybody home?" A deep unfamiliar voice called out softly, still gently tapping against a door.

I looked around my apartment, trying to figure out how to get out of the mess we were currently in.

"Caitlin, I-" Just then the door got kicked down and I gasped grabbing Micahs hand and taking a few steps backwards. In walked a man dressed in all black, it contrasted hugely against the silver hair on his head and the silver gun in his hand, already pointed directly at Micah.

"Drop it or I'm shooting him right in the fucking face." The man growled, glaring at me and I gulped. I slowly placed it down the table, right next to my wine glass. He had an accent, the same one like Dominic's.

"Good. Now step away for me." He instructed gesturing with the gun and I nodded raising my hands stepping away from the table. My inner-self was begging me to open my mouth to yell at him but that would be the worst idea ever.

I should've shot him as soon as he came in.

Suddenly he grinned, spreading his arms. "Micah! I wasn't expecting you to be here, thought I'd have to get that information out of your little sister. Thank you for saving me that trouble." He said, sounding completely genuine and innocent.

"Yurik. I'll get the money, I swear. Just don't hurt her, please." Micah voice was steady as he glanced from me to the man called Yurik. My heart was beating erratically at what could possibly unfold.

In that moment, I prayed that my asshole neighbour heard the noise But yet again, they would probably kill him too.

"Sorry buddy, you know I don't make the rules. My brother wants to have a chat with you so either you come with us or..." Yurik shrugged, flailing the gun around like it was nothing. Just then two other men stepped from behind him, wearing similar black clothes.

Definitely mafia.

I swallowed the lump that had formed in my throat. My hand was itching to reach for my gun.

One of the men behind Yurik eyed me up and down. His blue eyes landed on my bare legs and a revolting smirk formed his lips. I bit the inside of my cheek to stop myself from snapping at him.

Get your fucking eyes off of me.

"I'll come with you but-" Micah began but Yurik held up a hand stopping him.

"Nope. Go put shoes on, sweetheart." He instructed pointing down at my sock covered feet and Micah's eyes widened.

"She has nothing to do with t-" The gun was cocked causing him to snap his mouth shut instantly.

"I wasn't asking." Yurik stated. His voice was casual but his demeanour wasn't. Despite his playful tone, I could tell that he meant every single word.

"Micah, it's okay." I spoke for the very first time since they entered the apartment. We didn't have a choice.

I looked around for my white sneakers until I spotted them right beside the door. Yurik noticed me looking before gesturing at the man who had been staring at me the entire time to hand them to me.

"I'm going to fucking kill you." I whispered underneath my breath. Fucking Micah.

It was weird. Yurik was over there threatening to kill us but he cared enough to make me put my shoes on. Who the fuck was this guy?

When I was done and ready to go, the two men latched onto Micahs arms and started walking out of the apartment. Yurik didn't touch me, instead he let me walk alongside him and that's when the nerves really kicked in. My mind was reeling with every-thing they could possibly do to us.

My eyes scanned the area, hoping that anyone would see the suspicious activity. But it was nearly midnight and nobody was around.

"Get in and don't say a word." Yurik demanded opening the car door for me.

CHAPTER 6

C AITLIN

I've had it.

"Keep looking at me like that and I'll rip your eyeballs out." I snapped at the very same man who had been staring at me for the longest time.

I would much rather have a gun pointed in my face than his lustful, disgusting eyes practically eating me up.

We were in the back of a van. The air was thick with tension and the pervert was sitting directly opposite me. A mischievous grin formed on his thin lips and his tongue flicked out to move in one circular motion. My face scrunched up in revulsion.

Maybe I should bark at him?

"You sick-" I got up completely ready to throw my hands at his stupid face but Micah grabbed my arm and sat me back down. I looked at him with a fuming scowl but he just gave me a warning look.

"Leave me, Micah." I demanded trying to get out of his grip. I wanted to tear his face off.

"Control her before I do it myself." The creep muttered with a smirk and winked at me. A shiver of disgust spiralled through me and my face turned into the hardest glare I could muster. I thought of every single hurtful thing I wanted to do to him.

"Yurik - you better control your boy before I break his neck. Also, I don't understand why she has to even be here. She has nothing to do with this." Micah bellowed at the silver haired man who sat there twirling a small knife between his fingertips.

He looked at Micah with a blank expression. "She can help pay off your debt."

My body tensed and my blood ran cold at what he was insinuating.

"What the fuck is that supposed to mean?" Micah asked, his voice hard and cold. Yurik glared at Micah but didn't bother responding. His attention switched to the knife in his hands.

"What the fuck man? She's innocent!" Micah was persistent as his face turned worried. I could see him regret every single bad choice he's ever made.

"Look, I know what happened wasn't your fault. I'm trying to fucking help you here but you're being a pain in my ass." Yurik snapped, his fingers professionally twisting the knife around speedily. Help him? How the fuck?

"If you think you're going to sell off my sister just to pay my dumb debt, you can suck my-" At the speed of lightning Yurik jumped up and grabbed Micah by the collar of his jacket. He pressed the tip of his knife against the base of his throat and I gasped, my hands instantly going out to stop him.

"You remember who the fuck you're talking to, Micah. You and I are friends but you and my brother are not and he won't hesitate to put a bullet in your skull. This one," He pointed at me with the knife. "She's your get out of trouble ticket so shut the fuck up and stop pissing me off." He growled and pushed Micah away harshly.

Micah opened his mouth to say something but I pinched his thigh. He needed to listen and be quiet.

"And you," he turned around to the man that was still staring at me. "Lower your fucking eyes and stop making her uncomfortable before I kill you myself." Yurik said glaring at him and gave him a hard hit on the head. "I should get rid of you."

I couldn't understand but I guess he told him to leave me alone because he instantly looked away and mumbled something.

"Pavlo says sorry." Yurik said but I couldn't respond. Pavlo needs to die.

My body was frozen and a turmoil formed in my mind - were they going to sell me?

He sat down and took a deep breath in before looking at me. "Don't worry, it's not what you think. We're not going to hurt you." He assured and the tension in my shoulders disappeared. I knew I couldn't trust them but I couldn't help but feel somewhat slightly relaxed.

"Then why-"

"Micah! Can you stop? You're going to get us killed." I yelled at my brother. I swear if they didn't kill him, I would eventually.

"We don't kill women unless they're a witness." Pavlo murmured in his thick accent and my eyes widened. Am I a witness? Micah scoffed from besides me.

Yurik seemed to be younger than the two but I could tell that he was in charge. How did they expect me to help Micah get out of his debt? Who was this brother he spoke of and was he really as heartless as they made him out to be?

Of course he was, it's the fucking mafia.

The van finally came to a halt and that's when my hands began to shake with nerves. I was always confident - I was always in control but this, this was absolutely terrifying.

The door slid open and Yurik grabbed onto my forearm, dragging me out the van and onto the gravel. The ground crunched underneath my sneakers as my head spun around, taking a good look. I could see the whole city from where we stood.

It was dark but there were lights surrounding the gigantic house enough for me to see the two men carrying large guns walking around the perimeter.

"Don't even think about running unless you want to be chased by a Rottweiler." Yurik threatened lowering his head. He was so close I could smell his cologne and see the tattoo behind his ear. I squinted before my face dropped.

Very familiar tattoo.

"I wasn't going to." I retorted but bit my tongue when he looked at me amused. I had to remind myself that they were currently in charge.

"Good." He gave a cheeky smile and continued leading me to the front door. I turned to look at Micah and he was being escorted by the other two men, a permanent dirty look on his face.

This is very weird.

"Listen, whatever this is - I'm not selling my ass. You can rather just kill me." I stated looking up at his jaw. No way in hell.

"Relax, sweetheart. We don't do that over here, you'll only sell your pussy." He responded and my face turned completely horrified. Yurik laughed at my expression and I gaped at him trying to thrash out of his hold.

"You-"

"I'm kidding." He quickly added and shook his head. "I known Micah and even though he's dumb as fuck - I don't want to see him die when I know he wasn't at fault." Yurik explained. He greeted the tall man at the door with a nod and moved his hand to the small of my back, guiding me.

"However, that's not how my brother thinks and I'm taking a huge ass risk here so you better be fucking grateful. If he sees that we can use you two to make more money, he'll let Micah live. And that's what you want, right?" Yurik asked looking down at me seriously. I swallowed my words and hesitantly nodded. Of course that's what I wanted.

"What do you mean by 'make more money'?" I asked curiously.

"Work for us."

That's very ominous.

I turned my head to throw a deadly glare at Micah. I wanted to strangle him.

"Couldn't this wait until the morning?" I muttered quietly looking down at my too big sweater and loose shorts. Nothing made sense. Especially the way Yurik was treating me. I expected to be tossed around and yelled at considering who and what they are.

We walked through the modern foyer and I knew straightaway that it wasn't a home. It was empty, large and...just void. There was hardly any furniture and an echo bounced off the white walls. If it wasn't for the circumstances I would've been in awe.

We were led downstairs and into a concrete basement. It looked like an interrogation room that was recently cleaned spotless. The smell of bleach still lingered in the air and my nose scrunched up at the scent.

"Stop. That's adorable." Yurik said looking down at me with a small smirk and my face fell. You stop.

"Stop flirting with my sister." Micah threatened and shrugged his arms out the two men's hold. Yurik turned to him.

"Do you want me to flirt with you instead, sweetheart?" Yurik snapped back and cocked an eyebrow. Micah's eyes widened before he cleared his throat and looked away. Yurik bit back a smile and I looked at them both in confusion. Even with him literally threatening to end Micah's life back at my place, he seemed to have a soft spot for my brother.

"What the actual fuck is going on?" I whispered to myself, not expecting an answer but I was sure no one was going to give me one.

"Wait here - have a seat. I'll go call my brother." Yurik instructed and gestured for me to sit down at the table. I nodded and sat down alongside Micah - absolutely dreading meeting the 'boss'

He left the room and shut the door behind him, immediately I turned to Micah who appeared to be just as nervous as I was.

"I don't want to hear it, Caitlin. I already know." He shut my rambling off and I pressed my lips into a tight line. I crossed my arms on the table and buried my face in it, bouncing my knee.

My head was starting to throb and I winced in pain. The entire day had been exhausting since the second I woke up and I was starting to feel the effects of it.

I should be at home sipping on my wine.

The door opened but I kept my head down, willing the ache to stop.

"I don't understand why he's still breathing, Yurik." A very familiar voice growled out and a cold shiver travelled through me. My entire body stilled and goosebumps formed on my skin. I know that voice. I sat on that voice.

I have now resorted to manual breathing.

"He's-"

"Who the fuck is that?" Dominic asked, his accented voice deep and husky. Oh God. I heard footsteps approach me.

"Is she sleeping or what?" Yurik asked before a pinch landed on my arm and I jumped up with a yelp. My first instinct was to pinch him back but he swiftly dodged it, laughing at me in the process. I scowled at him.

"Dick." I whispered, rubbing the sore area with a frown. I froze when I realised how deadly silent the room had suddenly become. My eyes landed on Dominic and he was staring right back at me with the angriest glare.

My heart was throbbing in my chest as I received flashbacks from just three nights ago. He looked different- instead of his suit he was dressed in a plain black hoodie and grey sweats.

Dominic looked between me and Micah before averting the glare to Yurik who was busy smiling sheepishly.

"What is this?" Dominic asked roughly taking a step towards Yurik who backed away and raised his hands. Even he looked scared.

"Don't get mad at me, Domo. She's Micah's sister and I just thought-"

"What? That Micah will get some sort of immunity just because-" Dominic stopped himself from finishing the sentence. He looked at me slowly before narrowing his eyes suspiciously. I gulped. What is he thinking?

"You two, get out. I want to speak to Caitlin alone." He demanded pointing to Micah and Yurik before nudging his thumb towards the door.

"I don't remember telling you her name." Yurik taunted crossing his arms.

"You're fucking insane if you think I'm leaving you alone with my sister." Micah stood up from his chair and planted his palms onto the table. Big mistake.

The gun was drawn from Dominic's waistband, cocked within a millisecond and pointed towards Micah. Not an ounce of hesitation. "If I'm not mistaken - you shouldn't even be alive right now so I suggest you calm yourself and get the fuck out." He seethed, finger dangerously close to the trigger.

My heart nearly stopped. I was terrified for my brothers life and Dominic looked ready to kill.

"Wait," I stood up. "Its fine, I'll talk to him. Just please go." I practically begged. I could see the contemplation in his eyes before he sighed and left the room, Yurik followed behind him.

"He won't hurt her." I heard Yurik reassure before closing the door. Dominic locked it quickly. He snapped his head into my direction and I gasped when he started stalking towards me.

"What-" He dropped the gun on the table with a loud clatter and wrapped a tattooed hand around the back of my neck, lowering his head to my level. My eyes widened when I saw how cold his expression was.

"Angel, was this your little plan all along?" He asked lowly.

"What do you mean?" I asked in confusion, trying to step back but his grip was firm and unmoving. My lips parted when he tightened his hand and pulled back, making me look up at him.

"You gave me a feel of that sweet pussy so I won't kill your brother." Dominic murmured, but his eyes were softer as he scrutinised every feature on my face.

My breath hitched at the close proximity - despite literally being in the face of danger I couldn't deny how deadly handsome he was.

"Wait. You think I elaborated some sick plan to fuck you so you won't hurt Micah?" I asked narrowing my eyes at him. He moved his hand to my chin, holding it in the tip of his fingers and tilting it upwards.

"It's very convenient that here you are three days later with a man who owes me money." He stated looking at me suspiciously.

"I didn't know about any of this since an hour ago." I defended ripping my chin out of his hold and giving him the dirtiest glare I could muster.

"Oh yeah? Is that why you have a gun next to your bed? The very same bed where I fucked you? Is that why you felt comfortable enough to allow a mere stranger into your home?" His jaw clenched, an unreadable emotion dawdled in his brown eyes. I looked at him appalled and pushed him away roughly.

"I've had enough of this shit. I know how this looks but I didn't ask for any of it so you better believe me." I snapped feeling my irritation start to build up. Dominic stared at me for a few moments, trying to find a hint of a lie but I kept my gaze steady. Eventually he sighed and rubbed a hand through his hair.

"I'm sorry. You're either a really good liar or you're telling me the truth, angel." He said softly before glancing down at my bare legs, his eyes hardening. "Are you cold? I'm going to fucking kill Yurik. Why would he bring you here?"

I frowned at him. This whole family is weird. "I don't care about that right now. Tell me that you won't hurt Micah."

Dominic didn't say anything.

"Dominic," my voice took on a softer, more pleading tone as I pressed my hands against his chest. "Please tell me that you won't hurt him. Yurik said that if I work for you I can pay you back and you won't hurt him."

He looked down at my hands and his features softened. "I won't."

"Promise me." I gripped his hoodie in my fists.

"I promise."

I blew out a sigh of relief and instantly it felt like a weight was lifted off my shoulders. The relief was short lived when he spoke again.

"On one condition."

CHAPTER 7

CAITLIN

"Better not be what the fuck I think it is." I said, crossing my arms and looking at him sceptically. Dominic smirked before stepping away and picking up the gun he had carelessly tossed on the table. I watched him curiously as he held it in both hands, examining it.

He moved closer, achingly slow until his hand suddenly stretched out and firmly wrapped around my waist. I stumbled against his chest, nearly tripping over my own feet but he held me steady.

"You think very lowly of me." Dominic whispered, inching his face downwards. An unrecognisable emotion danced in his eyes as they narrowed at me, studying me.

"Shouldn't I?" I taunted back trying to keep my face as blank as possible. My attempt to hide how effected I was failed miserably when he lifted my sweater and started stroking my bare skin with his fingertips. He smiled - obviously pleased with himself when he saw me falter.

The man touching me gave me the best orgasm of my life and his mere touch had tingles rushing through me in spite of the dangerous situation I was currently in. I needed to get a fucking grip but the handsome specimen with a touch like wildfire made it impossible.

"Still as soft as I remember." Dominic murmured.

"Yeah, yeah. Are you going to tell me what your condition is?" I breathed out subconsciously moving my head back to give him more access to my neck. He ran his tongue over his bottom lip before leaning down and caressing his nose against my jawline. I stopped myself from reaching up and cupping his head in my hands.

"You are sworn to silence. You cannot speak a word of this to anyone. You die before you snitch." He responded before the tip of something hard was pressed against the middle of my stomach. I looked down at the gun and my mouth dropped. Dominic was staring at me expectantly waiting for an answer.

"You're going to fucking shoot me?" I asked in disbelief trying to step away but he gave me a look that said not to try him.

"I might. I might not." He said tilting his head to the side innocently. My eyes turned into slits as I glared at him. I could see that he was testing me - testing just how far I'd go to protect my brother but Dominic wasn't as slick as he thought he was.

"Do it." I muttered through gritted teeth. I grabbed the barrel of the gun with my fist and brought it higher, right above my pounding heart. Dominic's hard expression wavered for a split second before it was replaced by something even more...devious.

"You are not afraid to die?" He asked softly. He started moving it upwards, at a snail's pace until the cold tip stopped just below my chin. The gun was now pointed upwards - ready to blow my head off within a second. I stood my ground, looking right back at him.

"You wouldn't." I said confidently.

Dominic raised a perfect brow, pressing it further against my skin until it almost hurt. "What makes you think that?"

I smiled at him. "Because just five minutes ago you were concerned enough to ask if I'm cold or not."

"Observant, are we?" He seemed surprised at my answer before a devilish grin formed on his lips. My mouth suddenly felt dry but I wasn't about to show him how utterly scared I was. I wrapped my arms around his narrow waist pulling his body impossibly closer. My neck was starting to hurt from looking up at him but I was determined.

"Do it." I demanded, trailing my hands along his sides. I put my hands underneath the hoodie and his muscles tensed as I made bare contact with the smooth skin of his back. Dominic's lips parted and I was sure I saw him gulp. My legs involuntarily pressed together.

"You don't know me well enough to make this type of judgement, Caitlin."

"I guess not." I murmured with a casual shrug. Dominic chuckled before pulling the trigger.

The gun clicked, a resistance stopping it from releasing a bullet into my skull.

"Dumbass," I pushed him away. "If you wanted to do it you would've taken the safety off as soon as you picked it up."

Dominic looked genuinely impressed as he nodded his head with a small smile. His eyes glint with amusement. "You didn't even blink."

"So?"

"So? Like I said, you're observant. You're in."

"As if I have a choice." I rolled my eyes and pushed past him to sit down at the table, again. He looked at me one more time before walking to the door to leave, the faintest smile still playing on his pink lips. His back was turned to me but I could still his hand drop down to adjust something in his crotch area.

"Crazy woman." He whispered under his breath before opening it and stepping out. As soon as he was gone I leaned my elbows on the table and rested my head in my hands. My heart was still beating erratically as I took deep breaths in. I couldn't believe that I had the guts to do that.

A few minutes later Dominic returned with Micah and Yurik. I frowned at the pair who looked like they couldn't stand each other yet they were 'friends'

"Windy outside, huh?" I asked referring to their messy hair. Their hands flew up to smoothen it down and they both coughed simultaneously. I shook my head with a knowing laugh.

"Did he touch you?" Micah asked sending daggers with his eyes towards Dominic who looked like he couldn't care less.

"No he didn't. Now that all of this is cleared up, can I go home?" I asked stifling a yawn with my fist. My eyes were starting to sting. I wanted to be in my bed and forget that any of this happened.

"Actually-" Yurik began but Dominic stopped him.

"I want to go home. She wants to go home. We can talk tomorrow." I looked at him in surprise, not expecting me to go so easily. I could see the wheels turning in Micah's head as his eyes moved back and forth between me and Dominic. Yurik gave him a look that basically said 'I told you.'

"I'll get Kuzma."

"You don't need to walk with me, you know." I muttered in annoyance as Dominic followed behind me up the stairs. He didn't say anything and when I turned to look at him, his eyes were completely fixated on my ass. I clicked my fingers to get his attention and his head snapped up to meet my gaze.

I recognised that look. There was a primal hunger on his features and I couldn't believe that with everything that just happened, he had the nerve...the audacity to be horny. I shook my head in disapproval.

Stop lying to yourself, you want him just as bad even though he stuck a gun in your face.

"I thought you said you wanted to go home." I heaved out a sigh. My legs were aching from the stairs as it usually did because the elevator never seemed to be in service. When we finally reached the hallway my shoulders slumped.

"I just want to make sure you're safe." He responded unashamedly and I could just imagine the casual shrug.

"Thank you but I think being with you is probably the most unsafe thing right now." I gave him a small smile before opening the door and stepping in. I flicked the lights on and rolled my eyes when I saw my gun on the table - why do I have you if I'm not going to use you?

"So stupid." I breathed out rubbing my neck. The door shut and the lock was clicked into place. My body froze on its own accord as I felt Dominic's presence creeping up from behind me. My breathing suddenly became shallow as I kept my back to him.

I bit my lip. "Is this the part where you kill me?"

"Why would I do such a thing, angel?" He asked softly and the deepness of his voice nearly had me trembling on the spot. We were alone again but this time it felt different and it made me nervous.

"Because now I know what you are." I mumbled. His hands landed on my waist and he was so close I could feel his body heat radiating off him. My body jumped slightly when his grip tightened, almost painful but I nearly threw my head back because how much I shamefully enjoyed it.

"Does that change anything?" He asked leaning down to gently speak into my ear.

I groaned. "It's supposed to."

"I asked you a yes or no question." His voice hardened at the same time his hands did as a reminder that he wasn't playing around. I didn't know what to say. Of course the answer was meant to be yes but I couldn't bring myself to utter the simple word. His hands disappeared underneath my sweater and I had to physically prevent myself from sighing out loud.

"Caitlin. I need to know." He kissed the side of my neck and my face twisted into pure frustration. My mind was conflicted but his touch had my pussy throbbing desperately.

"Are you seducing me right now?" I asked leaning my head to the side to allow more space to land fiery kisses on the skin.

"I might be." I felt him smirk against me and my eyebrows scrunched together. I hated how he made me feel but at the same I was loving every second of it. I turned around in his hold and grabbed his cheeks in my hands. His eyes widened in shock before his bottom lip got pulled between his teeth. I looked away for a split second and that's when my mind was made.

"Fuck it." I growled out before tugging him down to press my lips against his in a deep, lustful kiss that had me moaning against him. His hands immediately went down to my ass to grip the fat in his palms. I felt my loose shorts bunch up before he lifted me to wrap my legs around his waist. He spun us around and pushed my back against the wall while keeping his lips planted on mine.

Just one more time and that's it.

He grinded his pelvis into mine and I gasped against him when I felt the huge erection in his sweatpants. It wasn't my first time feeling him but it sure felt like it. His tongue snaked into my mouth and the groan emitting from his throat was music to my ears.

Barely two minutes alone with him and I already caved in.

"It's just sex." I whispered into his mouth.

"No, it's fucking chess." He replied sarcastically and I bit his bottom lip harshly as payback.

He gasped before pulling away to glare at me as he removed one hand from underneath me. He ran his thumb over the lip that I had bitten to check for blood. There wasn't any.

"I liked that." Dominic admitted with a smirk, his eyes glazed over with pure desire and my eyebrows shot up in shock. He was so fucking handsome but devilishly beautiful at the same time and my mind couldn't grasp how badly I wanted him in that moment.

I wrapped my arms around his neck to pull him in for a hard kiss. I tugged on his hair and a deep baritone moan escaped him. He let me control the kiss and when I stuck my tongue into his mouth, he accepted it and sucked on it ferociously.

"Room?" I breathed out leaning my forehead against his. Our lips were swollen and plump but I could go on forever. I was so wet and I needed him inside me - urgently.

"I won't go so easy on you this time, angel." He whispered huskily and yet again, I looked at him in surprise.

"The first time was you going easy on me? Well fuck." I smiled cheekily at him and a grin lit up his face. Truthfully, I was scared because the last time nearly ruined me but I found myself biting my inner cheek in excitement and partial anticipation. I dropped my legs from around his waist to land on my feet before grabbing his hand and leading him to my bedroom.

Before we stepped out of my living room, a loud disturbing phone call rang through the room and I threw my head back in frustration.

I let go of his hand to pick up my cell from the table and I pursed my lips when I saw the caller. I quickly pressed decline and flicked my phone to silent. He immediately started phoning again but I put it screen down back onto the table. He can wait.

"Who the fuck is Blake?" Dominic asked harshly from behind me and my eyes widened. I turned around to make eye contact but he was frowning down at the phone. The previous glint in his eyes disappeared only to be switched to something cold and hard...jealousy? I scowled at him but I hated to admit that he looked ten times hotter when he was mad.

"He's a friend." I felt the need to explain myself even though I absolutely didn't have to. Dominic stunned me by grabbing my cheeks in one hand and glaring at me. My eyes widened when his jaw clenched.

"Why would you decline a friend that calls at midnight?" He asked lowly but this time his voice was deeper than before and the accent was extremely prominent. I clenched my thighs and pulled my lips into my mouth. Fuck, he looked so good. "It could be an emergency."

"I don't think so." I tried my best to sound confident but it came out as a mere whisper. His grip tightened and I was sure it would leave marks on the skin but I fucking loved it. Dominic finally let go after a few moments of a scrutinising glare and reach down to rip my sweater over my head. He grabbed the back of my thighs and threw me over his shoulder.

"You don't think so?" He questioned and gave me a small slap on the ass. I yelped at the pain but it sent a tingle straight to my pussy leaving me wanting more. A few seconds later I was thrown flat on my back onto the bed. I didn't have time to register it before my hips were grabbed and I was flipped onto my stomach by large tattooed hands.

I was living my very own fantasy.

My belly was pressed against the bed and my feet were firmly onto the floor. I fisted the sheets in pure excitement and slight nervousness.

"Dom-" He laced his fingers over the hem of my shorts and pulled it down my legs along with my underwear. My ass was now bare to his view.

"Look at how fucking wet you are. You're already making a mess." He growled gripping one ass cheek and that's when I felt his breath on my hole. When I looked back - he had dropped to his knees and was staring straight at my core with dark lusty features. He licked his lips like a starving man staring right back at a meal that he was about to devour.

"Dominic." I whimpered shifting around trying to find any sort of friction to release the ache. I needed to feel him. I was suffering.

"I'm going to touch you, okay?" He asked softly and started moving his fingers along my inner thighs. I shivered when the cold ring around his pinky gently caressed me. It felt so intense yet he was barely touching me.

"Yes."

"Stop moving, angel." He snapped using his hand to spread my legs even further. I groaned when his thumb became circling my clit in a tortuously slow manner. In that moment, I forgot about everything that I learned about him that night.

The pleasure racking through me was enough to give me an orgasm right there and when his warm wet mouth completely covered me I couldn't help but stand on the tip of my toes.

It felt so unbelievable good and I thoughtlessly started pushing back onto his face. Shit, at that rate I would cum right there. He moaned against me and dug his hands further into the flesh.

"Just like that. Oh fuck." I moaned pressing my face into the sheets trying to control my breathing but it was impossible when

I had the sexiest man I've ever seen lapping me up and down not just for my pleasure but seemingly for his too. His tongue, his lips, his hands, his everything contributed to the waterfall between my legs.

"Does that feel good?" He spoke against me, looking for affirmation and the vibrations made my lift my head from the bed. My hair covered my face like a curtain and I so badly wanted to move it away but my hands couldn't seem to stop holding the sheets in a tight grip.

"Yes it does. Shit, I love that." I said breathlessly and I could feel him smiling against me happy with himself. Dominic was a man who put my needs above his own and it was my first time ever experiencing something like that.

"Dominic, let me." I tried to sit up on my palms but he placed a hand on my lower back and roughly pushed me back down. The sudden movement made my core clench and an orgasm approached faster than I expected it to. Holy fuck.

"Cum for me." He whispered and that's when I released into his mouth. I could hear how wet I was. When I was done riding out the incredible orgasm with shaky legs and tensed muscles, I fell limp onto the bed.

My body was covered in a thin layer of sweat but I was ready for more. I heard Dominic's clothes fall to the ground and the clinking of his gun on the dresser before it was slid open.

"I'll stop when you tell me to but you have to use your words." He instructed and moved behind me again. I heard the sound of a wrapper before the hard tip was rubbed up and down my slit spreading the juices around. I moaned in agony trying to push back and sink himself into me. It felt like an itch that desperately needed to be scratched.

"Stop fucking moving." He seethed startling me by landing a loud smack on my ass no doubt bruising the skin. I groaned when red hot pain spread through me but it was the good type of pain. I swallowed hard - instantly going still.

"I like these." Dominic complimented softly moving his fingertips along my lower back where the two dimples were located.

"And these." His fingers moved to the sides of my ass where the stretch marks laid horizontally. His touch was so gentle that I sighed in content but nothing could calm my pounding heart.

"And this." With one swift movement he plunged so hard into me I couldn't help but let out a tiny scream at the sudden intrusion. His pelvis was flush against me and the massive dick currently inside me was overwhelming in the best way possible.

"Fuck," I heard him whisper under his breath. "You feel so good." His voice sounded strained as if he would combust at any second. When he started to roll his hips, waves and waves of inexpressible pleasure flowed through every inch of me.

He pulled out slowly before thrusting unbelievably hard back in hitting that spot that almost blinded my vision. "Shit." I groaned putting my arm underneath me to press my palm against my lower stomach. He was so deep.

Dominic was relentless, hammering into me with no mercy and gripping my hips to support himself. His groans and my moans filled the air along with the sound of skin slapping against skin. Suddenly I felt like I needed to see him. I wanted to see the expression on his face.

"Turn me around." I practically begged. Dominic wasted no time in pulling out and flipping me around onto my back, almost excitedly. He reached forward and grabbed a pillow to place underneath my head and I gave him a thankful smile. Why the fuck was he so nice?

"Holy fucking shit." I gasped out when he entered me again. It felt deeper - more intense and the eye contact made it even more overpowering. His pink lips were parted and his eyes were low as he stared down at me.

He leaned forward, grabbing both my wrists in one hand and pinning them above my head. I looked at him in confusion but he started rubbing my clit with the other hand and that's when I realised why he was holding me down. My entire body jerked as I desperately tried to thrash out his hold so I could move his fingers away from me. It felt too good.

"Bitch!" I hissed out before I could catch it. Dominic stopped.

"What did you just call me?" He growled at me. My eyes widened and my lips opened to speak but nothing came out. Dominic laughed humourlessly before letting go of my wrists and pulling my legs over his shoulders. Oh no.

"Fuck!" I yelled out when he started pounding into me again. I thought it couldn't get any more intense but it did and my eyes rolled back in pure bliss. He knew what the fuck he was doing to me and his face told me he enjoyed every second of it.

My body stiffened and my toes curled as I came, again.

Dominic didn't stop. He grabbed my thighs, clutching it hard and kissing my calf right beside his face. My eyes fluttered closed but a large hand wrapping around my neck and squeezing hard made them fly open. His jaw was clenched and sweat made his already tan skin glisten underneath the light of my room.

My pussy clenched around him and he groaned slowing down. I was exhausted and on the brink of passing out right on the spot.

"I'm going to cum." He croaked. I already did. Twice.

Finally he released himself into the condom and I let out a long sigh when he pulled out. That was the most intense sex I've ever experienced and yet again I found myself curling into a foetal position. I raised my fist to Dominic and he chuckled before touching his fist with mine. I smiled into the sheets.

"I'll get you cleaned up." He whispered before moving my hair out of the way and giving me a kiss on the forehead.

CHAPTER 8

C AITLIN
Dominic and I were talking.

We were actually cuddled up in the middle of my bed having a conversation.

He was on his back, staring at the ceiling and I had my head on his chest with a leg draped over his. It felt more intimate than any of the times we fucked but I wasn't complaining. After two rounds I was drained and needed the rest. Dominic, on the other hand, could fuck for hours if I'd let him.

"Ma'am, are you blind? Of course they're fucking." Dominic laughed and his body shook slightly. I gasped and pinched his nipple. He winced and grabbed my hand, his large one covering mine completely. He surprised me by bringing it up to his lips and kissing it softly. My cheeks turned beet red and I pulled it away, hiding my face in his chest. That felt...a bit too nice.

"What did he mean when he said I have to work for you? What would I have to do?" I asked curiously.

"Okay, listen." He sighed. "Yurik knew that I know you and he completely used that to his advantage to save Micah's ass."

"How did he know?"

"Yurik can find out anything about anything. Nothing surpasses him but I'm convinced that my drivers car was traced back here. He found out who was at the bar and you...a stunning woman who just so happened to be the only one from this complex there that night. You and Micah have the same surname and he just knew. Yurik has fucking superpowers." He explained and his voice softened. I could tell that he loved his brother deeply.

"Such a coincidence." I whispered before pushing myself away from him to lay on my stomach. I rested my head into the palm of my hand facing him.

"But you didn't answer my question. What would I have to do? It better not be me selling my pussy." I narrowed my eyes at him. The joke Yurik made was still lingering on my mind.

"Why would you even think that? I don't expect you to work for me. Micah can fix his mess himself." Dominic said before pulling me on top of him. Our naked bodies pressed together and I could feel his dick hanging down his inner thigh. "As long as you keep your pretty mouth shut about any of this, you're good." He muttered but I could hear the underlying threat in his voice and see it in his eyes. I was a risk and Dominic was making sure I wasn't going to run my mouth.

"I'm not going to." I assured. "Just keep your promise of not hurting Micah."

"And risk my brother killing me? I like sleeping peacefully at night." He chuckled and I caught myself smiling softly.

"Wait but," I adjusted myself on top of him to get more comfortable. "Working for you lowkey sounds exciting." I mumbled and watched his eyebrows shoot up. I couldn't believe what I was saying. I must have gone mad.

"A little vixen, I tell you." He shook his head. "This is a dangerous environment and once you're in, I don't think I'll let you go. You need to change your mind about that, angel." Dominic shut me down instantly and I looked at with a blank face.

"Alright then." I muttered and let the subject go. It was insane anyway. Dominic was quiet for a short while before he sighed deeply.

"What do you do for a living?" He asked and my eyebrows scrunched together at the random question.

"Odd jobs. Right now I'm a freelance journalist." I shrugged. I hated the job and I hated the unstable income but work was hard to find considering the useless philosophy degree I obtained. I would forever have regrets about it and a shitload of student debt.

"Journalism? Is that something you like doing?" He asked and I felt him start to stroke my hair. We were cuddling like a couple and it started to unnerve me but I kept my composure.

"No but I don't really have a choice. The lights have to stay on." I murmured.

"So you're broke." He deadpanned and I removed my head from his chest to glare at him. He was blunt but it was also very true.

"Utterly fucked is a better way to put it but I'm doing okay right now. Kind of. Hey, maybe I should actually start to sell my nudes or pictures of my feet. Men live for that shit." I said nodding my head. Dominic chuckled.

"You know what - I will completely understand why. Money is very important." He said. I shifted my legs and I felt his dick rub against my thighs. Our stomachs were squashed together and I could feel him harden slightly. He ignored the look I gave him.

"It is." I agreed and pressed my lips into a tight line. Money was the reason why my father was no longer with us and I shook my head to get rid of the morbid thoughts. Dominic must have noticed the shift in my mood because he frowned at me but I spoke before he could say anything.

"So, Dominic," I smiled at him cheekily. "What do you do for a living?" He gave me a bored look but I just bit my bottom lip looking at him expectantly.

"You just told me you're a journalist and now you want to know everything I do. Angel, you guys are worse than the cops." He said raising a brow and my face dropped.

"Freelance." I corrected lifting my pointer finger. "Also, why would I risk my whole life to snitch on you? That's a one way ticket to heaven...or hell."

"It's a one way ticket to the bottom of a lake." He responded and my mouth dropped while my eyes widened.

"That sounds like way too much effort. I heard the best way to get rid of a body is to drop them into molten metal. No fuss and no mess." I said grinning at him and he looked at me weirdly before seemingly thinking about it. Finally he nodded his head.

"That's actually brilliant. Nobody would find you ever. No body, no evidence." He muttered thoughtfully and I narrowed my eyes at him. Me?

"I will literally haunt you. Do not try me." I poked a finger into his chest and he chuckled grabbing my hand. He brought it up to his lips for a second time that evening and once again I blushed embarrassingly like a school girl. I felt the urge to break the comforting atmosphere we have created and I couldn't fathom why.

"Okay fine, I won't." He said in annoyance and rolled his eyes.

"Wow, thank you so much." I said sarcastically. Dominic's fingers started trailing down my spine until they landed right on the curve of my ass.

"You ready for round three?" He whispered and kissed me softly on the neck. I shivered when his tongue darted out to lick the skin. I definitely wanted another round but I doubt I could handle it. So

I pushed myself off him and pressed my lips against his. He kissed me back with the same amount of urgency and palmed the back of my head.

"My pussy isn't but..." I said softly against his mouth and he pushed me away to look at me in confusion.

"Anal?"

I laughed and shook my head. "No you fucking idiot." I bent down to kiss his chest and started trailing wet kisses down his tattooed abs. He tensed underneath my touch before relaxing completely. My mouth watered at the thought of me filling it up with him.

I looked up to meet his eyes and the excited smile disappeared from his face as if trying to hide it but I caught him and I couldn't help but chuckle. The dick underneath me was now hard as a rock.

He groaned when I reached just below his belly button and I sensed that he was beginning to get fidgety and impatient. I wanted to tease him a little more.

"You're killing me, angel." He whined and buckled his hips. His open hands hovered over my head before they turned into clenched fists. Dominic was stopping himself from grabbing me and pushing me down.

I kissed both hipbones before wrapping my hand around him. My eyes widened when my fingers could barely touch. That was inside of me?

"Handsome." I whispered against him. He really was.

I looked up at him and just as my mouth was about to wrap around the massive tip, a disturbing knock came from my front door. My lips pressed together and I frowned. I waited a while, hoping that whoever it is would go away but the knocking only got gradually louder. Who ever that was was going to wake everyone up on the damn floor.

"Who the fuck..." I muttered before climbing off him. Dominic grabbed my hand, a similar frown on his features. He was irritated by the interruption and I could understand why.

"Are you expecting anybody?" He asked before getting up and pulling on his boxers. I shook my head no but I had a feeling about who it was and I swallowed hard. It better not be.

"Then I'll go check." He said but I grabbed his forearm.

"No!" I said and he looked at me weirdly. I sighed.

"It's probably Blake. He won't leave me alone but stay here and I'll get rid of him. Please." I begged and grabbed his hoodie to slip over my head. I wanted Blake to know I was currently fucking someone else but not who so he could finally get the hint to leave me alone. Ever since ending things with him he's been constantly texting me and calling trying to get my attention.

"Your friend? Nice." He said, voice lacing with displeasure.

"Stay." I pointed a finger at him and he raised his hands innocently and shrugged. I eyed him warily before finally leaving my room and towards the persistent knocking.

I peeped through the hole in the door and there stood Blake, leaning both hands against the doorframe. As soon as I opened the door, he leaned in for a kiss and I backed away. He scowled at me in confusion but I looked at him unamused.

"I miss you, Lin." He mumbled and I could see the sincerity in his hazel eyes. My face twisted into disgust at the nickname I've always hated.

"Its two o clock in the morning. Why are you here? Please leave." I asked and he pushed past me into my apartment. I took a deep breath so I wouldn't snap on him. His light brown hair was ruffled into messy curls and he was dressed in his usual jeans and olive green bomber jacket. He looked good but it suddenly didn't appeal to me anymore.

"Blake, you can't just show up here when you feel like it. Go home." I said exasperatedly throwing my hands up in the air. My eyes darted to my room's door where Dominic was waiting and I chewed on my lip nervously.

Blake looked at me up and down before he narrowed his eyes at me. "Whose hoodie is that?"

"It's mine. Can you leave?" I walked behind him and started pushing his back towards the door. He stood still, not moving an inch. Of course he didn't move - he was an ice hockey player. I pressed further into his hard back to no avail.

He turned around and I took a step back when I saw how angry he was. "Why the fuck have you been ignoring me?" He asked furiously. I glared at him.

He needed to leave.

"We," I gestured my hand between us. "Ended things."

"It wasn't a mutual decision." He argued and it wasn't a valid argument at all. He had agreed with me but a day later he decided it wasn't what he wanted anymore. Things didn't work like that.

"That doesn't matter."

"Why would you open the door if you didn't want me to stay, Lin?" He asked reaching out to grab my waist but I took a step back again. I pinched the bridge of my nose in utter annoyance.

"Because you were making a fucking noise." I yelled out and then clamped my mouth shut.

"Why won't you let me touch - oh that's why." He suddenly said with a slow realisation nod. Blake was looking directly at Dominic who stood there leaning against the wall with crossed arms, bare chested and sweatpants low on his hips. He was glaring at Blake and I grit my teeth.

I was beyond annoyed by the amount of testosterone in my apartment.

"Yes, that's why. Leave." I said casually and walked to Dominic who wrapped an arm around my shoulders, almost protectively. Blake's face faltered and my heart clenched at how broken he looked.

I sighed - I shouldn't have felt as terrible as I did but I couldn't help it. He turned around to leave and I frowned at how easy that was. I was angry that Dominic's mere presence was enough to drive him away.

"Typical," I scoffed. "He respects a man who just stands there more than he respects me."

Blake muttered something under his breath and I couldn't make out what he said but the way Dominic tensed besides me told me he fully understood. He let go of me.

"What the fuck did you just say?" Dominic growled and walked to Blake who turned around with wide eyes before rushing out and shutting the door behind him. He hadn't expected anybody to hear him. I grabbed Dominic's forearm to stop him from taking another step.

"Don't. What did he say?" I asked curiously watching how his jaw clenched.

"He said 'one day I'll get you alone.'" He fumed. "That's a fucking threat and I won't take it likely so don't even try to convince me otherwise." Dominic stated shaking his head. I scowled and removed my hand wrapped around his arm.

"He said that?" I muttered hesitantly. "The little shit actually said that? I'll kill him myself."

Dominic opened his mouth to speak but I stood on the tip of my toes to kiss him. "Just forget it - shower with me?" I asked hoping he'll just drop it and accept my offer.

He sighed. "Of course."
Dominic agreed but the mood was already ruined.

CHAPTER 9

D OMINIC

"Hi sweetheart. How are you today? Do you want to make two thousand?" Yurik grinned into the phone while scooting towards the opposite end of the table. He was side eyeing me and I glared at him, immediately shutting my laptop. We were the only two in the boardroom and he better not be talking to who the fuck I think he's talking to.

"Two thousand cash yes." He said nodding his head.

"That was a fucking joke! You wouldn't need to sell any of your body parts." Yurik yelled and leaned back into the chair spinning around before looking up at the ceiling in frustration.

"No. I promise it's not a trick." He continued speaking and I narrowed my eyes at him. Yurik was yet again doing whatever he wished to without consulting others.

"You're fucking broke but you're saying no to an easy 2K. That makes no sense. Haven't you got any ambition?" Yurik asked looking extremely annoyed at the rejection. My shoulders relaxed the tiniest bit as I watched his face crumble.

"You have a degree? Then where's the stable job, sweetheart?"

My jaw dropped as he placed a sickly sweet smile on his face and cooed into the phone. I shook my head - my brother had absolutely no filter but I guess it was one thing we had in common. I could hear the voice of Caitlin speaking ever so faintly but I wasn't able to make out what she was saying.

"Stop yelling at me!" He shouted before pulling the phone away from his ear and looking at me with a shocked expression. "She's the first girl to ever yell at me. She's amazing." Yurik complimented softly and I rolled my eyes.

Caitlin would yell at anybody.

"All you'll have to do is put a little honesty drug into a little man's drink and learn a little information. Easy." Yurik muttered casually with a shrug. As soon as I darted out of my seat, his eyes widened and he jumped up. He pressed his back into the wall and held a hand out to me. He was pointing a knife at me and I glared at him - how the fuck did he manage to get that out so fast?

"She's not doing that." I said through gritted teeth. It was far too dangerous.

"Take one more step and I'm telling her your dirty little secret." He threatened still pointing the tip of the knife in my direction. He looked at the phone for a split second and that was my opportunity to lunge forward. I grabbed his wrist hard and locked his arm underneath mine until the knife was pointing at his neck instead.

Yurik was good with knives but agility was my strength. He stood no chance as my grip on him tightened and his face contorted into pain.

"You wouldn't fucking dare. Tell her you change your mind and that it's too dangerous." I growled at him before grabbing the knife out his hand and pushing him away from me. I flipped it closed and shoved into my pants pocket. Yurik scowled before he smirked.

"Hey Caitlin, did you know Domo over here likes to-"

"Shut the fuck up. God, you're so fucking annoying." I said in complete irritation and plopped down into the seat. I rubbed my hand over my face and took a deep breath in.

Yurik grinned and straightened his suit jacket wiping away the creases. "So, you're in?"

Please say no.

"Good! We'll come over in an hour to discuss everything."

He put the phone off and looked at me with a smug expression. I wanted to shoot him in the face.

"Yurik - please explain to me why you're doing this?" I spoke in my mother tongue. My English failed me when I felt in any way upset or bothered.

"Did you know she's 30K deep in student debt and you're just going to let her struggle? Shame on you, Domo." He sighed and sat down alongside me. I didn't bother asking how or why the fuck he knew that in the first place.

"I was going to- you know what, never mind. It's far too dangerous. She's not trained." I argued giving him a pointed look but Yurik was as stubborn as an ox once he set his mind on something.

"Oh, you're one of those bosses who want experienced workers but won't give non-experienced workers the chance to gain the experience they need to find work so how is anybody ever supposed to find work if no one is willing to give them a chance." Yurik rambled on and I looked at him in utter confusion. My brain nearly malfunctioned.

"Are you on crack?" I asked slowly.

"Dominic," he sighed and him calling me by my full name told me he was serious. "You can't tell me that you don't see potential in her. She's exactly what we need."

"We don't need anything."

"You're wrong. I see a fucking queen and I know you see it too."

Yurik was right. Caitlin wasn't like any other woman I have met and I knew the second she pulled my gun out of my pants and placed it next to her own. She was strong willed and I had no doubt that she could achieve greatness but the thought of putting her at risk was enough to drive me up the wall. Just thinking about her getting hurt in any way made rage fill my veins.

I still had to deal with that Blake boy.

"The target on her head would be enormous if anyone finds out we're using her to get closer to our rivals."

"Nobody will find out. Can't you see that Caitlin isn't a weak little girl who'll crack under pressure?" Yurik asked tapping his fingers on the glass table.

I exhaled deeply, thinking about it for a second. "You want to assign her to Lucas. Anybody can give him the truth serum."

"The man has five bodyguards around him 24/7. The only way anybody is getting close to him is if they have tits and a pretty face."

"You want to use her body? Do you not understand the risk? The danger? What if it goes wrong and Lucas ends up sexually assaulting her? He's a lowlife who won't think twice about it." I stated feeling my blood start to boil at the mere thought. I cracked my knuckles to relieve some of the tension.

"That won't happen." Yurik reassured and I looked at him unconvinced.

"You don't know that for sure."

"You have very little faith in me, Domo. It won't happen because we'll have a sniper team ready if he does try anything and she'll have a weapon attached to her thigh." He said opening the laptop and going straight into the encrypted website only the Romanov mafia had access to. I sat back into my seat pursing my lips.

Yurik sighed at my silence. "She's a grown ass woman who needs a little financial help so stop being a baby about it and let her decide for herself. We're not forcing her and if she says no, then so be it."

At the end of the day, my decision was final so I slumped in the chair and thought about it again for a moment.

She did say working for me sounds exciting.

"Okay. Make it 5K." I muttered after a brief moment of quiet. That amount of money is nothing compared to what we would receive if Yurik's plan worked. He grinned, happy that he had received the go-ahead.

"□□□□□□□." He thanked me and I nodded my head leaning my elbows against the table.

I loosed the tie around my neck moving my head side to side - it had been two days since I last laid my eyes on her. I could feel myself start to heat up as images of her naked body sprawled on the bed bouncing as I pounded into her came to mind. Fuck, I thought about her constantly and she had no idea. Her moans, her groans and the way she trailed her nails down my back played like a broken record and my attempts to get rid of it was useless.

"Shit." I mumbled to myself as I tried to think of anything besides her soft body and how her ass looked in my grip. I wanted to press my face between those cheeks and suffocate. I would die a happy man.

Just as Yurik raised his fist to knock on the door, it was opened and an unfamiliar face nearly walked into straight into us.

A young woman - probably in her early twenties with short red-hair and a freckled face stood there with wide eyes and a dropped jaw. Her eyes moved to Yurik and she unashamedly checked him out from head to toe. She did the same to me and I exhaled in annoyance tapping my fingers on the doorframe impatiently. Her eyes scanned the tattoos on my neck and hands and I could see the judgement in them.

"Sorry, I think you have the wrong place." She chirped and I almost winced at her high-pitched voice.

"Does Caitlin live here?" Yurik asked ignoring her blatant ogling.

"Yes but why-"

"Leah, its fine. Let them in." Caitlin's sultry voice came from the living room and I swear I felt my heart speed up. The redhead seemed unconvinced and didn't step aside as Caitlin just told her to. Obviously our presence felt like a threat to her as we towered over her frail looking body.

"But-"

"Leah, I said its fine. Let them in, for fucks sake." Caitlin yelled out as we stood there waiting for her to move. I knew her for all of two seconds and she was already annoying me. Who was this girl?

"They-" She was cut off by Yurik rolling his eyes and pushing her aside and entering the apartment like he owned the place. She gasped, looking completely offended watching us walk right in. I glared at her, just wanting her to fuck off.

"Girl, shut up." He muttered and her face turned bright red - matching the fierce colour of her hair.

"Okay, I'm going. Be safe and call me if you need me." Leah spoke keeping her eyes on me cautiously and I frowned as she closed the door behind her. Did she think we were going to hurt Caitlin? The thought alone nearly made me laugh out loud.

I finally looked at Caitlin and she was sitting on the floor at a small glass table, leaning her forearms on it with a scissor in one hand as she cut up...weed?

"Hi, angel. Your friend is annoying as fuck." I mumbled and shrugged my jacket off before sitting on the couch facing her.

Yurik went over to her side instead and crouched down closer to Caitlin's hands watching as she expertly and casually cut it up into the tiniest fragments on a piece of paper. She was dressed in a plain white hoodie that was way too big for her and her legs were bare showing off her thick thighs. Her head was covered in the hood but her long brown hair fell out the sides and down her stomach.

So simple but yet she still managed to be the most beautiful woman I've ever seen.

"Hey, you're twenty minutes early. Also, don't mind Leah - she's just paranoid." She muttered distractedly.

"Purple haze? Where did you find this? Dealers don't just sell this to anybody." Yurik asked leaning down to pick up a small amount between his fingers and studying it closely. I tilted my head to the side watching them interact - everything suddenly felt...normal, more normal than it should.

She grinned. "Well, my dealer has the fattest crush on me so I get all of this for free."

I clenched my jaw looking away from her. I had no right to suddenly feel the amount of jealousy I felt in that moment and I scowled at myself for being irrational. I shook my head and clasped my hands together willing myself to stop thinking about it. It was just weed.

"Free too? He must really want a piece of that ass." Yurik murmured and I felt myself tense again. He sat down alongside me so now we both faced Caitlin as she just sat there casually doing her thing.

"Oh, he does." She agreed with a nod and I leaned back into the couch rubbing a hand over my face. I had no reason to feel so stressed.

"Are you okay?" I looked up to see Caitlin speaking to me and I nodded silently. Was I that transparent?

"Yes, let's talk about the assignment and if you're willing to do it." I said clearing my throat and trying to get straight to the point. I couldn't believe that I was about to have that conversation and potential put her in danger.

"I'm in." Caitlin said without second thought and I watched her start to fill a brown piece of paper with the weed. Her long nails were painted a light blue and she had a silver ring around her pointer finger.

"Let us explain and-"

"Two thousand? I'm in." She mumbled before bringing the paper up to her lips and sticking her tongue out to give it a lick. I groaned and shifted in my seat - how am I supposed to focus when everything she did turned me on? Surely this is unhealthy.

"It's five now because-" Yurik started but I sent him a look. Caitlin did not need to know that I was the one upping the payment. Her eyes widened and the rolled blunt dropped from her hands and onto the table. She was so good at that.

"You're fucking lying." Caitlin said in surprise and abruptly stood up.

I chuckled shaking my head. "We're not but sit down so we can explain everything."

Caitlin grabbed a chair and sat down adjacent to me, her bare thighs squashing down onto the seat as she folded her ankles and leaned back. She gestured with her hand to let me continue, almost impatiently and I cocked an eyebrow at her with a small smile. This woman...

"If," I emphasised. "You're willing. Your target would be Lucas Trevino, software engineer and owner of Godfather nightclub."

I paused for her reaction and she simply just nodded her head waiting for me to continue.

"Every Friday night, he sits in the open VIP area of his club seeking beautiful women to join his side. The area is right in the corner, overlooking the floor of the club from above. Your job is to be invited in. Subtlety is key." I explained and watched her carefully for any sort of doubt.

"He has five bodyguards protecting the area but their backs are usually faced to him watching for danger from the entrance. That is why being besides him would provide the best outcome." Again, I waited for any reaction but she just nodded her head in understanding.

"We will give you a powder, hidden in either a bracelet or ring. It will make him drowsy, give him the sudden urge to lay down but at the same time it will make him want to spill his heart out to you.

"Above the club is his glass penthouse - you need to suggest finding somewhere quiet and hopefully this would lead to the both of you leaving and being alone. You don't need to worry about this because some of my men and I would be on the opposite building ready to blow his brain out if anything goes wrong." I announced, feeling myself start to get riled up at the thought of him touching her inappropriately.

I felt like I was sending her straight into the lion's den.

"Why can't you just kidnap him?" She asked scrunching her eyebrows curiously after a few moment of ingesting the information I had just given her.

"He is protected by highly trained guards but we know his weakness. A pretty face." Yurik intervened and I nodded my head in agreement. "You find out what you need to and then leave. He won't remember a thing." He said.

"We will do our utmost best to ensure your safety but if you're uncomfortable with this in any way, you really need to let me know, angel. We could try and think of something else you could do and-"

"What? Are you kidding?! Of course I want to do it." Caitlin said looking at me flabbergasted. Yurik grinned shaking his head, obviously she wanted to do it. "What makes this guy so special?" She asked.

"Lucas is the second in command to a cartel drug lord. He's smart and he's the only one who knows the password and location for a large sum of cocaine hidden in an unknown deserted location." Yurik continued explaining and Caitlin's eyes widened - as if just realising how serious it actually was.

"And you," she pointed between Yurik and I. "Think I'm right for the job?"

"We think you have potential and obviously we'll teach you a few things. You're a freelance journalist, right? Perhaps those skills could come in handy."

"I need coffee and then we can talk more. You want coffee, tea, whiskey?" She asked getting up from her seat and walking to the kitchen. I watched her legs and tilted my head to the side before Yurik punched my arm and mumbled, "stop being a perv."

"Tea for me, please." I cleared my throat.

"Same, thank you." Yurik said and she nodded her head, switching on the kettle.

What am I getting her into?

CHAPTER 10

C AITLIN
  I must have gone mad.

"Thank you." Dominic muttered after taking the last sip of his tea. Cute.

The two men screamed power and money but yet they made themselves at home in my tiny apartment. Yurik was laying on the couch with his head on the armrest, lounging lazily as he watched the television. His tea was long gone and he had taken it to the kitchen himself after he was done.

Both of their guns were on the glass table, right next to my weed. I would smoke but sativa made me way too horny to be around Dominic when I knew I couldn't have him.

"You're welcome." I said and took the empty cup from Dominic's hands, stopping him from getting up. My fingers just barely brushing over his but I could feel the slight warmth he was radiating.

If Yurik wasn't here...

They managed to explain everything to me in finer detail but before they did that, I had already drawn the conclusion that I wanted to do it. It was possible that I had too much self-confidence but the thought of it excited me in ways I couldn't explain.

It made me feel good that Dominic and Yurik had faith in me, well, Yurik more than Dominic I could tell. He was a bit hesitant and he had a sceptical look in his eye that only fuelled the need for me to show him otherwise.

They went into detail about how I would need to act, talk...seduce. That was a topic that really got Dominic clenching his jaw and I couldn't help but smirk at the jealousy he was very obviously trying to hide but no doubt failing.

Little did he know that he had ruined every single man for me.

I was convinced nobody would exceed the standard that Dominic had set but would I admit that to his face? Probably yes. Unapologetically so too.

"Wait, what does this guy look like?" I asked sitting down on the couch and facing my body towards him. I didn't know what I was expecting but when Dominic opened the laptop and showed me a mug shot, my eyes widened.

He looked to be in his late twenties, sporting a dark buzz cut and a neatly trimmed beard. He had a black eyebrow piercing and I could see the tattoos sneaking up his neck stopping just below his jawline. Lucas was smirking with his head tilted up slightly, almost mockingly and that alone told me the man feared no one.

"Holy shit, he's fine." I blurted without thinking. The laptop was slammed closed and I jumped.

Yurik let out a loud laugh and shook his head. "Be careful, sweetheart. This one is about to go all woof woof snarl grr on your ass."

I looked at Dominic and he was glaring, not at Yurik or me but at the laptop. "This won't work if you're attracted to him." He said but something in his tone was harder and I narrowed my eyes at him. Yurik was watching with his mouth formed in an 'O'

"I never said I was attracted to him. There's a difference." I defended.

"It's written all over your face, Caitlin." Dominic said still avoiding my gaze and I looked at him appalled.

"You should know what my face looks like when I'm attracted to someone and that was not it." I snapped and this made his eyes finally meet mine. Wait, I shouldn't be defending myself.

"Should I?" He teased.

I opened my mouth to speak but a loud ringing through the silent living room stopped me. It was Yuriks phone on the table and a picture of...Micah popped up. I frowned - the little fucker doesn't even call me.

Yurik's eyes lit up and he hurriedly picked it up before excusing himself and leaving my apartment closing the door behind him. Dominic was still sitting there, deep in thought so I did the first thing that came to mind. I sighed and threw one leg over his lap, straddling him. His eyes widened the slightest bit and his hands went straight to my ass.

"You're cute when you're upset." I whispered leaning closer to him and his face turned cold. I guess the big mafia boss didn't like being called cute.

"I'm not upset." He snapped through gritted teeth and I smiled biting my lower lip, unmoved. You're not as good as hiding your feelings as you think you are.

"Oh, yeah? Relax your jaw," I trailed my fingertips along his jawline. He listened.

"Good. Get rid of this frown." I moved toward his forehead and I watched the wrinkles disappear.

"Finally, loosen these tense shoulders." I said softly and placed my hands on his broad shoulders and I felt them sag beneath my touch. I grinned at him and Dominic sighed nearly in relief.

"Better?" I asked massaging his hard muscles. Suddenly it was like a switch was flipped and a menacing look formed in his eyes. Dominic's hand flew up gripping my cheeks so hard I thought the bone would break. He squeezed my lips into a pout and it hurt but it did something to me - something I couldn't quite describe.

"Do you like teasing me, angel?" Dominic asked leaning his head to the side and keeping his eyes on my mouth.

"Yes." I admitted gulping hard. His grip tightened and I gasped trying to pull away but he held me in place, glaring at me hard.

"Tease me again and I'm fucking that pussy raw." He muttered before placing an open mouth kiss on my awaiting lips. I moaned and it took every bit of self-control to push him away when I realised Yurik could walk in at any second.

"Get rid of this." I whispered pressing my palm against the bulge forming in his pants for a quick second as I climbed off him. I wiped the saliva off my lips with the back of my hand and smirked at him.

He gets hard way too easily.

His black slacks had tightened around the groin area and it seemed to be growing by the second. Dominic stood up before adjusting the erection, keeping his back towards the front door. I watched him carefully, my mouth watering. The hottest man I've ever seen and I had him inside me.

Maybe I should continue teasing him.

The day had finally arrived.

It was Friday and I was getting ready for the night. I had been instructed to wear something sexy, so I opted for a black tight fitting spaghetti strap dress with a slit. My curves were accentuated and my cleavage looked good. The dress was short, high on my right leg while my left was nearly covered completely by the soft material.

I pursed my lips looking at myself in the mirror. Was it enough? I turned to the side, seeing the curve of my ass and my bare back.

Hair up or hair down?

I used my hands to move my hair into a make-shift bun, tilting my head as I watched myself carefully.

Hair up.

I picked up my brush and proceeded to put my hair into a high bun, allowing my neck and collarbones to be bare. I chose silver medium sized hoops to add some life into the look, deciding on not wearing any necklace.

Next was the shoe. I slid open my closet door and scanned the heels I had neatly packed on the wall shelf. My eyes immediately landed on my favourite black pair Leah, my university friend, had gifted me for Christmas. It was simple, opened toe with a strap and a long thin heel. It was a good thing I had painted my toenails white just that previous night.

I couldn't help but feel slightly anxious about the whole ordeal.

Wait, can I go to jail for this? The smile fell from my face. That would be fucked up.

A knock erupted from my door and I immediately knew who it was. I walked to the living room while stumbling trying to get my last heel on. It was a success and I breathed out before unlocking the door and opening it. Dominic was standing there and the second his eyes landed on me, his jaw dropped.

"Angel. You look beautiful." Dominic said in awe before stepping in and grabbing me by the waist. I smiled and pulled him down for a peck without thinking. I froze when I realised that kissing Dominic non-sexually and platonically was crossing the invisible line. Although, he didn't seem to mind it at all.

"Thank you. You look handsome." I said honestly, a grin on my face. Dominic always looked neat but that particular night, he looked a little bit different. A good different. He was dressed in a black suit and tie, tailored for his large body. The tattoos trailed down from his neck down to his hands and onto his fingers. At first glance, one would know not to fuck with him.

He looked ravishing and despite telling myself it wouldn't happen again, I knew it would because I wanted it to.

"Thank you." He said and shut the door behind him. Dominic shrugged his jacket off, revealing the suspenders and two gun holsters on both sides.

"I got something for you." He announced, pulling out a relatively small blade with a black handle. It was pretty. Yurik had shown me the basics. He taught me how to flip, twirl and throw. I wasn't a pro but with the knowledge I gained from him, I was confident in protecting myself.

Although I wished it wouldn't get to that point.

I watched as Dominic dropped to his knees in front of me. He gestured for me to lift my dress and I trustingly did so. I heard him take a sharp breath in when I revealed the red lace thong. It wasn't for anyone but myself, it made me feel good and capable of accomplishing anything I set my mind to.

"I would have your name engraved but I don't want it to be traced back to you." Dominic said before using his hand to separate my thighs, lingering a moment longer than necessary.

He removed a strap from his pocket. It was round and had a tiny pocket attached to it, just big enough for the blade.

"Am I really doing this?" I asked as he tied the strap around my thigh placing the blade inside. It was tight, secured and well hidden when my dress fell back down.

Dominic stood up. "Yes you are. You're going to do it because you can and you're strong." He said seriously grabbing my cheeks and staring at me intensely. I nodded my head. It was the confidence booster that I needed.

"You remember everything I told you?" He asked and I hummed.

"Words." He demanded tilting my head back to look up at him. He was so tall.

"Yes, I remember." I breathed out.

"Good. You got this, angel."

I had to drive myself to the club, to avoid arousing any suspicion. Albeit I was given a brand new Mercedes with a fake number plate for the night so I wasn't complaining. Apparently my Mini Cooper could be 'traced back' to me. Dominic was going to the extremes to make sure I was protected and he took literally everything into consideration.

When I parked, I sat in the car for a while taking deep breaths in. I played with the ring around my index finger, it seemed like an ordinary innocent gem stone but inside held a dangerous substance. I shook my head, I had to get into the mood. I couldn't afford to be slacking.

I stepped out, closing the door behind me and locking it. The car seemed more expensive than my whole life. A group of men standing close to the entrance shot a few wolf whistles my way when I passed them and I refrained from rolling my eyes, not wanting to start something. Any other day and my mouth would've been running wild.

Fucking men.

The club wasn't what I expected. It was big, open planned and sort of resembled a fancy casino without all the machines. Right in the centre was a large circular stage with two poles, currently occupied by topless women dancing to sensual music. I smirked.

I took a seat at the bar and almost instantly a bartender was opposite me taking my order.

"Double whiskey with ice, please." I said, getting comfortable on the stool. I had no idea how long I would be here but Dominic had instructed if I wanted to leave at any time, I could.

I wasn't going to.

I avoided looking up where I knew Lucas was sitting and watching from above. I checked my phone, a feign disappointment on my face as if I had just read a message from someone telling me they 'weren't going to make it.'

I sighed throwing my head back and shoving my phone back into my purse with an unnecessary force. The barman handed me my drink and I thanked him before taking the smallest sip. It tasted like the first night I met Dominic but this time it wasn't his eyes on me, it was a specific short haired man sending eerie shivers down my spine.

I turned in my seat, leaning my back and elbow against the counter as I watched the women dance. They were doing a damn good job. A brunette dancer winked at me when she caught me watching and I grinned cheekily.

I sat there for fifteen minutes.

"Whoever stood you up is a fucking idiot."

I glanced up, stopping myself from showing any reaction when I saw it was Lucas. I was told that Lucas would send one of his men down but there he stood in the flesh with a chilling smirk on his face. That sentence told me that he was watching me the second I stepped foot in the club.

That was way too easy.

I shrugged. "I'm used to it."

Lucas slid onto the stool besides me, a confused expression on his face. "You shouldn't be. I would never do that to you." He said still holding the smirk and I almost laughed.

I turned my body to face him and his eyes immediately went to my cleavage. "I highly doubt that."

"Lucas." He stretched his hand out to me and I eyed it sceptically.

He laughed. "I don't bite."

"Nice to meet you, Lucas. I'm Sophia." I placed my hand into his and he immediately brought it up to his lips, kissing it while maintaining eye contact. I swallowed down the grimace making its way to my face. Ew. He was handsome but I still felt disgusted that he was touching me. I smiled at him, hiding my distaste.

"Nice to meet you, Sophia. Care to join me?" He gestured up to the VIP area and that's when I noticed the two guards standing behind him - the man went nowhere without protection.

"I don't know about that, Lucas." I said pursing my lips and looking at him unconvinced.

"Come on, you can't sit here on this uncomfortable chair." He said trying to persuade me and I mentally shook my head. My goal was to not show a hint of emotion that would awaken any sort of suspicious from him.

"Okay, sure. Why not?" I said standing up and fishing for a few notes from my purse. Lucas put his hand over mine stopping me before gesturing something towards the bartender who nodded in return.

"Don't worry about that. Just come with me." Lucas held his palm and I took it without hesitation. There was something off about him. He wasn't bad looking, quite the opposite actually and I was sure he wouldn't have trouble finding a woman for the night.

"Thank you."

Just like that I followed him up the stairs right into the deserted and empty area.

CHAPTER 11

CAITLIN

Lucas was very touchy.

Any chance he got he would be touching my shoulder, my waist and even once his hand would hover over the bare part of my cleavage. I knew this was what I signed up for but that fact didn't stop me from nearly gagging at his touch.

Luckily he hadn't picked up on anything yet.

He wanted to take me to bed, it was obvious in the way his eyes would glaze over with lust and he would squeeze me closer to him. We were sitting side by side on the couch, his arm draped over my shoulders and a weirdly proud look on his face as if I were some sort of trophy.

While I was hauled up into his side, his eyes would still wander the club floor at all the women. My patience was wearing thin, the need to get it over and done with hit tenfold. I was sick of him. I wanted to be within arms that made me feel warm and comfortable, not uneasy and unnerved.

While he continued chatting my ear off about something pointless, I eyed the small table besides him, occupied by a wide and shallow glass filled with brown liquid and ice. I looked towards the guards and they had their back turned towards us, the exact way Dominic had explained.

"You interested in one of my men?" Lucas asked suddenly and my head snapped towards him. The prior conversation came to halt as he caught me apparently checking out one of his guards.

I laughed. "No, of course not."

"Really? Who are you interested in?" He asked licking his lower lip and I let my eyes fall down to his mouth, enticing him. Man, I really didn't want to kiss him.

"Let me show you." I whispered trailing my fingers down his hard chest. He wore a white shirt with the first few buttons undone, giving me a peek of the gold chain around his neck. Lucas was gorgeous, in a dark daunting way and any other scenario I wouldn't have minded getting with him.

Dominic better not be watching.

His body tensed and for a second I thought he had finally caught onto the act but he smirked and before I knew it I was being pulled into his lap. I yelped in surprise when I sank onto a really hard bulge.

"Show me." He said softly and leaned back, resting both arms onto the back of the couch.

I didn't hesitate when I bent down, wrapping one hand around his head and pushing my lips against his. His lips were soft and he tasted like my favourite drink but the kiss did nothing for me. No chills, heart palpitations or the faintest pussy throb. Just nothing.

"Open your mouth." Lucas demanded against me and I obeyed. I stopped a dry heave forming in my chest when his tongue pushed past my lips and swirled around with mine. He was rough, dominating and left me no room to catch up.

It wasn't like Dominic's kisses at all and the brat in me wanted to bite his tongue off for being too controlling.

Both his hands reached down to my ass groping it and grinding me against him. While he did that, my arm reached out to his drink. In a split second the ring around my index finger was flicked open by the nail of my thumb and the contents spilled into his whiskey. To the naked eye, or camera it would've seemed like I was just casually picking up the glass.

I pulled away, pretending to take a sip even though it just slightly wet my lips. "Let me show you in private, does that sound good?"

Say yes.

Lucas smiled, taking the glass from my hand and downing the whiskey until only ice remained. "That sounds perfect. I can't wait to fuck you." He whispered setting the glass down and kissing my neck. I moaned throwing my head back and allowing him to do whatever he wished to.

He stood up with my legs still wrapped around his waist before setting me down. I had a terrible feeling but I swallowed it down and followed him towards the elevator. He motioned for his men to stay and I bit my lip in anticipation.

When the door slid closed, I was instantly pushed against the wall and Lucas' lips were on mine again. I groaned when he grabbed the back of my leg and hoisted it around him pressing his body flush against me.

"You look so sexy, I might just fuck you right here." He croaked and continued grinding into me. He turned me around, shoving my front against the wall and pressed his erection into my ass. When is that fucking drug going to kick in? Is it going to kick in?

I felt his fingertips lift my dress and I panicked.

"Not here. I want to be on top." I mumbled the first thing that came to mind trying to prolong it as much as possible. The thought of having him inside me dried my pussy up like the Kalahari Desert.

He groaned and backed away from me, relief flooded through my veins. "Shit, I bet you're so good at that." Lucas muttered and pressed the button to get the elevator moving again.

"Where are we going?" I asked although I already knew.

"My loft. It has all the privacy we need."

Privacy.

I smiled. "Perfect."

The door slid open, exposing the breathtakingly beautiful penthouse. The first thing I noticed were the floor to ceiling windows and the dark shape of a building on the opposite side. Dominic's words echoed in my mind.

'Some of my men and I would be on the opposite building ready to blow his brain out.'

Could he see me right now?

The night was a midnight blue, an array of stars littered the sky and complimented the bright orange city lights. I didn't have time to marvel at the view when I froze suddenly comprehending that I was alone with Lucas, a man who had been described as infamous.

I whirled around, catching his eyes on my ass. When he looked up, his lids were droopier than they were a few minutes ago. Is it working?

I sat down on the couch, spreading my legs and a smirk formed on his face. I watched him stumble until he was only a foot away, looming over me with his impressive height.

"I want you to fuck me with this view."

Lucas shook his head, the leer still apparent on his lips but I could tell that he was a bit confused. I grinned watching him unbutton his shirt, slowly exposing the tattooed skin underneath and the gold chain with a pendent that looked expensive enough to pay off my debt.

He was still standing, trying to get his shirt off with clumsy hands as I kept my eyes on him. I hid my reaction when I saw a red dot flicker twice on his forehead before it disappeared entirely.

Dominic was letting me know he had my back.

"Come on, what's taking you so long?" I whined scrunching my face and titling my head. I leaned back onto my flat palms and spread my legs even further. Lucas eyes were bloodshot, he aged about ten years in the span of five minutes.

"Sorry, I-I think I drank too much." He whispered clutching his head before swaying but I got up and wrapped my arm around his waist to steady him. If he fell and got knocked out then all of this would have been for nothing. I rolled my eyes when his head dropped - it was supposed to make him spill his heart out, not unconscious.

"Point me to your room so you can lay down." I instructed him and he just lazily lifted his hand pointing towards an open door in the far corner. I started leading us towards it and sighed when I saw the ceiling to floor window. Lucas wrapped his arms around me from behind before falling onto the bed, cuddling into me.

"Hey, are you okay? Should I leave?" I asked furrowing my brows.

"No, stay with me. You're warm and soft." He said, his voice muffled by my hair. I almost growled in frustration. The man loved cuddles definitely but I needed to get the information out of him before he fell asleep. I reached into my purse and pressed record on the recorder in pen form.

"So...Lucas..."

Thirty minutes later and I had everything I needed to know, plus more. I don't know what magic that powder contained but Lucas answered every question without hesitation or suspicion. He just continued cuddling into my back and sighing in content.

Lucas was singing like a canary about his job, how he had an ex-wife who cleaned out his bank accounts, to one of his bosses he was planning to murder so that he could take over, to the newest business transactions regarding the large amount of coke being shipped in and the location.

Everything.

"Speaking of coke." He slurred before pushing himself up. I turned on my side, watching him open the pendant around his chain and holding it out to me. My eyes widened when I saw the bright white powder in the centre. I should've fucking known.

"Have some." Lucas urged bringing his body closer to me, still holding the pendant vertically so it wouldn't spill out. I shook my head no and his face dropped, a look of anger replacing his previous playful expression. My heart sank.

"I said, have some." He growled at me before grabbing the back of my head trying to push me down.

Lucas was still weak and his strength seemed to have vanish along with his balance so I had no trouble escaping his hold and standing up. I needed to leave. I picked up my purse that had fallen and looked up, catching Lucas holding one nostril closed and taking a deep sniff of the white powder.

I hurriedly turned around. I knew what cocaine did and I needed to get out of there before he regained his power. My heels clinked on the tiles as I rushed through the large loft and just as I was about to reach the elevator, a hand wrapped around my arm.

"Where are you going? I feel better." It had only been a few seconds but I could already tell the difference in his voice. I whirled around. Through the dark brown tint of his glassy eyes I could see how massive his pupils were.

"We still need to fuck, remember?" Lucas snapped, the grip on my arm tightening painfully. I wanted to hit him so fucking hard in the face but I didn't want him also questioning the bruise the next day, wondering where it came from.

Yurik said Lucas wouldn't remember a thing or be sceptical about the lady he had met the previous night and I wanted to keep it that way.

"Give me your number. I'll call you." I said smiling trying to convince him. He shook his head, not buying it.

"No. Now." He sneered before grabbing a hold of my hair so hard I could feel the prickling pain of the strands being pulled.

I grit my teeth and reached my hand down to his crotch. I grabbed his balls through the thin material of his pants so hard I felt the tender flesh squeezing in my palm.

"Let go of my fucking hair before I rip your balls off." I snapped putting all my strength into the squeeze. Lucas released my hair and let out a blood curling scream. He dropped to his knees, clutching his groin and coughing. He fell onto all fours before gagging with nothing coming out. I watched in disgust as he pathetically tried to stand up.

I put my heel on his shoulder and kicked him down again.

"You bitch." He hissed rolling onto his back. The effects of the cocaine plus the drug Dominic had given seemed to be fighting a war with Lucas as his eyes rolled into his head. He let out one strangled groan before falling limp. I froze - is he dead?

I bent down and pressed two fingers against his neck. I sighed in relief when I felt that he was still very much alive, just unconscious.

I couldn't leave him on the floor, so with much difficulty I managed to drag him all the way to his bed and undress him. The man weighed a fucking ton and by the time I was done I was breathing heavily and my throat was parched.

For good measure I gave him one last smack on the face for all the trouble.

I blew a kiss at his men and they grinned, probably thinking that I had just fucked the shit out their boss. Of course I had intentionally ruffled my hair and messed up my eye make up to give that idea. When I was out of the club, I breathed out a sigh of relief and headed to the Mercedes.

I couldn't wait to get out of there.

Once I was inside the car I dropped my forehead onto the steering wheel, taking deep staggering breaths in as an attempt to calm myself. That was way more difficult than I had expected and I needed to shower...urgently. I stopped the recording on the pen.

I switched the car on, putting it in reverse and rushing out of the parking space. My destination was the mansion and after a few minutes of driving, a familiar van was trailing behind me and I smiled at the rear view mirror.

When I pulled up to the large house, the gates slid open allowing me in. I parked and stepped out, instantly feeling more relaxed than I did a few minutes ago as Yurik, Dominic and a few unknown faces stepped out of the van.

Yurik grinned before rushing over and giving me a rib-crushing bear hug. I squealed when he spun me around before setting me down and inspecting my body for any injuries.

"You okay?" He asked concerned and I nodded looking over his shoulder at the man who was reluctant about the situation from the very beginning.

My face fell when Dominic walked right past me, ignoring my existence completely.

CHAPTER 12

"What's wrong with him?" I asked Yurik while rummaging through my bag for the pen. Dominic didn't even look at me but I could clearly see that he was unpleased. He disappeared into the large house, not before yelling out orders in Russian with a scowl on his face. He looked beyond upset and I frowned watching how his men scattered out of his way. I felt bad I found him so fucking hot when he was angry.

"Do you have any idea how many times I had to stop him from shooting Lucas? He's mad at himself for putting you in that position. He can't bare the thought of you getting hurt." Yurik explained as I handed the tiny object to him. Mad at himself but taking it out on me? Zero sense.

"But he didn't put me in any position. I allowed it and I'm perfectly fine." I uttered in confusion.

"You did fucking amazing, sweetheart. You were almost...too good." Yurik said narrowing his eyes at me and I gave him an unamused look. If I was so good then why was his brother acting like I fucked up?

"It's not my place to explain this to you so go talk to him." Yurik muttered before giving my shoulder a slight nudge with his own. I shook my head.

"No. Where's my car? I need to go home and shower that man off of me." I said determined to just head home and be in my own space, alone. We could talk some other time.

"Your car is in that garage," he pointed to the triple door garage. "and your key is in Domo's office."

"Fine, I'll just take-" before I could finish the sentence Yurik snatched the Mercedes' immobiliser out of my hand and hurried away. I let out an exasperated groan watching his uncaring retreating form.

That fucker.

I straightened my shoulders and walked into the partially empty mansion, immediately swamped by the scent of disinfectant. It smelled like a hospital and I couldn't help but scrunch my nose. I walked to his office situated down a hall and at the very end. Sighing, I knocked on the slightly ajar door but made no move to enter.

"Yeah?" His voice reached my ears and I pushed the door, barely peeking through. Dominic was standing by a built in steel door safe collecting cash. I had a view of his side profile as he counted the money and I stepped in fully.

"I need my keys, please."

His head snapped up to me and if I wasn't a mistaken, another flicker of anger flashed through his eyes. "They're in that drawer but you can't go home."

I crossed my arms. "And why the fuck not?"

"Because you're coming home with me."

I looked at him incredulously. "You have to ask. Stop acting like an alpha male, we're not in the bedroom." I snapped scowling at him. Dominic shut the door of the safe with an unnecessary force and clenched his jaw. That sort of behaviour was only acceptable when he was fucking me, not right now.

"I just..." He muttered through gritted teeth, not finishing his sentence.

"What? You just what?" I asked throwing my hands in the air. "You're acting like an overgrown child." I walked over to his desk and opened the drawers, looking for my fucking car key so that I could leave. I had no idea what his problem was.

"Where is it?" I questioned still looking through the papers and pointless items, not finding it. I looked at Dominic and he was standing there watching me carefully. I walked up to him until we were only an inch apart.

"Where is it?" I asked again, this time my voice was angrier than before.

"Dominic!" I almost stomped my foot in annoyance when he didn't answer me and just continued looking at me with that unreadable expression.

He grabbed my fists that were about to push his chest and next thing I knew I was being pulled in for a tight embrace. My body stilled in confusion as he wrapped his arms around my shoulders. What the fuck is going on?

"I'm sorry for acting like an asshole." He whispered leaning his chin on the top of my head. I didn't respond.

"There was a moment when I couldn't see you and Lucas and it scared me so much, angel." Dominic said softly and I physically felt his body relax against mine. I sighed dropping my forehead against his chest and the tension escaped my muscles. He was just worried about me.

"I'm fine, I promise." I assured him circling my arms around his waist. I relished in the feeling of being within arms that made me feel contented, instead of the unnerving feeling Lucas gave me. Dominic's familiar scent was comforting at best and I held on tighter, as if I wanted him to climb inside me.

"I know that now but...never mind. I'm so proud of you and my apologies for ignoring you outside but if I looked you, I knew I would have tackled you to the ground." He said and I laughed shaking my head. I would never understand how men worked and I could tell that Dominic was starting to care more than what we both intended.

"I wouldn't mind being tackled by you." I said, my voice soft and his body shook with a slight laughter. A tackle from Dominic would probably break all my bones.

In that moment I allowed myself a sliver of vulnerability.

"You're forgiven but if you ignore me again, I'll strangle you." I threatened, my voice muffled by the thin material of his shirt as I squeezed tighter. I could feel the guns on his suspenders digging into my stomach.

"I'll probably like that." Dominic mumbled and gave me one last bone-crushing squeeze before letting go. He gently grabbed my wrist inspecting the dark blue lines already forming from where Lucas had grabbed me. His eyes darkened.

"Piece of shit." He muttered.

I chuckled and shrugged. "Well, I did kind of drug the guy."

Dominic gazed at me and I could still see the slight worry behind his eyes. "That's true. You did good." He reached to his desk and grabbed a large stack of cash wrapped in a black rubber band. He opened my purse and dropped the money inside. My eyes widened at the size of it.

"That looks like more than five thousand." I mumbled and closed my purse just in case he changed his mind.

"Don't tell anyone." He said with a slight cock of his eyebrow and a small smile. After that brief hug we shared, he looked ten times more relaxed but there was still a slight fire blazing in his eyes and I couldn't quite understand it yet.

"When are we going? I need to shower, like right now." I stated rubbing my arms and goosebumps arose on my skin as I shivered slightly. Dominic noticed this and shrugged his jacket off to drape over my shoulders. Warmth immediately invaded me and I gave him a thankful smile.

"We?" He asked in confusion.

"We're going to your place, right?" I asked imitating his confused face. He smirked before pulling my key out of his pocket. Of course he had it in the entire time and I messed up his once neatly packed drawers for nothing.

"I'm driving though." Dominic said dangling my key in front of his face.

"My car is manual." I told him, scared that he'll fuck up my motor by not knowing how to drive stick.

"Okay, and?" He rolled his eyes and started leading us out of the office.

"Your place is beautiful." I complimented as we entered his home. It wasn't what I expected at all. It was located in the forest, away from civilisation and surrounded by greenery. It was secluded and the air was crispy, a breath of fresh air from the usual city pollution. A heavy layer of fog hovered over the cobblestone driveway leading towards the one-story house.

Dominic had parked my car next to his own. It was fun seeing the large man driving my small Mini Cooper but it didn't seem to faze him at all.

"Thank you." He said before walking behind me and sliding the jacket down my arms.

"You live alone?" I asked turning around to face him. We were in his living room. It was minimal, accents of white and grey. I would have pegged him for a dark themed man but his house was, in a way, very homey and relaxing but also modern.

He shook his head. "Yurik lives here too but he's majority of the time at the compound, or wherever. I don't really know."

I walked up to a glass door cabinet, filled with medals, certificates and everything academic. "Woah, is this all yours?" I asked bending down to inspect them further.

"This might come off as a surprise but most of them, yes. The others belong to Yurik." He replied and I saw his reflection on the glass as he slowly walked up behind me. I nodded my head, who would've known...

I squinted my eyes to read some of them and my mouth dropped. It ranged from high school, all the way to university.

Dominic Romanov. Top of the class in Physics, Mathematics.

Dominic Romanov. Top of the class in Latin.

Dominic Romanov. Gold medal, Horizontal Bar. Gymnastics.

"What the fuck..." I mumbled. "You're a prodigy." I whispered skimming through the list of all his achievements, it went on and on and seemed never-ending. Yurik had a spot of his own accomplishments, medals and trophies for tennis.

I wanted to ask questions but I bit my lip to stop myself.

Dominic wrapped his arms around me from behind and rested his chin on my shoulder. "I can see you're dying of curiosity. Don't be afraid to ask." He said gently and moved my hair to one side of my neck.

"Why did you stop?" I asked and pressed my back further into his chest. His lips gentle grazed the skin and my eyes fluttered closed at the contact.

"My father wanted me to take over the family business. My life basically got put on hold." Was his blunt response and I frowned. That's not fair.

"You didn't have a choice?"

"No."

"That sucks."

"I know."

I turned around in his hold. "Where's your dad now?"

"He's travelling the world with my mother. Somewhere in East Asia, probably Japan but I can't be too sure." He responded and stroked my cheek with the back of his hand. I cleared my throat and took a step away. Dominic was making my heart tremble with just a simple touch and I needed it to stop.

"Enough about me. What about you...where are your parents?" He asked genuinely interested and I pursed my lips looking away from him. I sighed, it would make no difference if he knew or not.

"My mother lives with my grandma about an hour away, she takes care of her. My father...he's in prison for...wait, I should rather say what is he not in prison for." I stated sarcastically with a small shrug. My dad was a...mess, to say the least.

"That bad, huh?" He said and I nodded. Just speaking about it angered me to the point of no return because he always promised me he wouldn't get caught and that he knew what he was doing. He promised he wouldn't leave his 'babygirl.'

"Organized crime is my life and I should probably be in-" I cut him off right there.

"I swear if you go to prison too, I'll be very mad at you." I said sternly and narrowed my eyes at him. He chuckled before pulling me towards him by the waist. Very affectionate man.

"Right, I wouldn't want you to be mad at me." He said, his dark brown eyes twinkling with amusement. I had a feeling Dominic probably owned the prison.

"If I get locked up for what I did tonight, will you bomb me out?" I asked playfully and his smile widened, the deep dimple penetrating his cheek. My question seemed to humour him.

"Without another thought, angel."

My face turned warm at his answer and Dominic took a step back to observe me with a curious expression.

"Wait, you're blushing because I said I'd bomb you out of jail? Is that what you're into?" He laughed and I ducked my head. What the fuck is wrong with me?

"No!" I defended.

"So," he tilted my chin up with the tip of his fingers and bent down eyelevel. "If I said I'll kill any motherfucker who tries to hurt you, what then?" Dominic tilted his head to the side and bit his lip, his gaze engrossed on my mouth. I wanted to jump his bones right there.

"Stop..." I mumbled pushing him away but he held his ground. "You shouldn't care so much."

"If I said, I'll kill any man who tries to touch you. What then?" Dominic was looking at me intensely and I swallowed hard letting my hands drop to my sides.

"I'll tell you that I'm strong enough to take care of myself." I breathed out.

"And I'll tell you that I don't doubt that at all." He whispered and I felt his breath fan my face ever so gently. My insides were turning to mush.

"You can't say stuff like that because I'll believe you." My voice cracked and I don't know why. There was something about the way that Dominic was looking at me that made my heart ache. He looked at me as if he sincerely meant every single word.

"Believe me then, baby." He whispered.

Fuck.

"Because I mean it. You have my protection for life, whether you like it or not." He continued and a chills flowed through me. My abandonment issues were resurfacing and even at the age of twenty-two, it still felt the same as when I was a thirteen year old girl crying because I felt so alone in the world.

"No, stop. You don't mean that. Uh-uh, I don't want to hear it." I emphasised when I saw his mouth opening to defend himself.

"Can I use your shower?" I asked cutting off that conversation right there while rubbing my hands along my arms. My skin was starting to feel itchy from the night. Dominic sighed.

"Sure, use the one in my room. Down that hall and the last door on your right." He pointed towards it and I offered him a smile. Please join me.

He didn't move and I rolled my eyes before making my way to the direction of his room. It was nice, like the rest of his house and I beamed in awe. The bathroom, however, was by far the nicest and biggest bathroom I've ever seen. His shower was square shaped, big enough for at least five bodies and with a flat head in the centre.

"I'll leave clothes on the bed." Dominic yelled out and I closed the door to his en-suite. I unstrapped my heels, peeled off my skin tight dress and eventually my underwear. I sighed in relief, already feeling a million times better. I noticed a mouth wash at the basin and I quickly rinsed my mouth out with it.

Once I was in the shower, the hot water released all the stiffness in my muscles and I groaned in pleasure watching the droplets fall down my naked body. Flashbacks of when Dominic and I showered together at my apartment came to surface and I clenched my eyes shut. My body was tingling, my mind a hazy mess.

The glass door slid open.

Lips landed on my shoulder.

I felt his naked body press against mine and I inhaled deeply. His tattooed hand reached around me and onto my stomach, the other covered one of my breasts, softly moulding it. I hated to admit how grateful I was that he joined me.

"No." I said quietly and instantly his hands left me.

"I'm sorry." He apologised but I spun around grabbing his hand and stopping him from leaving. Not wasting a second, I dropped to my knees and filled my mouth up with him. A startled gasp erupted from his throat and his body went rigid.

I wanted to suck his dick for the longest time. I wanted him to feel good. I wanted him to ruin me.

"Oh, fuck." He hissed and the water got switched off allowing me to hear his shallow breaths clearly.

He wasn't fully hard yet. It wasn't difficult to place him inside of my throat. However, when blood started pumping to his dick, he grew inside of me and my eyes widened as my throat muscles got forcefully expanded.

I pulled out, hallowing my cheeks in the process to provide him the best pleasure that I could. I looked up at him through watery eyes. Dominic eyes were lust-filled, low and dark. He leaned both hands against the wall of the shower and looked at me as if he was in pain. My eyebrows got pulled together, my mood instantly dampening.

"What's wrong? Do you want me to stop?" I asked laying my palms on his thighs.

"No, don't stop. Nothing's wrong." Dominic's voice was husky, a deep baritone as he shook his head. I eyed him for a few moments.

"You're holding back, aren't you?" I asked and his face faltered slightly.

"Yes." He croaked and closed his eyes.

"Well, don't." I insisted and pulled his tip into my mouth again, swirling my tongue around and tasting his pre-cum. I sucked hard, enjoying the feeling of his bare skin against me. I grazed my teeth very gently and teasingly over the length and he grunted in response, his left leg shook slightly.

"Fine." He growled and gripped my wet hair, a pleasurable pain filling my senses and I hummed around him. I gave him consent to literally fuck my face up and Dominic didn't take it lightly, he did what I wanted him to.

Ruin me.

I relaxed my jaw, held onto his thighs for support and tried to breathe through my nose while bobbing my head in rhythmic pace. His moans were fuel to the fire, motivation for me to keep going. Anger was being released as his dick continued throbbing in my mouth and bruising my lips. My throat was going to be absolutely wrecked, I just knew it.

"Fuck, angel. You're amazing." He groaned. Dominic slipped his dick out, catching me off guard when he bent down and placed an open mouth kiss on my wet lips. I moaned, stretching my neck upwards and welcoming his tongue against my own. It was unexpected but exhilarating.

I was wet, and it wasn't because of the shower.

He bit my lip harshly before releasing himself from me and immediately his cock was shoved into my mouth again. This time, he held my head still and jerked his hips forward, long and deep strokes that had my eyes rolling back into my head.

"Yes, baby. Take it all." Dominic whispered and I nodded my head probably looking stupid doing so but in that moment, I didn't care. Not one bit.

The tip of my nose reached his pelvis and I wrapped my hand around my own neck, feeling it bulging as he penetrated as deep as possible. I knew I had no gag reflex and I couldn't be more appreciative of that fact on that occasion.

Dominic held me there, not giving me room to breathe and when I tried taking air into my nostrils it got pinched closed by his fingertips. The near-death experience had my core throbbing, my skin chilling and deep lustful moan erupting from my throat. I fucking loved every fucking second of it.

I tapped his thigh when I felt close to passing out and he pulled out, a long string of saliva still attached from my mouth to his dick. I panted loudly, taking in big gulps of air.

"I don't like it when other men touch you." He grunted and pulled my head back by gripping my hair, forcing me to look up at him. I knew he was jealous but he tried so hard to hide it and he was finally letting go of that pent-up frustration.

I let him.

His jaw was clenched and a deep scowl on his forehead as he glared down at me. I gasped when he grabbed the base of his dick and rubbed the tip along my lips, bruising the already raw and swollen flesh.

I bent down and sucked his balls into my mouth, showing him that I enjoyed it just as much as he did because I truly was. He let out a small cry and his knees buckled before he caught himself.

"Such a good girl. On your knees for me. I love it." He stroked my face, moving my wet hair away from my eyes. I already lost all my dignity a while ago, not that I cared much but being praised by Dominic made me lose all my senses entirely.

My hand continued stroking the long and thick shaft while I fondled his sac with my tongue and eventually I let go before placing him inside me again again. His movements were becoming sloppy and I knew he was close when he throbbed even harder.

With a moan that sounded like heaven, he released himself into my mouth and I swallowed every last drop like the good girl that I was.

Dominic held out a hand to me and helped me off my knees. I grinned at him despite my aching jaw and he laughed placing a kiss on my lips. He pulled away.

His fist collided softly against mine.

CHAPTER 13

DOMINIC

I didn't expect to wake up alone.

To say I was disappointed would be an understatement. I wanted to roll over to my side and slide into her warm pussy but the empty space besides me diminished that thought instantly.

For a second I was hoping that she had gotten up to use the bathroom or anything of the sorts, but the house was dead quiet and the sheets felt cold. I was more annoyed than upset and I breathed out exasperatedly letting my face fall back onto the pillow. Of course she would leave. I don't know why I was surprised.

I glanced at the clock on my bedside table, 9:15am. There was a small note resting on the black machine and I shot up from the mattress to quickly grab it.

You are the shittiest sleeper ever. Your side is your side for a reason, Dominic. Stay on it. I'm kidding, I don't mind. I just got shit to do but come over whenever you want and I'll give you a fat kiss to make up for it.

The smile that formed on my tired face was fucking embarrassing and my dick twitched against my thigh. I looked down at my naked body and all I could think of was Caitlin's beautiful eyes as she sucked the life out of me. Literally.

I had to remember to let her know how ugly her handwriting is.

With a loud yawn, I rubbed my eyes with both fists. I wasn't an early riser, quite the opposite but that specific morning I felt a little bit more hyper and a certain brunette was the sole reason. I got out of bed, neatly made it up and proceeded to get ready for the day.

Yurik didn't come home, as usual.

An hour later I was stepping out of my front door ready to face the dozen of responsibilities that lied ahead of me.

Just as I opened the door, Natalia was standing there with a flirtatious smirk. She wore a trench coat, hiding what I knew was underneath. Her light honey brown hair framed her sharp features and I could see her blue eyes already mentally fucking me. I crossed my arms and looked at her expectantly.

"What? No morning kiss?" She asked, pouting her pink lips and I sighed leaning forward.

"Get the fuck off my property." I whispered in her face, not in the mood for her. She gasped, taken aback by my bluntness. She shouldn't be. I had ended things with her a while ago, way before I met Caitlin but there she was, standing in front of me with the strap from her red bra peeking through the coat.

"What's wrong with you, Nick? You love morning sex." She whined and placed her palms on my chest. I frowned at the awful nickname. Suddenly, Domo didn't seem that bad.

"Nothing is wrong and don't call me that." I pushed past her and closed the door behind me, locking it. I felt her hands on my shoulders and I grit my teeth spinning around to push it away from me. Natalia was a small woman but her confidence was through the charts, it was probably why I liked her in the first place but right now it was just annoying.

"Stop it." I snapped.

"You're hot when you're mad. Why don't you take all that anger out on my pussy?" She smirked and reached down to grab my dick but I gripped her wrist just as her fingers grazed my zipper. Who the fuck does this woman think she is?

"You're testing my patience, Natalia. Maybe I should take my anger out on this wrist of yours?" I asked lowly watching her grimacing face. Whimpers left her parted lips as she tried escaping my vice grip hold.

"You're hurting me!" She gasped.

"And you're irritating me. Don't touch me again." I said throwing her hand away from me. Natalia scowled rubbing her aching wrist, a red mark already beginning to form. I didn't want to hurt her but she needed to get a hint and leave me alone. I walked past her and headed to the driveway where my Audi was parked.

"I took a taxi all the way over here and this is how you're treating me." Her voice saddened but guilt failed to find its way to me. I ignored her and climbed into the driver's seat, shutting the door after me. As soon as I started the car, Natalia was entering the passenger's side and I looked at her disbelievingly. The sheer audacity.

"Get the fuck out." I was fed up. I pulled my gun out, pointing it at her head. She wasn't Caitlin - I wouldn't hesitate to shoot her in the fucking face if she continued to try me but I was worried about my car...the mess would be horrendous.

"Fine! All men are the fucking same!" She shouted hurrying out and I gave her a look when she tried to slam my door. She slowed it just in time before gently closing it. I sped away, not sparing her another glance.

It wasn't until later that night when I was finally parking in the lot outside of Caitlin's apartment. My duties kept me busy the entire day - everything ranging from interrogation to the planning of intercepting the location Lucas had given Caitlin.

I would love to believe my jealousy was irrational but just the thought of her touching any man besides me made me want set my claim on her.

A familiar man walked past me and I narrowed my eyes at him.

Why are so many people trying me today? Can I just fucking live?

I jumped out of the car and followed behind Blake. His hands were stuffed into his jeans pockets and he hadn't noticed me yet. He was about to. Just as he rounded the corner, I caught him off guard shoving him against the wall and pressing my forearm against his neck. His eyes widened before a look of recognition passed on his features.

Blake pulled his hands out of his pockets to push my arm away and something fell to the ground. I looked down and breathed out a humourless laugh. Condoms.

I was already in a fucked up mood and two seconds away from snapping his neck.

"Are you going to be a problem for me? It seems that you don't listen." I asked softly, not an ounce of emotion in my voice and the blatant fear in his eyes spoke volumes.

"Look. I like Caitlin, okay? You can't keep me away just be-cause-"

I punched him so hard that my knuckle cracked and his head snapped to the side. I gripped his collar and pushed him against the wall when his legs nearly caved in. Blood poured out of both nostrils, staining his lips and chin. Blake mewled in pain. He had a deep gash on his nose where my ring had cut him. Good.

"Listen to me and understand. Don't think I forgot about that little threat you made. Wanting to get her all alone?" I repeated his words and shoved him against the wall so hard crumbles of red brick fell to the floor.

"You weren't supposed to hear that! I didn't even mean anything by it!" He pleaded and I looked at him in disbelief. He was more stupid than I initially thought.

"I don't give a fuck. If I see you around here again or anywhere around Caitlin, I will kill you. Stay the fuck away." I sneered, completely meaning every single word. Blake adams apple bobbed up and down as he gulped before he hastily nodded.

"I wasn't going to do anything. I-"

"I don't care. Leave." I stepped back and he quickly ran in the opposite direction, not before picking up the condoms he had dropped. I shook my head and pulled my phone out - going straight to Yurik's contact.

He answered on the very first ring.

"Blake needs your attention. You keen?" I asked leaning against the wall and shoving my hand into my pants pocket keeping my eye on Blake's retreating figure. I wasn't going to take any chances.

"I've been waiting, Domo." He laughed and I smirked. Was I overreacting? Probably. Did I care? Absolutely not.

The tantalising pull I felt towards Caitlin made me want to protect her with my life, keep her away from any harm and make sure she was always okay. I'll be dammed if I allowed a bitch boy to get in the way of that.

"I knew I could count on you. Make sure he fully understands." I said before hanging up. Yurik had a soft spot for Caitlin too - I don't know why - it was almost concerning but I relished in the fact that he would care for her if I was not around.

I sighed and walked up the stairs into the lobby. My day was rough, and I needed a cuddle. Drastically.

The amount of times I've been to her apartment allowed me to completely memorise the intricate way to her doorstep so within two minutes I was knocking on the brown wood.

The door opened and my heart utterly sank upon taking in her state.

Her eyes were bloodshot, as if she had been crying and she was dressed in clothes that were way too big for her. I closed the door behind me and instantly Caitlin walked into my hold, still clutching what seems to be a hot water bottle in her arms. She pressed her cheek against my chest and I wrapped my arms around her. A sigh of content emerged from her lungs.

Just like that every fraction of stress from the day vanished within a millisecond.

"Thank you for coming." She mumbled and I just barely heard her.

"Angel...what's wrong?" I asked although I already had an idea.

"Blood. Pain." She stated, her voice muffled by my shirt. I could feel the warmth of the bottle against my stomach.

"Do you need anything?" I asked softly stroking her hair and leaning back to look at her. A weird feeling formed in my gut as she clenched her eyes shut, grimacing in pain and I felt her body tense. My face softened.

"Pizza."

"I'll order some pizza, okay? Anything else?" I asked, already knowing I would do anything and everything for her.

"Chocolate."

"Of course. Anything else?"

"You."

I couldn't help but smile as she picked her head from my chest to gaze up at me, trying to subtly pout her lips indicating she wanted a kiss. I bent down and placed a soft kiss on her lips. It was gentle but the fireworks erupting behind my eyes were not.

"Is this the fat kiss you were talking about?" I asked against her mouth before moving my lips with hers. I felt her nod and a small smile stretching across her face before she stood on the tip of her toes to deepen the kiss.

This was another side to Caitlin. A softer, more vulnerably side that I had finally gotten the privilege of witnessing. I hated that she was in pain but I loved that she was seeking comfort from me. As fucked up as that sounds.

"You have me, angel." I whispered before pulling away. "I'm going to make a call." As soon as I backed away from her she shook her head and stepped with me. I bit my lip to stop myself from smiling like an idiot. She was so fucking cute.

With Caitlin still in my arms I picked my phone from my pocket and called Kuzma. On the call, I asked for everything she wanted, also added some extra goodies. A man could never be too sure.

"It's on its way." I informed her. "Let's go sit down." I wrapped an arm around her shoulders and guided us towards the couch. When we sat down, she was cuddling into my side again with her head on my chest and an arm around my stomach, the hot water bottle between us.

It was kind of surprising, Caitlin was usually the one backing away when we got too intimate - besides fucking - but at that moment, she held me as she was scared I'd disappear. I would be lying if I said it wasn't one of the best feelings in the world.

"Smoke with me? It helps." She asked softly after a few minutes of silence. I nodded and she climbed off me, removing all the warmth that I wanted back immediately. I watched as she picked up the blunt from the glass table and a light blue bic.

45 minutes later

"Caitlin! Sshh!" I whisper yelled staring wide-eyed at her. She was laughing, tears pouring down her cheeks as she bit down on a slice of pizza. If she carried like that she was going to choke and my concern grew when she coughed.

"Shut the fuck up!" I hissed and she completely ignored me, cackling like a maniac.

"You're going to die!" I shouted and tried to grab the slice but she dodged me. How the fuck is she so fast?

"Your dirty little secret is....Oh fuck, I can't breathe. I can't breathe. I can't breathe." She gasped and finally gave up on taking a bite of the pizza. She threw it down in the box and slapped her thigh, nearly screeching with laughter.

She has the prettiest smile.

"Don't judge me." I scowled at her. She was now laughing so hard with no noise except the odd wheeze and hiccup.

My jaw dropped and I picked up a jelly bean to throw at her head.

"Don't fucking laugh at me!" I snapped. I winced when the jelly bean hit her straight in the forehead and her eyes went crooked. I didn't mean to actually hit her and she didn't know that because her face turned into a sharp glare and she lunged at me full force. My eyes grew in fear. She was so fucking scary.

"You bastard!" She shouted and her tiny fists went to grip my hair, tugging and pulling at it.

"Okay. Okay. Okay." I grabbed her wrists and flipped us over so her back was against the couch. I got off her and walked backwards but I tripped over my shoe and fell straight back on my ass.

"Ow." I whined rubbing my tailbone. That hurt like a bitch.

"Good. I hope it's broken." Caitlin declared and picked up a cushion to throw at my head. I didn't have time to dodge it before it smashed straight into my face and slid down onto my lap. My eyes turned into slits as I frowned at her.

"I can't stand you, I swear to God. I should never have told you. It's not even that big of a deal." I said and stood up, dusting my pants off.

I was a mess - I don't know what the fuck type of weed that was but I felt like I was in the best but worst mood ever. My black shirt was completely unbuttoned and untucked and I don't know when that happened.

"It's really not a big deal. We all have our kinks. Yours just happen to be cartoon porn." She shrugged.

I gasped at the disrespect. "It's called hentai, you uncultivated woman."

"Uncultivated?" She mocked with feign shock. "Oh, I know big words because I'm a big mafia man who watches cartoon porn." She deepened her voice to imitate me and my jaw went slack. The fucking nerve!

"Hentai!" I corrected her.

I slumped down on the couch besides her. I placed my finger on her lips when she opened her mouth to speak. "No. Let's play the silent game."

She opened her mouth and bit my finger. Hard. My face turned into pure horror when she didn't let go.

"Stop! What the fuck is wrong with you!" I yelled and tried to pull it out but she just clamped down harder. Pain radiated through my whole hand.

"Say sorry." She mumbled around my finger. Sorry for what?!

"Okay. Okay. I'm sorry." I breathed out and sighed in relief when she finally released me.

As much as it didn't seem like it, I was having the best night.

"I'm too high for this." I groaned rubbing my hand over my face. My mouth felt dry, my lungs felt weird and my stomach felt hallow despite already stuffing myself full.

"Don't worry," she laughed. "We're almost out of the first phase."

"What's the next phase?" I asked.

She grinned. "You'll see."

Ten minutes later.

"Angel, please hold me." I begged and crawled on top of her.

She was laying on the couch on her back. I laid besides her but rested my cheek against her soft breasts and one leg over both of hers. I sighed when she wrapped her arms around me. Felt like home.

"Oh, this feels good." I groaned and shifted to get more comfortable. The space was tight but we made it work.

"I love this so much." She whispered and ran her fingers through my hair. I closed my eyes as my body relaxed. I could stay there forever, breathing in her comforting scent and hearing her heartbeat.

"You know one of my secrets. It's only fair that I know one of yours." I said softly trailing my fingertips down her arm.

She took a deep breath in. "Promise not to judge me? Nobody knows this."

"I promise."

"I lost my virginity to the captain of a cruise ship while on vacation with my mother. I was 17, he was 30." She muttered and my eyebrows shot up.

I bit my lip. "Like, on purpose?"

Caitlin laughed. "Yes, on purpose."

"I want to ask where..."

"In the cockpit, pressed against the window with a view of the beautiful ocean." She whispered still dragging her fingers through my hair.

"Your story is way more eventful than mine." I stated. It was true, mine was boring and anticlimactic.

"How did you lose yours?" She asked.

"My girlfriend at the time when I was 15, ten years ago. It was horrible. I didn't even cum." I complained with a scowl. I remember it being so awkward and rushed.

"Me neither." Caitlin chuckled.

"How are you feeling?" I asked and traced my fingertips over her stomach. I was in the best position.

"I feel way better than earlier. Thank you for everything. For the food, the snacks, for being here. Mostly the food though." She said and I smiled sleepily.

"You don't have to thank me." I mumbled and her fingers stilled before continuing.

"I do. It's a Saturday night and you're here with me." Caitlin responded and I bit my tongue to stop myself from saying anything. It didn't matter what day it was, what time it was, I'd always want to be in her company.

I was falling so fucking hard for her.

CHAPTER 14

C AITLIN

I woke up to the smell of cooking.

An aroma of something delicious wafted through my room's door and I sighed into the pillow. The cosiness I felt was short-lived when my stomach cramped so hard I was forced on my knees with my forehead still against the mattress. I breathed in deeply and squeezed my eyes closed.

I needed a shower so I willed myself out of bed. A soft smile formed on my lips when I saw the two painkillers with a glass of water on my dresser. Dominic...I needed to show him my appreciation when my period was finally over.

I downed the tablets, groaning in satisfaction when my dry throat got quenched. I could hear the sound of pots and pans clinking and as much as I wanted to join him, I needed a bathe.

One cold shower later and everything necessary, I was dressed in comfortable clothes and feeling way better than when I woke up. Entering the kitchen, my heart swelled as I witnessed Dominic standing by the stove, bare chested and his gaze fixated on the pan in front of him. His back muscles flexed as he moved the spatula.

I couldn't help but feel bad that he didn't leave like I did. Instead, he was making breakfast.

I padded towards where he stood and wrapped my arms around him, resting my palms against the top of his toned stomach.

My first instinct was to give him a kiss on the middle of his back and his body tensed slightly. I felt him place his hand on my forearm. He smelled like my body wash and shampoo and I grinned at the lavender scent radiating off him.

"How do I say 'good morning' in Russian?" I mumbled against his skin.

"Dobroye Utro." He said, his voice still husky and deep with sleep.

"Nevermind." I muttered and felt his chest shake with laughter. I let go of him and stepped back - we were acting like a couple but I realised in that moment, there was absolutely no harm in doing so. I had to stop allowing my issues to ruin a potentially good thing.

"Did you sleep well?" Dominic asked tilting his head to look at me. I smiled when I saw the sleep lines on his face and his slightly damp messy hair. Last night was rough, we were up until nearly 3am watching terrible low quality movies and laughing at the horrible acting. It was fun. At one point Dominic fell asleep on top of me and I was nearly squashed to death.

"Yes, thank you. You look like you did too."

"Oh, it was amazing. You have a really nice bed." He said and averted his attention to the pan in front of him. We didn't cuddle in bed, he understood that I needed my space because of my period and surprisingly he stuck to his side the whole night.

There was a moment when my cramps were so bad that it woke me up and I was groaning in pain. Dominic didn't say anything, instead he just quietly passed me a fresh hot water bottle and went back to sleep.

"I have to go, just thought I'd make you something to eat before I leave." He said while folding up the dish cloth, his eyes trained on me.

I pursed my lips. "You're not going to eat with me?"

"I wish I could..." Dominic picked up his phone and stared at it for a few seconds, his mood darkened the smallest bit but I immediately caught it.

"Okay," I tried to hide the disappointment I felt. "Thank you."

He smiled but the stress in his eyes was obvious. I had a feeling Dominic was carrying a lot more on his shoulders than he let on and I could only imagine the immense amount of pressure he was under.

He placed the cloth down and bent down to give me a hard, passionate kiss on the lips. My eyes momentarily widened at the force of it before my entire body relaxed and darkness succumbed my vision. The feel of his lips on mine and his hand on my hip drawing circles with his thumb was almost overwhelming but all too soon he let go.

While I was still trying to wrap my head around what just happened, Dominic was collecting his things.

"See you, angel." He gave me a kiss on the forehead and two seconds later he was out of my apartment. I frowned - what the fuck is going on?

"Hi, dad." I sat down on the cold metal chair, feeling slightly uncomfortable from the looks I was receiving - especially from the guards who were supposed to be protecting the visitors.

I was dressed in the baggiest clothes with a hood over my head but still predatory gazes seemed to find my way.

I hated coming to the prison, it almost always fucked up my mood and I left feeling more hallow than ever. It was a Sunday, however, so I thought I'd pay my father a visit after a very long time.

"Hi, baby girl. Micah didn't come with you?" He asked and looked around before he slumped in his seat in disappointment. I smiled to hide how hurt I was just by that simple question.

"No, he didn't. You know Micah can't stand seeing you in here." I said shaking my head. I could see he was trying to hide how unhappy he was that his son never visited him.

"You've always been the strongest one even though he's older." He smiled warmly, his almost faint Colombian accent coming through. I remember how angry he was when my mother went and changed our surnames to her maiden name, instead of Valencia.

If I just mentioned visiting him, she would throw a massive fit and practically forbid me from seeing my own dad. But there I was...

"You look...healthy." I said trying to brighten the mood. It was true, my father was in his mid-forties with a head full of black hair, not a grey in sight. His green eyes were dull and through the orange jump suit I could see he had gained a lot of muscle over the years of being locked up.

"How are you?" I asked twiddling my thumbs. Why the fuck was it so awkward? I wanted to get up, leave and never return.

"Don't worry about me. How are you? How's your mother? I haven't heard from her in ages." He asked leaning forward and placing his clasped hands on the table separating us. As soon as he did that a guard stepped forward and gave him a warning look.

My father scoffed and rolled his eyes, not giving a fuck. The guard backed up and raised his hands. I looked at them in confusion - I was aware he had connections in jail, but not to that extent.

"She's fine. Taking care of grandma and doing her embroidery. You know how much she loves that." I mumbled, stopping myself from mentioning that she was currently seeing someone else. He would go absolutely berserk at the fact.

My father smiled, his eyes lightening up at the memory. "I know, she's very talented. How's Micah? Is he still dating that boy, what's his name...Oh yes, Evan?" He asked looking at me genuinely interested.

"No they broke up a few months ago. Something about him going away for college." I replied shaking my head. Micah would absolutely have my head if he knew I was talking about him to our dad. I shut my mouth, stopping myself from saying anything else.

He nodded. "Mi hija is the only one who comes to see me. Thank you. You're keeping me sane." His voice saddened and I felt my heart clench. My father didn't know how much responsibility and pressure he was setting on me with just that sentence.

"Of course." I smiled.

We continued to speak for about 30 minutes. I kept my private life out of it despite him prying for information. I left with the same empty feeling I always did and stopped to get ice cream on my way home. I sat in my car, facing the pier and watched the rough waves while munching on something that I thought would make me feel better. It didn't.

After an hour drive, I was walking up to my apartment ready to have the most amazing nap.

My tracks faltered when I rounded the corner and saw two men standing in front of my door. Relief flooded through me when I realised it was Micah and Yurik, currently pushing each other around and making a heck of a noise.

"Shut up." I muttered and pushed past them sticking the key in the hole and opening my door. I didn't bother saying anything when the both of them entered my apartment and made themselves comfortable on my couch.

"Caitlin, what's your Wi-Fi password?" Yurik asked pulling his phone out and looking at me curiously. I gave him a bored look. Micah switched the tv on and started flicking through the channels. They really made themselves at home.

"Why are you here?" I asked opening my fridge and grabbing a slice of leftover pizza.

"What's your Wi-Fi password?" He asked again, ignoring my question.

"Just look on the router, dumbass." Micah said giving Yurik a small push. Yurik frowned before he launched himself at Micah and proceeded to place him in a chokehold. They were wrestling each other like little kids in the middle of my floor. I rolled my eyes and placed my pizza in the microwave.

"Tap." Yurik demanded tightening his hold around Micah's neck. I crossed my arms and leaned on the counter, observing them fighting with an unamused expression on my face.

"Never." Micah gasped, his face turning red as he struggled to get out of the restraint Yurik had him in. That's when I noticed how freshly bruised Yurik's knuckles were.

If the silver gun on his waistband wasn't a huge reminder about who he was, the red and purple marks on his hands certainly were. Despite being playful majority of the time I knew how dangerous he was. Just like his brother.

It was actually scary.

"Tap, bitch." Yurik snapped. They were now on the floor, Yurik was lying flat and Micah's back was pressed against his stomach. I swear if they broke any furniture...

"Never, bitch." Micah croaked, looking on the verge of passing out while grasping at Yurik's forearm in a desperate attempt to escape. I pulled my pizza out of the microwave and took a big bite shaking my head at the maniacs in my living room.

"Oh, really. How about now?" Yurik said before his grip tightened so hard that Micah's red face looked ready to burst. I smirked - that's amazing.

"No! I'll die before I tap, you stupid little - okay, okay I tap." Micah breathed out as he viciously hit Yurik's arm. He let go, grinning in victory while Micah held onto his neck panting heavily and letting out loud coughs.

I sighed and joined them on the couch when it was safe to do so. Yurik got up and went to my router in the far corner, he flipped it over and started putting the password in. Micah was still dying alongside me.

"You good?" I asked taking another bite and he glared at me. I stifled a laughter when he shifted the glare at Yurik's back, looking completely violated. I still wanted to know why the fuck they were here but I had to admit, they lightened my mood a bit.

"Thank you." Yurik said with a cheeky smirk on his face. "Do you have more of that? I'm starving." He asked and I nodded gesturing my head towards the kitchen. Micah turned his body towards me while Yurik was getting himself some food.

"Where do you come from? It's a Sunday." He asked gazing at me sceptically. My brother hardly spoke to me and barges into my apartment with the nerve to question where I've been. I gave him a dirty look and switched my attention to the TV.

"Caitlin, where were you?" He asked more prominently and I let out a deep annoyed breath.

"I was visiting our father." I stated with a shrug. Micah's face softened and a small smile formed on his lips. I knew he missed him, he was just too stubborn.

"How is he?" He asked scooting closer to me.

"Why don't you go and find out or at least call him?" I responded finishing up my slice. Yurik plopped down next to me with a satisfied grin - he had also grabbed a can of coke.

Where is Dominic and why are these two acting so weird?

"I should. I miss that old man but it's just so hard." He said furrowing his brows slightly. My lips pressed into a tight line and refrained from telling him to stop being so scared. Micah will deal with it on his own time.

I turned to Yurik. "Are you going to tell me what you're doing here?"

"We missed you." Was his blatant response but I wasn't buying it.

"Sure. Where's your brother?"

"Working."

"What-"

"Stop with the questions, sweetheart." He interrupted giving me a pointed look, one that said I really needed to stop. The hint of playfulness he had still lingered in his eyes but I could tell that he was serious.

"Okay. I'm going to nap." I said before getting up from the couch. I put my plate in the sink and rolled my neck, my eyes feeling slightly heavy. I wasn't about to let Micah and Yurik ruin the planned sleep that I had. I was tired. With that I left them in my living room.

They better not fuck on my couch.

CHAPTER 15

CAITLIN

"Why did you send Yurik and Micah over to my place?" I asked Dominic over the phone once I was settled in my bed. I could still here them fighting about what to watch and I was on the brink of yelling at them to shut the fuck up. I needed my peace and quiet.

"What do you mean?" He faked confusion and I could immediately sense it.

"Dominic, come on. Don't lie to me." I said softly and rolled over to lay on my side. I put the call on speaker and let it rest next to my head on the pillow.

He sighed and I heard him shuffle around a bit. "How did you know?"

"Because my brother never comes to see me unless he needs something. So tell me, why?" I asked again, more firmly. Dominic should know better than to lie to me.

"Those idiots suck at making a girl feel better." He mumbled after a few moments. "I just thought you needed some company."

I didn't buy it. Not one bit.

"Okay, sweet. Now what's the real reason?" I asked keeping a neutral tone. Dominic didn't say anything and my bottom lip got pulled between my teeth at the nearly deafening silence. I wasn't mad at him - I just wanted to know why. All three men were obviously hiding something from me.

"I don't need a babysitter, Dominic." I stated putting my arm underneath my head to get more comfortable.

"Stop. Why the fuck are you so good at this?" He asked and I could just picture him pinching the bridge of his nose in annoyance and then raising his hand questioningly. "It's only for today, angel. I'm just making sure Blake won't try anything and I know you can take care of yourself but-"

"Wait, wait. What do you mean? What does Blake have to do with this?" I asked frowning. I was aware that he said something weird but I haven't seen him since he showed up to my door after Dominic and I had fucked.

"I caught him walking to your apartment last night. I told you that I won't take that threat lightly so-"

"Dominic. What did you do?" I asked sitting up, suddenly very more aware and alert. For all I knew, Blake could be laying in a ditch...or thrown into molten metal.

"Interrupt me one more time, angel. Please do it." His voice went an octave lower and I could hear the threat underneath. I stilled and kept quiet.

"That's what the fuck I thought." He scoffed and I smiled, letting him continue. Dominic was the only man I'd let getting away with talking to me like that. Partially because he was the finest man I've ever seen, and mainly because I knew how kind and soft he could be.

"Yurik spoke to him last night. I'm making sure he won't show up again but I doubt he will." He stated and I choked on my spit. I coughed, my eyes watering.

"He beat the fuck out of him, didn't he?" I asked quietly. My thoughts were reeling with every possible scenario.

"A little..." he said slowly and I sighed dropping my head on the pillow again. I clenched my eyes shut and pressed my palm against my forehead. Did Blake deserve that? He was always so nice to me -it was just when I broke things off with him then he started to act out of character but did he deserve to get his ass handed to him on a silver platter?

"Are you mad at me? I was just trying to make sure you're safe and I know you're a grown woman who's very much capable of doing it herself so don't even start that shit, okay? I already know but I told you that you have my protection for life." Whether I like it or not, I remembered.

Free protection? Who am I to deny such a pleasure?

"I'm not mad at you. Just don't lie to me ever again or you and I are going to have a huge problem." I warned him.

"What are you going to do? Spank me with those little hands that can barely wrap around my dick?" He laughed and I gasped. Dominic was making fun of me.

"I will do exactly that. Perhaps even pistol whip some sense into you." I muttered and drew the covers over me feeling the pain killers I took start to take effect as heaviness laid on my eyes.

"Alright but we're taking turns. I've been meaning to let off some steam on that pretty ass of yours." Dominic said and I let out a loud laugh almost startling myself. My cheeks turned bright red and even though he couldn't see me I hid my face in the pillow. There he goes again making me blush like a teenager.

"Aw, you're getting shy." He cooed when I didn't say anything and I groaned.

"Stop! Goodbye, Dominic." I said in finality and he chuckled.

"Goodbye, angel. Sleep tight."

"Wait, how do you know -" Before I could ask how he knew I was about to sleep, he hung up. I narrowed my eyes.

"Stop telling your brother what I'm doing!" I yelled out, hoping that Yurik would hear me and he did because I heard a faint 'Fine!' in the distance. I shook my head and pulled the duvet up to my chin.

One week later

"That stupid, perverted, disgusting, old piece of shit." I fumed exiting Mr. Luro's office. I hated this job so damn much - I, once again, interviewed a man in the position of CEO who apparently only thought with his dick.

'Touch me and I'll give you all the information you need, darling'

I wanted to gauge his eyes out with my bare fingers. I looked down at my palm - it was a bright red and slightly stinging from when I slapped him in the face. He laid his hand on my breast and my vision blurred into pure anger - I snapped.

When I arrived back at the headquarters after a brief drive, my blood was still boiling. All I wanted was for the interview to run smoothly with not a single bump in the road but of course the bald headed man who looked old enough to be my grandfather had other plans.

I knocked on the door trying to control my rage. I understood now why David, my boss, had told me to wear a skirt. Not that I listened because nobody tells me what the fuck to wear.

"Come in." David called out and I pushed the door open, already giving him the hardest glare I could muster. His eyes glanced down to my pants covered legs before meeting my own. I'm going to fucking kill him.

"Caitlin, how did it go?" He asked, looking slightly frightened. I stepped closer and leaned my fists against his desk in an attempt to stop myself from reaching over and slapping him silly.

"You sent me there knowing Mr. Luro is a fucking perv. You told me to 'wear a skirt' knowing what he would want from me. Did you think I was going to accept it? What the fuck is wrong with you?" I asked loudly.

David shot up from his seat and walked over to me, grabbing my arm. "Lower your fucking voice." He hissed softly and looked through the door for anyone who might hear.

"Don't touch me!" I ripped my arm out of his hold. I was pissed - so very pissed that I felt like I could hit something. Both men disgusted me. I was angry at David for condoning such behaviour and I was angry at Mr. Luro for just having the fucking audacity.

"That was a very important interview and you ruined it. Why didn't you just entertain him?" He asked bending down slightly. My mouth dropped - how dare he?

"Why would I do that, ever?" I asked coldly. I wanted to smash his head against a wall.

"That's what girls like you do, right?" He said in a condescending tone and reached around to grab my ass. He didn't get the chance. My hand had a mind of its own as it stretched out at the speed of lightning and hit him in the face. It was loud and left my palm stinging, again. I couldn't believe he had the nerve to try and fucking touch me.

In the span of one afternoon two men tried to lay their hands on me without consent.

David's head snapped to the side, a red hand print already form- ing on his pale cheek and his jaw clenched. I stood my ground, scowling at him. He slowly tilted his head back to gaze at me while holding his cheek. I could see the unmistakable anger blazing in his eyes as he took a daunting step closer to me.

"You're fired. Get the fuck out before I make you." He sneered and I scoffed at his attempt to be intimidating. Did this bitch think I was afraid of him?

"You are disgusting." I said blatantly and turned on my heel to leave. As soon as I exited the building and I was on the route towards my car, I picked my phone out of my purse and went straight to Dominic's contact.

Those rats deserved to lose absolutely everything. How many women have they sexually assaulted and ended up getting away with it? It seemed like a regular thing for them and the abuse stopped right there with me. I was going to make sure of it.

"Hi, angel. You done with the interview?" Dominic's deep voice floated through the phone and I squeezed it so hard fearing it might crack in my hand.

"David White from JournaCo and Andrew Luro, CEO of GamingHord. Both men tried to touch me inappropriately today." I stated getting into my car and throwing my bag onto the passenger seat. I closed the door and held the phone between my ear and shoulder as I stuck the key into the ignition.

I didn't give a fuck about what happened to either of them.

Dominic didn't ask anything before I heard him yelling out those names to someone in the background and giving orders that I couldn't quite understand. He didn't waste a second.

"Done. Are you okay?" He asked, voice lacing with concern and slight anger. I breathed out deeply, feeling myself relax as he spoke to me. I grabbed the phone and rested my head against the steering wheel trying to control my pounding heart.

"I'm okay." I muttered.

"Are you okay to drive?" Dominic asked and I could hear him trying to stay composed. In a way, it helped calm me down as he uttered his concern to me.

"I am now. Thank you." I said and looked out the window at the building I never wanted to step foot into again.

"I got you, angel." He said and a soft relieving smile formed on my lips.

Dominic got me.

I stepped into my apartment and instantly kicked my shoes off. My jacket was shrugged off next as I walked in the direction of the bathroom. All of my clothes were discarded along the way and I let it fall wherever, deciding to care about it some other time.

My period ended two days ago and I was sex deprived and affection deprived. I wanted Dominic to come over so I could fuck the shit out of him and release the built up tension.

I was naked by the time I reached the shower and I stepped inside, letting the water cascade down my back. I exhaled and inhaled deeply, leaning my palms against the tiled wall. The hot temperature of the water aided in me finding my serenity and by the time I was done washing myself and shaving everywhere, I felt like a whole new person.

The wonders of a shower.

I applied lotion to my body and enjoyed the distinctive scent of vanilla and cinnamon. Once I was completely satisfied, I wrapped a towel around me and walked to my room. A knock coming from my door halted my steps and I immediately knew who it was.

But just to be safe, when I reached the living room I peeped through the hole in the door and grinned when I saw it was Dominic - looking sideways down the hall. He had the most beautiful profile and he was painfully attractive.

I opened it, allowing him inside. He took a step forward and when his gaze snapped to me, he stopped and let his eyes travel down my towel cladded upper body until they landed on my bare legs. His jaw clenched and an unadulterated animalistic lust formed on his face when he licked his lower lip.

He shut the door behind him and locked it.

"It's getting take care of right now." Dominic was the first to break the silence with a husky voice and I nodded, knowing what he meant. Serves them right.

"You good? Do you need anything?" He asked stepping forward and his hand reached up to my cup my cheek. He was gentle - more so than usual and I frowned.

"Dominic. You are not about to treat me as if I'm fragile." I said sternly. In that moment, I didn't want to be treated like a porcelain doll. I wanted to be ruined - again. I wanted to be fucked so hard that even days after, I would feel a reminder about who was inside of me.

His grip tightened before his hand trailed to the back of my neck, pulling me towards him for a hug. It took me by surprise and I went stumbling into his hard chest with a startled breath. Dominic held me tightly and bent down to bury his face in my neck. I wrapped my arms around him and caught a whiff of his intoxicating scent.

"I'm so glad you're okay. Don't worry, they're going to pay for what they done. I missed you so much, angel." He mumbled against my skin and both hands reached down to grab my ass over the towel, squeezing it softly.

I hadn't seen him for days and I was aching for his touch. I wanted to take my anger out on him...in a good way.

"I missed you, more." My voice was slightly muffled by his shirt. It was a simple hug but I felt his bulge growing against my stomach and my tongue swept over my bottom lip. Fuck - I wanted him so badly.

I felt one hand leave my ass, caressing up until it landed right on the part where my towel was tucked in the corner above my left breast. He pulled away to look at me - looking for any sort of protest - but I kept quiet, silently willing him to continue. I felt my pulse start to quicken, my senses were overwhelmed and he was barely touching me.

Dominic had the ability to make me want him by just standing there. His dark brown eyes were glazed over in desire and I could see how much he wanted me too.

I wanted to be in control. I wanted to be the one to settle the pace. I wanted to be the one to fuck him while he just accepted it.

With one tug my towel went falling to the floor and my naked body was completely exposed to him. I was so ready.

CHAPTER 16

CAITLIN

"Oh, fuck!" I screamed when I was thrown onto the couch like a rag doll, landing on my back and bouncing a few times. As soon as I tried to get up, inked hands were pushing my shoulders back down and a glare was directed my way.

"Behave." He warned me. I obeyed.

Dominic was hovered over me, looking down at my naked body with a fiery hunger that made me nervous...but excited at the same time. The moment my towel dropped, his entire demeanour changed and thoughts of me being in control went flying out the window.

He started unbuttoning his shirt with quick, desperate movements and eventually he got so fed up that he tore it open, sending buttons flying everywhere. My eyes widened and my heart started pounding against my ribcage. I felt like I had to brace myself for the impact he was about to bestow on me.

I gulped when his shirt was discarded across the living room and his impressive abdomen was open to my view. Today, he wore a silver chain around his neck complimenting the silver watch on his wrist.

Dominic wasn't making eye contact, his gaze was fixated on my bare pussy as he licked his bottom lip. He looked at me as if he was the predator, and I was his prey. I was quite comfortable in my skin but the way his eyes scrutinised every inch of me made my blood pressure rise.

"Dominic-"

He bent down to kiss me, so hard that my head was pushed onto the back of the couch and a moan emerged from my throat. With one hand on my waist and his lips pressed against mine, I heard him start to remove his belt.

The sound of the leather getting pulled from within their loop restraints made my body jump. Dominic noticed and broke the kiss to look from me, to the belt in his hand with a curiously cocked eyebrow.

I swallowed hard staring at the black item with an uncanny lust. Generally, I wasn't a submissive person at all but when it came to fucking - I wanted to be hurt, grabbed and pounded until my legs shook.

Why did I want to be spanked until my ass was raw?

"Oh, you dirty little..." He murmured in realisation and paused, seeking any sort of objection to him finishing that sentence and when he didn't find any, he bent down eye level and whispered, "slut."

I breathed out, feeling a strange euphoric feeling wash over me. My hand reached down to my pussy, desperate and aching for any friction. Dominic grabbed my wrist hard, almost bruising the skin but successfully stopping me.

"No. You're not allowed to." He was stern with his words and I nodded even though my core was frantic for a form of release.

"Turn around, on your knees." He said softly, caressing my cheek with his knuckles. I knew what was coming - and I could sense he knew exactly how badly I wanted it.

I followed his instructions and got on my knees, still on the sofa. I leaned my forearms against the backrest and arched my back. Dominic took a deep breath in as my most intimate part got exposed to him. My body was nearly shivering with anticipation as I sat there, awaiting what he had to offer.

"Safe word." He didn't ask, he demanded.

"Red." I said the first thing that came to mind. I heard Dominic chuckle, a deep baritone noise that warmed my insides and made my lips tilt up slightly.

"Of course." He responded and rubbed his palm against my bare ass cheek, soothing the skin for what was coming. I sighed and dropped my head onto my forearms waiting for the blow to come and when it didn't, I looked back at him with a frown.

"Are you sure?" Dominic asked and me being the impatient little brat I was, I gave him a 'really?" look that he didn't appreciate at all.

"Why? Are you sca-" There wasn't a chance in hell that I would finish that sentence. Dominic's hand flew down onto my right cheek so hard that a yelp escaped my lips and I jumped forward. Hot pleasurable pain resonated through my skin and I groaned moving my hips. I wanted more.

"Chill with the fucking attitude, angel." He repeated the same words from the first time we fucked but this time, it held more power and I felt obligated to submit.

He slapped the cheek again, sending waves of rippling desire through every crevice of my body. My skin was tingling as a sheer layer of sweat began to form. Dominic was teasing me and I hated being teased.

"Good girl." He said and gave me a kiss on my lower back. The praise made my eyes squeeze close as I stopped myself from reaching down to pleasure myself. I was in agony but the ecstasy of being spanked overthrew it completely.

He soothed the warm skin with his fingertips and I whimpered at the sensitive sensation. My ass throbbed as blood rushed to it, turning the skin from its usual tan to an angry red.

More.

Dominic took a deep breath in and sighed out. It sounded like he was enjoying it just as much as I was and I stopped myself from turning back to look at him even though I badly wanted to. The creaking of the leather belt reached my ears and I found myself clamping my bottom lip between my teeth in eagerness.

"Touch yourself, angel." He gave me the go-ahead and I wasted no time in grasping at the opportunity. My middle finger and ring finger was shoved into my wet hole without another thought and my eyes rolled back in dreamy, overwhelming exhilaration.

I heard the whip through the air before I felt the impact on my skin.

"Shit!" I screamed out when the leather collided on my ass. It was ten time worse than his hand and I moaned out loud, moving my fingers in and out of me at a pace I struggled to keep up with. I circled my clit with my thumb and a teeth gritting feeling formed in the pit of my belly.

More.

The pure pleasure emitting from deep within my core and the pain coming from my exterior was overpowering in the best way possible. Dominic did it again, and again until all my senses were being overloaded and nothing existed besides me, him, and the leather in his hand.

By the time he was done, my ass was numb with pain and our heavy breaths filled the entire living room.

"You're taking it like a good girl, angel. So perfect, so beautiful. I cannot wait to fuck this pussy." He whispered breathlessly and kissed me right in the middle of my back. His compliments were the final straw. My toes curled and my fingers hit that spot inside me that activated the impending orgasm.

"Not yet." Dominic pushed my hand away and I whimpered at the sensation of being edged. Fuck - I needed my release and I needed it urgently. He brought my fingers up to his lips and sucked them clean.

"You taste good." He said before getting on his knees and shoving his face between my ass cheeks. His expert warm tongue entered my pussy and I groaned pushing my hips back. My skin was still aching and I was aware I would struggle to sit for days but in that moment, I did not care.

As soon as he started to swirl his tongue around, my mind was blown. My legs weakened and I clenched my eyes shut so tightly that when I opened them, my vision was nothing but a messy blur.

What the fuck happened to me being in control?

Within a minute of Dominic pleasuring me with his mouth, I came so fucking hard that my body convulsed and a white noise consumed my hearing. An unfamiliar moan came from my chest and I gasped when he started placing kisses along my back and eventually reaching my neck.

For a few seconds, I couldn't think straight.

I hadn't noticed Dominic sitting on the couch until my waist was grabbed and I was pulled to straddle him. He was naked, his erection was standing to full attention and I rolled my hips against the length of it. I wanted him. No, I needed him.

"Ride me, baby." He murmured softly and I put my hands on his shoulders, lifting myself up and sliding down his rock hard dick until I was filled to the brim. It stretched me out as if it was our first time and I couldn't help but let out a strangled gasp.

"Oh, God." I said looking down at our adjoined pelvises. Dominic grabbed my ass hard, squeezing it and moulding the flesh between his hands.

Without the separation of latex, we were skin on skin and I couldn't grasp how it managed to feel a million times better. It enhanced the sensation and the way Dominic's eyes rolled back was evidence that he felt it too.

"Fuck, you feel so good." Dominic croaked when I started to move my hips, gradually going faster and faster. I was in pure bliss as a result of the beautiful man beneath me allowing me to sink down on him and feel things I never knew was possible.

My legs were on either side of his waist and my arms were around his neck when I leaned down to kiss him hard, enjoying how soft his lips were. At that point, Dominic decided to crank it up a notch. He held the back of my thighs, holding me in place and started slamming upwards into me at a brutal continuous speed.

"Holy fucking sh-." I screamed out, my breath hitch with each syllable as the air left my lungs and I was rendered incapable of finishing the sentence. Dominic was relentless, thrusting into me until it felt like I was floating on a cloud of untainted pleasure with the inability to grip reality.

It was the best high ever.

Our parted lips were barely touching as our breath mingled but I couldn't find it in me to pull away. I was looking directly into those brown eyes as Dominic showed me exactly what he was capable of and also who the fuck he was.

"□□ □□□, □ □□□□□□ □□□." Dominic muttered and I frowned at the foreign language. I didn't care about what he said as I pulled his bottom lip between my teeth and eventually sucked the plump flesh into my mouth. [translation: you are mine, and only mine.]

Before I could comprehend what was happening, Dominic was standing up with him still inside me and my back was slammed onto the couch. My legs were pulled over his shoulders and I gasped grabbing my breasts when he started moving again.

"Angel, you feel amazing." Dominic whispered and pressed his nose against the crook of my neck. I circled my arms around him and enjoyed the cooling sensation his chain had to offer.

"I'm going to cum." I whimpered, feeling that build up start again. He wrapped a hand around my neck and squeezed the sides hard, no doubt leaving his mark.

"Don't you fucking dare." He snapped glaring down at me. My breath was temporarily restricted and it was only when I started to grasp at his hands when he loosened his grip but still kept it firmly in place.

"Please." I almost cringed at how desperate I sounded but I needed to fucking cum. Dominic was ruthless. He pulled out until just the tip was inside me before slamming back in so hard that both of us groaned out loud. He hissed through his teeth when I clenched around him, orgasming again for the second time.

He wasn't done.

Dominic grabbed my hair in his fist and pulled my head back, scowling at me unimpressed. "I thought I told you not to cum."

"I-I had to."

"I'm going to let it slide, just this once." He responded and continued pounding into me ruthlessly. I was over-stimulated to the max and I closed my eyes shut. The angle we were in allowed me to feel every single inch of him and he was so deep I nearly fucking cried.

After another few minutes, Dominic pulled out and came on my stomach.

He still wasn't done.

We fucked for over an hour. By the time he was finished, I was completely and utterly drained. Dominic had the stamina of a horse and the ability to cum three times in a row. We were both sweaty and exhausted, me more than him even though he did majority of the work.

He carried me to my bed and proceeded to wipe me clean with wet-wipes and tissue. I smiled tiredly, still trying to come down from the high of having the best orgasms in the world.

"That was nice." I whispered. My pussy was sore, my legs were shaky and my ass still stung.

"Nice? That's it?" He asked looking slightly offended and my eyes widened. If I didn't correct my mistake, Dominic was going to fuck me again until it was no longer considered just 'Nice.'

"No! I mean- it was perfect. You have good dick." I mumbled quickly and Dominic laughed at me shaking his head.

"I know you're tired, baby. Relax." He leaned down and kissed me on the forehead. A warm flutter formed in my chest, far from anything sexual and I smiled softly.

"Angel..." Dominic sounded slightly nervous as he grabbed my hand and brought my knuckles up to his lips. "I would like to take you on a date...if you allow me to."

Definitely.

I chuckled. "You are so cute when you're nervous. Of course, Dominic."

Dominic's eyes lit up and a wide grin formed on his lips. He pulled me in for a hug and nuzzled his neck into my shoulder.

"Thank you. I'm going to go make a call, okay?" He said and started to get up to leave my room. I sighed and dropped down onto the pillow, pressing my face into the soft material.

When he reached my door, he stopped as if remembering something and rushed back to me. He grabbed my wrist and brought my fist up to his with a stunning, dimply smile on his face that I couldn't help but return.

"Almost forgot." He said before turning around and leaving.

CHAPTER 17

C AITLIN

I might have regretted saying yes to the date.

Not because I was afraid of my feelings but because I didn't know what the fuck to wear. I was comfortable enough around Dominic to not care much about my appearance but that specific night I was nervous because I wanted to get it right.

I sighed in frustration and dragged a hand through my hair. Clothes were scattered all along my bed in a messy sprawl as I looked through them with the intention of finding the perfect dress. What type of date was it? A wine and dine or were we going for a casual meal? What sort of attire suited both occasions? Why am I overthinking?

"Fuck this." I picked my phone and dialled Dominic's number. I rested my hand on my hip and tapped my phone impatiently waiting for him to answer.

"Hi, angel." He greeted and an unfamiliar feeling of calmness washed over me.

"You are stressing me out, Dominic." I stated bluntly. Why was I so nervous? It was a date...with a man who fucked me so hard

I couldn't walk straight for a whole day. With a man who choked me so hard he left bruises on my skin.

With a man who was sweet and caring and always went out of his way to make sure I was okay.

"I'm not doing anything." He laughed.

"Tell me what I should wear." I demanded and sat down on my bed with a small huff. He was supposed to pick me up in about an hour and there I was still debating over what to wear.

"You look good in anything." Dominic said and I rolled my eyes. That was the issue!

"What are you wearing?" I asked him and fell down onto the mattress to look up at the ceiling. It wasn't my first time going on a date with someone so there was no reason for me to be acting like a teenager.

He chuckled. "Angel, stop. Wear something...I don't know...sexy and revealing."

"Wow that's a first." I stated in shock. Flashbacks of my conservative boyfriend in high school resurfaced and I shuddered at the memory.

"You wear whatever you feel good in and I'll be there to make sure no one lays a hand on you." He said as if it was the most obvious thing in the world and I sighed.

"Okay fine, I'll see you in an hour."

"An hour?" he asked and I heard a car door slam shut. "I'll be there in half an hour."

"What?! Bye!" I quickly put the call off and jumped from my bed. I dropped the towel and started looking through the many pieces of clothing.

My eyes landed on the deep red satin material that I never wore before and I instantly made my mind up. I decided not to ponder on it any longer as I picked up the dress.

"Please fit me. Please fit me." I chanted as I held the soft dress to my naked body.

Once I stepped into it and pulled it up my body, relief flooded through me. It fit perfectly. It was short, spaghetti strapped and tight around the hips. I smiled as I smoothed the material down with my palms deciding to keep my hair down tonight.

"Where are we going, angel?" I asked Dominic and he sent me a side glance while keeping one hand on the steering wheel. I noticed that he had gotten a haircut and I smiled admiring his handsome face.

Dominic's entire appearance screamed dominance and power, all the way from his expensive shoes to the tattoos on his neck and I couldn't help but notice how good we looked together.

"Don't call me that. I call you that." He responded with a slight scowl.

"What should I call you?" I asked curiously and leaned back into the seat but still kept my body angled in a way that I was facing him.

"Dominic." He stated bluntly and I gave him a bored look even though he wasn't looking at me.

"That's boring. I'm thinking babe? No wait, never mind. That sounds fratboy-ish." I muttered and then hummed in thought.

"Honey? Nope, sounds too marriage-ish. How about cutie?" I teased him and the frown on his face deepened in a very cute manner. If I wasn't mistaken, a slight blush formed on his cheeks as he stopped himself from smiling. I knew Dominic well enough to know that he was secretly a giant softie.

"Dominic is just fine." He deadpanned but I wasn't having it.

"How about...sir?" I asked softly.

Dominic's entire face dropped and the grip on the steering wheel tightened visibly. "I'm driving." He said keeping his eyes trained on the road ahead.

"Master?" I continued teasing him and I bit my lip to contain myself. Dominic's face was flushed red and he was avoiding looking at me. I decided to take it a step further and place my hand right above this crotch.

"I am driving." He repeated through gritted teeth but made no move to remove my hand. I slowly started massaging the growing bulge and his breath noticeably quickened. It was fun seeing him quiver because he always wanted to be in charge.

I was aware that Dominic could pull over at any time and possibly teach me some manners but I wanted to enjoy the little control I had while I could.

I leaned forward until my face was just inches away from his ear and whispered, "daddy?"

The car swerved to the side and I fell back onto my seat with a mischievous chuckle. Dominic's eyes were hard with brief restraint and in a blur he pulled over to the shoulder of the road, unbuckled his seatbelt and grabbed my face between his fingertips. I watched him with wide eyes wondering what the fuck I got myself into.

"Call me any of those names again and we're not making it to the restaurant." He threatened glaring at me and I raised an eyebrow at him.

"Oh, so we're going to a restaurant?" I asked cheekily with a grin. Dominic's hand tightened as he studied my expression with a playful glint in his eye.

"You look beautiful tonight angel, don't let me fuck up that make-up of yours." He whispered and clasped his hand around my neck just below my ear.

"Waterproof..." I said before leaning forward and giving him a peck on the lips. "Baby." I whispered and kissed just below his jawline. I was probably going to regret it but I loved seeing Dominic squirm.

He groaned and shifted in his seat with a painful look on his face. I watched as he pulled away to look around the secluded road before averting his eyes back to me. Dominic seemed to be contemplating something as he pulled his bottom lip between his teeth. He eventually shook his head.

"You're teasing me, aren't you? Stop before I fuck that face." Dominic sounded like he was in agony and I finally decided to let him breathe. I returned to the seat with a shrug and looked straight ahead. Dominic didn't move and I looked at him expectantly while gesturing for him to carry on driving.

"You little..." He scoffed looking completely unimpressed as he put the car in drive and started the route to the restaurant, again.

"Dominic...you're joking." I whispered in astonishment and took a step out of the elevator.

I was expecting a casual area with other patrons, not an entire empty rooftop with the most stunning view of the city lights and a personal fully decked table right in the centre. My heart threatened to burst out of my chest as I took in the dazzling scenery.

There was a bed too.

"That's a bed." I stated trying to overcome from the shock of witnessing what Dominic had planned. It was beautiful and the slightly warm and calm weather definitely played in our favour.

"Why not?" He replied nonchalantly and circled his arm around my waist to pull me to his side. My face softened and tingles spread through my entire being. The sky was clear as the stars crystallised with a captivating beauty. It has been a while since I admired the night.

Dominic began guiding me towards the table and pulled the chair out for me. The soft orange hue emitting from the candles created a shadow on his features highlighting his already too-beautiful face.

Nobody had ever gone through so much effort for me.

"Thank you." I said sincerely and straightened the back of my dress before sitting down. Dominic shrugged his jacket off and placed it around his own chair opposite me before sitting down.

"Don't thank me. I wanted to make tonight special and I know you weren't in the mood to be around a lot of people." He said leaning his elbows on the table and grabbing my hands in his own. He was absolutely right. I only wanted to be around him and enjoy his company.

"That's very thoughtful. Do you own this place?" I asked and circled my thumb over his fingers. My feelings were on a low simmer but I had a hunch it would turn into a full-blown boil quicker than I anticipated.

"Yes, actually just bought it from one of my good friends. He moved back to Italy." Dominic said and covered my hands with his. I used to think I hated affection until Dominic came along and changed my mind completely.

"Moved back to Italy? Aren't you supposed to hate Italians?" I chuckled and his eyes lit up as if seeing me smile for the first time.

"Generally yes but there's no point. We established peace and we've helped each other out with favours ever since." He responded and I nodded my head in understanding.

Mafia...it wasn't something I thought about often. I should be scared for my life but I wasn't. Dominic had proven to me over a dozen times that I could trust him and he also made me feel ironically safer and protected.

"There are five cuisines. Japanese, Italian, Mexican, Indian and Thai. Take your pick." He said before tapping his phone and almost instantly the door was opened and a young red-headed waitress approached us with menus.

Five cuisines?!

She smiled politely and proceeded to hand us the menus. Her almond shaped eyes dropped to my cleavage and she stumbled over her feet before catching herself. I laughed when her cheeks splotched red.

"You're cute." I complimented with a grin and her eyes widened.

"Thank you, ma'am. I'm Holly and I'll be your waitress for the evening. Let me know when you are ready to order." Holly said hastily before turning her back to us and leaving. Poor girl looked utterly flustered.

"That's something I'll have to get used to." Dominic mumbled before grabbing my hand and bringing my knuckles up to his lips. I smiled when the plump flesh gently grazed my skin causing a blazing fire to spread through my hand.

"Dominic, I know you said I shouldn't thank you but-"

"I don't want to hear it." He interrupted and shook his head, stopping me from expressing how grateful I was.

I sighed and let go of his hand to look through the menus. Authentic and traditional meals littered the laminated paper in beautiful cursive and my mouth watered as I went through the list.

"Oh my God, that was fucking amazing." I groaned and rubbed my stuffed belly. I had everything from sushi to enchiladas and it was by far the best meal I've ever had.

I was in a food coma as Dominic joined me on the bed and together we stared up clear blue-black sky. We were alone and soft music played in the background breaking the silence.

"I'm dying." Dominic grunted and rubbed his stomach as if it was aching. I smiled tiredly as I adored the beautiful and peaceful atmosphere and view.

"You're not dying. Stop being dramatic." I told him and stopped myself from wincing. I was already full and Dominic still wanted to get dessert.

"No, I'm being serious. I ate so much." He croaked and clenched his eyes shut. I shook my head - you would've sworn he was really dying the way he was acting.

"Yes but you're not dying. Just jog it off."

Dominic startled me with a loud laugh. "Hah! You think I have energy to get up. That's so cute."

"I think the bed was more for you than me." I muttered and rolled over my side to look at his profile. I rested my head on my palm and studied his intricate tattoos. The one behind his ear was one of my favourites but nothing could beat the spirals and letters on his hands. It was art, beautiful and very painful looking art.

"I've always wanted to get a tattoo but I'm so indecisive." I said and trailed my fingertips over his neck. I scooted closer to him until my front was touching his side.

"It doesn't have to be anything significant. Just get whatever you like." He shrugged. I didn't say anything and continued tracing the dark ink with not a single trace of colour.

The evening was perfect and I didn't want it to end. I leaned my head down on his chest and sighed as my body relaxed. He wrapped one arm around me and pulled me closer until our bodies were flushed together.

There was something pleasant about laying on a mattress outside enjoying the fresh air and the incredible view but one thing for sure...the man besides me was by far the best part about the night.

CHAPTER 18

CAITLIN

"Are you ever going to tell me what you did with Andrew and David?" I asked and took another spoonful of my ice-cream.

Dominic complained about being full but still ordered a choco-cara-nilla sundae with extra toppings. Just the thought of it made me want to gag out loud so I opted for a simple vanilla scoop with a drizzle of chocolate sauce. The ice cream was made by an elderly Italian man called Riccardo and it was the best thing I've ever tasted.

Besides Dominic's cum.

"Let's just say they're not putting their hands on anyone...ever again." He stated and popped a glazed cherry into his mouth. How he managed to stay fit was beyond me.

"Why not?" I asked and crossed my legs underneath me. My underwear was open to his view but it wasn't like he hadn't literally been inside me.

"Because they don't have any." He said and I choked on the ice cream.

"Nice!" I high-fived him and he grinned before grabbing my hand and giving my palm a kiss. I didn't feel a sliver of guilt because I was entirely sure they deserved it.

Dominic did his research and figured that the both of them were working together to lure women in to try and prey on them. It was done before but the charges were dropped for whatever reason and Dominic made sure they were going to pay for what they did.

"I was so happy that you told me instead of being all secretive about it and wanting to fix it on your own," he said and then raised his hand defensively. "not that there's a problem with you wanting to do it on your own because, you know, independency and shit. But I liked that you came to me."

With a shake of my head, I smiled. "It's nice knowing there's someone who cares about me the way you do."

"It's nice having someone to care for." He shrugged and put his spoon in his mouth. Dominic was a provider, a giver and an excellent supporter. He didn't push and he didn't force his emotions on me. He allowed me to go at my own pace and I was so fucking grateful.

"Dominic, you're always giving and giving. What have I given you?" I asked solemnly and then looked up at the sky.

"That mouth does wonders, angel." He said with a flirtatious smirk and I gasped giving him a playful hit on the arm.

"I'm not talking about that! Look at this incredible date you planned. Sometimes I push you away and you take a step back but you're still there. You're...really fucking amazing." I said honestly. Dominic set his bowl down and sat up right. He was looking at me with a soft expression and for a moment I feel myself crumble.

"You don't push me away. We're just taking it easy, right?" He asked and I nodded before taking another bite. I was scared of getting attached but I was already long past that point. If Dominic stepped out of my life and decided that he had enough of me, it would hurt.

"You never take it easy on me." I muttered and winced as thoughts of him fucking me came to mind.

"Because you like it." Dominic responded and placed his hand on my inner thigh, really close to the lace fabric of my underwear.

"I do." I admitted. "One day I'm going to tie you up and I'll be the one to fuck you and show you whose boss."

He chuckled. "You are already the boss, angel."

"I am?" I asked with a frown.

"Yes. You're the one who decides how far I go, how hard I go. You're the one who chooses the limits and what's acceptable and everything in between. I just go with it." Dominic said and gave my thigh a gentle squeeze.

"I never thought of it like that." I said.

"I'm the one fucking you but you're in control all the time." He said softly and leaned forward to give me the gentlest kiss. The second his lips touched mine, my mind went blank and my vision darkened as my eyes closed automatically. It was a taste of heaven and everything good in the world.

Dominic was making me fall so fucking hard for him and I couldn't stop myself.

"Will you come home with me?" Dominic asked but he didn't have to. Of course I would.

"Yes."

"What the fuck are you doing here?" Dominic asked the second we stepped into his home. Yurik was sat on the couch wearing a black sweatpants leaving his upper body bare. My eyes didn't fail to notice the silver piercings in both nipples and the dragon tattoo on his rib.

There was no denying that both brothers were hot as hell.

"I live here." He shrugged and in that moment Micah strolled into the living room ruffling his wet curly hair with a towel. My eyes darted between them knowingly and I scrunched my nose up feeling like we interrupted whatever they were up to.

I guess that debt was paid off.

"Caitlin." Micah gasped when he saw me and stopped in his tracks. He had love-bites all over his chest and neck and it was something I definitely didn't need to see. He inherited my dads brown skin but the red marks were still very visible.

Yurik had a smile on his face as he got up to give me a hug and a kiss on the cheek.

Micah looked like a child who just got caught stealing a cookie.

"Hi, sweetheart. You look absolutely beautiful." Yurik gushed and then grabbed my hand lifting it to twirl me around. I smiled at the compliment and Dominic glared at his brother before pulling me towards him protectively.

"Thank you, you don't look too bad yourself." I beamed giving him the softest punch on his shoulder. He clutched his chest in mock surprise and awed out loud.

"Really, Yurik? You couldn't go fuck somewhere else?" Dominic scowled and my head snapped towards him.

"Where else would I go to fuck besides my home, Domo?" Yurik rolled his eyes and I laughed out loud. Micah was still standing there awkwardly with the brightest blush forming.

"Is Micah homeless?" Dominic asked brazenly and my mouth dropped. I always forgot how blunt and straight-forward he was until he said something to remind me.

"You know what, don't answer that question." Dominic raised his hand when Yurik opened his mouth to speak. "Angel, let's leave these two alone." He grabbed my hand and started leading us towards the back of the house. I could still hear Yurik chuckling and then a slap was heard when Micah hit him with the towel.

"You could've told me that they were coming." He hissed sounding pissed but nobody seemed to care besides him.

"Sorry, my love. Don't be mad at me, come here." Yurik's voice softened and Micah sighed. They were in love and it could be spotted a mile away.

It was a bit awkward - the only time I saw my brother was when either Yurik or Dominic was involved. We acted like we weren't related, hardly spoke and never kept up to date with what's happening in each other's lives but we also knew that we could always count on one another. It was an odd dynamic but it worked for the both of us.

To think Dominic was on the verge of killing Micah when he was in debt by thousands. The whole situation was strange convenience that we had somehow ended up connected.

"Where are you taking me?" I asked Dominic as he guided us downstairs. His hold on me was tight and comforting as he completely engulfed my smaller hand in his much larger one. I couldn't help but feel at peace with it being there.

"My garage. You love cars, right?" He pressed a pin into a keypad and the steel door unlocked automatically and quite loudly. I nodded.

Growing up my dad owned a mechanic shop and I would spend nearly every Saturday morning in his vicinity watching him work on cars and handing him whatever tool he needed. It was a bitter-sweet memory but I cherished it with my entire heart.

I picked up a few tips and tricks of my own. My father used to say 'no daughter of mine is going to drive a basic ass car.' and ended up getting someone to modify my Mini Cooper to be faster and more powerful. The fact that it was manual only made me love it more.

It was gifted to me in my final year of high school and up until recently I was so close to selling it to pay my student debt. I changed my mind last minute - that car was my life and despite it being small and dainty, there was power underneath that hood.

"So choose one angel and we'll go wherever you like." Dominic said and the bright lights flickered on. My jaw dropped to the ground. Garage? More like airplane hangar.

Rows and rows of various sports cars, both modern and vintage, were parked with just enough space between them to allow an easy exit. There was an all-black superbike parked at the very end and my eyes widened as I took in the magnificent sight. It was literally paradise.

"Whoa." I gawked and took a step inside. "This is all yours?"

"Yes, except that one over there," he pointed to a Mustang. "that's Yurik's baby."

I could feel my inner-child resurfacing as I gaped at the shiny cars illuminated by bright spot lights. My heels clinked on the floor as I took a step closer to the one that caught my attention immediately. It was the most beautiful car I've ever seen in my life.

Dominic chuckled behind me when he saw me admiring the predatory Audi. "I had a feeling you would have chosen that one. Here." He handed me a sleek matte key and I cautiously took it in my palm.

"You want me to drive?" I asked hesitantly clutching the immobiliser in my hand. Dominic was putting a lot of trust in me.

"You don't want to?" He asked looking slightly confused and I grinned before jumping up to wrap my arms around his neck. Of course I wanted to - I could already feel the excitement building up and I made no effort to contain it.

Dominic circled one arm around my waist and one hand went to lift up my dress to squeeze my ass. It felt amazing but I was beyond eager so I pulled away and walked to the driver's side.

"Come on, don't just stand there." I urged him on and opened the door.

Once I was seated on the cool leather seat, my heart started hammering in my chest. It was majestic and very expensive look-ing. It still had that fresh car smell but once Dominic entered from the passenger's side his slightly vague cologne wafted through my senses and it was the best scent ever.

"Don't mind me, I'll just sit here." He relaxed in his seat and pulled the seatbelt over his chest with a nonchalant expression.

I started the car and it growled to life. My thighs were shaking as it idled and for a second time, my jaw dropped.

"No way." I ran my hand along the steering wheel and took a deep breath in. Within a few minutes of adjusting everything to be more comfortable, I was speeding out of the garage and turning into the road.

I half expected Dominic to be frightened - to yell at me to slow down but when I spared a glance at him, he was already looking at me with a small smile on his face.

"What?" I asked laughing slightly.

"Nothing." He said but the smile still played on his lips and I felt every single nerve in my body relax despite the speed I was going at.

It was dark out and the roads were brightened by soft orange lampposts. It lit up the inside of the car and I opened the window to allow the wind to flow through my hair. I felt free - I felt invigorated and I felt at harmony just driving down a straight road with a handsome man alongside me in a beast of a car.

"You are so beautiful, angel." Dominic said softly besides me but there was just something about his tone that had every fibre of my being wanting to pull over and hug the fuck out of him.

"Thank you." I responded and resisted the temptation to look over at him.

The destination in mind was one of my favourite spots that I went to whenever I felt like I needed a breather. It was on a hill overlooking the sea and it was always vacant.

Once we arrived, I stopped the car and leaned back into the leather seat still feeling the adrenaline pumping through my body. That was one of the best feelings I've ever experienced.

"Wow. That was...wow." I whispered and ran a hand through my now tangled hair.

"You like?" Dominic asked.

I looked at him in disbelief. "Like? I fucking love!"

He grinned. "I'm glad you enjoyed that. This view...how did you find this place?"

"One night I was just driving aimlessly and came across it. I've been coming here for a few months now." I said and unbuckled my seatbelt. Dominic did the same but we stayed seated while I attempted to calm myself down.

When I felt at ease, I leaned over and kissed Dominic as if it was the last time I would ever feel his lips on mine. It was passion-filled but simultaneously platonic and had every nerve in my body lighting up. It was sweet and a reminder about how my emotions were starting to get the best of me.

I smiled into the kiss and I felt Dominic doing the same. I pulled away for a gulp of air but he followed along with me, not breaking contact. My heart started to beat faster but this time, it was a different form of adrenaline.

I wanted Dominic to be mine - I wanted him to call me his. I wanted him in more ways I could describe.

My hand palmed the back of his head and I pressed my lips against his own harder, and harder until my tongue was invading into his mouth tasting him and enjoying him. The world behind my eyes was beyond chaotic and a straight thought couldn't be formed. I couldn't think of anything besides how excruciatingly desperately I wanted him.

It scared me. It terrified me. But I didn't allow it to control me.

I stepped out of the gym into the fresh cool air the night provided. I went a bit harder than usual and I was utterly exhausted by the time I was done. My muscles were aching for a cold shower and my legs felt wobbly.

The parking lot was now empty except the odd stray cat or dog. The wind was starting to pick up but my body was still overheating from the intense session I had. I headed to my car at the very end - when I arrived a few hours ago the lot was completely full.

As I always did, I clutched my key between my fingers in case anyone decided to jump me. It was a sad reality but it had to be done.

I was so caught up blasting my music through my headphones and going all out that I didn't realise how late it was getting until a worker tapped on my shoulder to remind me that it was nearing closing time.

Once I was inside the safety of my car, I sighed in relief. I was tired and I contemplated heading over to Dominic's so he could massage my thighs. I was sure he wouldn't mind.

Just as I was about to stick the key into the ignition something cold and hard pressed against the back of my neck instantly causing shivers to run through me. The blood drained from my face and I immediately realised how fucked I was. Someone was pointing a gun at me.

"You should really check your backseats, Caitlin. Or is it Sophia?"

CHAPTER 19

CAITLIN

Lucas.

"Not so fucking smart as you think, huh?" He growled and pressed the gun further into my neck. The cold metal hurt the delicate skin but I grit my teeth not giving him the satisfaction of seeing me wince.

I cursed my dark window tint to the depths of hell.

"Do not fucking move or I'll blow your brains out all over this fucking seat. Who do you work for?" Lucas asked harshly and the small hairs on my nape arose. Dominic's words came to mind instantly and I clenched my fists. You die before you snitch.

"Myself." I said confidently and the gun was removed from my neck. For a second I thought he believed me - but he grabbed my cheeks with one hand and turned my head to face him. I kept my composure when my eyes landed on him. Lucas was scary and he was impulsive. A bullet could be released into my skull right there and nobody would know.

"Don't play cute with me. Tell me who the fuck you work for." He snapped and tightened his grip on my face. I didn't say anything and he roughly let go of me. I grabbed my jaw and moved it side to side. That hurt. I watched as he climbed over to the passenger seat while keeping the gun pointed at me.

It was almost comical.

He grabbed something from his jackets pocket and began screwing the object onto the tip of the gun. It was a silencer and that's when my heart started pounding even harder. Was I going to be killed in the parking lot of a gym? I had imagine my death to be a lot less eventful than that.

"I would say we can do this the easy way or the hard way...but honestly, both ways would be easy." Lucas said slowly and leaned forward once again. My keys were still in my hand and if I was quick enough I would get him right in the carotid artery but I didn't want to take the chance.

"Speak." He demanded.

I didn't say anything.

Lucas reached over at lightning speed and pulled the back of my hair exposing my neck. He pressed the gun right below my chin and he was so close I could feel his breath. I made the mistake of whimpering when agony shot through my scalp and Lucas smirked at seeing me in pain.

"Drop that." He nodded his head to the key in my hand and cocked the gun. A sick feeling formed in my chest and I hesitantly let go of it feeling all hope of me getting out alive diminishing.

"I'm not going to ask again. Who the fuck do you work for?" You just did, you dumb fuck.

"Myself." I said through a clenched jaw while maintaining an unwavering stare with him. Lucas groaned out loud before pulling the gun away from my neck. My eyes widened when it was re-placed by his lips and a tremor of disgust racked through me.

"Get the fuck off of me!" I yelled and tried to push him away but he was too strong - too powerful. I reached to the handle of the door and shakily tried to open it.

"Open that door and you're dead." He warned and I could see he meant every single word. His eyes were glossy and his pupils were heavily dilated - he looked high on something.

"You think you can steal from us and get away with it? You little bitch. Who the fuck do you think you are?" Lucas laughed but the humour was lacking. He reached to his pocket and pulled out his phone while aiming the gun in my direction.

"Yes boss, I have her. Do you want me to take her in for questioning or kill her right here?" Lucas held the phone to his face and tilted his head to the side as if he was asking a simple casual question.

Fuck - I was in trouble. I was either going to be shot dead or tortured until I spoke. Dominic words kept ringing in my mind and I clenched my eyes shut. He would want me to speak, right? My mind was hazy and a feeling of morbid hopelessness washed over me.

"Take her in and smack her around until the bitch speaks. We need to know who the fuck she's working for." A man responded and I felt my entire body rush cold. No fucking way. No fucking way.

"Papa?" My voice was cracked as I stared wide-eyed at the screen refusing to believe the very familiar voice I just heard. I would recognise it anywhere.

He was in jail. It wasn't possible.

"Caitlin?" My father sounded just as surprised as I was as he confirmed that it was in fact him. For a few moments I completely forgot how to breathe as the air got caught in my throat.

Dominic mentioned that Lucas was the second in command to a cartel drug lord and it turned out to be...my own flesh and blood. My throat felt like a golf ball had miraculously formed in it.

"What the fuck...you're his daughter?" Lucas asked in shock and quickly sprang away from me putting space between us.

The fire in my chest was blazing but at the same time I felt like I had no reason to be angry. I breathed in heavily and the back of my hands fell down to my lap.

"She's my daughter." My father...the Colombian cartel boss spoke hastily and sullenly.

"What the fuck..." I whispered.

How could I have been so oblivious? Why was I surprised? The more I thought about it the more it made sense.

My mother changing our surnames from Valencia to Haynes, obviously wanting to cut all ties with him. My mother forbidding me from seeing my own father because 'its dangerous' My mother demanding that we only speak English in her household.

Did Micah know?

"Caitlin? I swear to fucking God if you lay a hand on her." What the hell can you do? You're locked in a cell.

How could I have been so fucking blind?

"Boss I won't touch her." Lucas said shakily and I looked at him slowly. These were the type of men working for my father? I wasn't completely innocent - I drugged the man and they had obvious reasons to want to kill me but...but nothing. We were all fucked up.

"Caitlin, baby girl. Let me explain to you, okay? Your mother didn't want me to-"

"I'll come see you when I can." I interrupted him. We needed to talk but I had an idea that it wouldn't be anytime soon. How did this even happen? What were the fucking chances? It felt like everybody I knew was involved in some sort of criminal activity.

"Get out." I said and gripped the steering wheel tightly in my fists. I was overwhelmed by the newfound information and I wanted Lucas out of my presence. He seemed to be coming down from his high as his pupils returned back to normal but he could easily snap again.

He sighed. "Leave her alone Lucas and don't bother her again."

"But she stole-"

"Do you want a bounty on your head, boy? Don't fucking test me. Let her go." He said sternly and Lucas' eyes widened. My father was obviously very powerful to be able to make demands from inside a prison. I just couldn't understand why it was kept a secret from me.

Lucas got out and I felt my body finally slump down onto the seat in relief. How was I going to explain who I worked for without causing more complications?

I collected the fallen key from the floor of the car and stuck it into the ignition not wasting a single second before speeding out of the lot. Part of me wanted to rush to Dominic so that he could make me feel better like he always did...but that would be leading them right back to his place.

I felt like I couldn't go back to my apartment either.

My phone rang from inside my gym bag but I ignored it. It stopped but rang again and again until eventually I pulled over to the side of the road to answer whoever was calling.

"What?!" I yelled at the private number feeling beyond irritated.

"Ouch." Dominic said sounding hurt and I sighed letting my head fall back on the headrest.

"Why the fuck is your phone on private?" I asked a bit more harshly than I meant to. Don't take it out on him. He doesn't deserve it.

"I'm sorry," I apologised before he could say anything. Guilt consumed me - I was never the one to let my anger get the best of me and Dominic was not about to be my punching bag. "I didn't mean to speak to you like that." I said dejectedly.

"It's fine. What's wrong? Are you okay?" Dominic asked worriedly.

"I just...where are you?" I asked and watched the cars speed past me.

"I'm at your apartment waiting for you, angel." He said and I felt my heart sink. Dominic...he was always there for me.

"Okay. I'll be there soon." I muttered before switching the call off and getting back onto the road. Every five seconds I kept glancing at the rear view mirror or side mirrors in case anyone was following me.

When I finally reached my apartment door, Dominic was leaned against it and when he saw me he pushed himself off it and a smile formed on his face. It calmed me instantly but I unlocked the door and quickly stepped inside. I shut it behind Dominic and locked it before throwing myself into his arms.

"Baby...what's wrong?" He asked and stroked my hair as I firmly wrapped my arms around his waist. The warmth of his body and his scent was all the comfort I needed.

"Lets talk." I took his hand in mine and led us to sit on the couch. He was looking at me with concern in his eyes and underneath the dim light of my living room it almost seemed black.

"Ah fuck, you're done with me, aren't you?" I thought he was joking but the seriousness on his face said otherwise. My lips tilted up slightly and I shook my head.

"No." I reassured him and turned my body to face him. I was momentarily distracted by how good he looked in his grey sweatpants and plain black hoodie but I rid those thoughts immediately.

"What's the name of Lucas' boss?" I asked already knowing the answer.

He looked at me in confusion. "Alarico Valencia."

"You are rivals?" I questioned feeling dread and anxiety gush through me.

"We have been for years, angel. Can you tell me what's going on?"

Oh for fucks sake.

Chapter 20

CAITLIN

"Wait, you're telling me that you had no idea the cartel kingpin was your father?" Dominic eyed me with a hint of suspiciousness. I had explain the situation to him thoroughly and his scepticism seemed to be growing by the second as each word left my lips.

It looked like he didn't believe me and if I didn't know any better, it seemed like Dominic thought I played a part in the whole ordeal. That wasn't the case at all and I was just as shocked as he was.

I sighed in slight annoyance. "Yes, that's what I'm saying."

"How did I miss this?" He whispered to no one in particular and clasped his hands together. I could see the gears whirling in his head as he kept his gaze plastered on my dull tiles. A frowned formed on my eyebrows and I scooted closer towards him on the couch.

The same couch where Dominic completely obliterated me.

"Dominic," I placed my hand on his shoulder. "I know what you're thinking but I promise it's not like that." I said sincerely. The last thing I needed was Dominic thinking I was some sort of spy. For as long as we knew each other, an unexpected bond had formed between us and it was starting to manoeuvre into the depths of unforeseen romance.

I was finally allowing myself to accept it and cherish every moment of it.

"I know." He managed to respond after a few moments and a small smile of relief shaped my lips. Dominic grabbed my hand from his shoulder and held it in his own allowing me to feel a sense of security that calmed every inch of my body.

"You'd be dead by now if it actually was like that, angel." He said and I could tell he was feeling more relaxed when he threw a cheeky smirk my way. It was heart-wrenchingly beautiful despite the turmoil of emotions I was feeling.

"Thrown into a pot of molten metal?" I asked teasingly and he let out a breathy laugh.

"Yes." He confirmed with a nod and continued tracing his thumb over my palm. "It does sound very fun. We should try it on some-one one day."

"Preferably Lucas." I said in disgust and scrunched my nose up at the thought of his unpleasant touch.

"Don't worry - he won't come near you ever again. From what you've told me it sounds like your father will do anything in his power to protect you and I know he has a lot of power." Dominic said and his tone sounded convincing enough.

"I don't get why he would hide that from me. Am I not good at keeping secrets?" I asked feeling slightly offended.

"I think you're the best at keeping secrets. I feel like I could tell you anything and you'll do whatever to make sure it stays a secret but," He turned his upper half to face me. "To ensure your safety, I will be tracking your phone and your car."

"But-"

"No buts, angel. That's final." He said sternly and tightened his grip as a silent warning. He held an expression of seriousness that left no room for argument.

I heaved a sigh. "Okay."

"You know, I'm probably going to have to stop seeing you." Dominic muttered and soothed his hands onto his grey joggers. It straightened out to emphasise the bulge in the crotch area which left very little to the imagination. I was momentarily distracted by the sight until I registered what he had just said and my eyes shot up to meet his own.

"That's unfortunate," I scowled. "I'm actually starting to like your fat ass."

Dominic's mouth fell open in mock offense. "Starting to? I thought we were way past that stage."

"You're the one who wants to stop seeing me." I said and shrugged before getting up from the couch. I needed to shower and my skin was starting to feel tacky from my workout.

Dominic followed behind me. "Nobody is going to keep me away from you, angel. Not even your father."

Good.

"Better not." I responded and stepped into my bathroom. The thin hoodie was pulled over my head and with help from Dominic, my sports bra was peeled off my skin to reveal my bare chest. My arms were still weak and I groaned in relief when they dropped to my sides.

"You need help?" He asked but his eyes were captivated by my breasts and his breathing switched to uneven puffs. I smirked when his cheeks reddened the slightest bit while he shifted from foot to foot in an attempt to hide his excitement. It was adorable.

"You can help me shower but you're going to have to get naked." I mumbled and in a split second his own hoodie was discarded to the bathroom floor. He hurriedly started fumbling with the lace tie around his sweatpants before dropping it. I chuckled in amusement and started twisting the knob to achieve the perfect temperature.

"God damn." Dominic muttered once my cycling tights were pooling around my feet. I swear every time he saw me naked he acted like it was the first time ever.

His dick hung freely between his strong thighs and regardless of the fact that I've seen him way too many times to count, it still left me stunned each time.

"Don't just stand there. Come on." I gestured for him to join me. After having showered with Dominic a few times, he seemed to quickly catch onto my routine. Like how I washed my hair and face first and foremost with cool water instead of the blistering and damaging heat.

"This one, right?" He asked and collected my shampoo from the rack. I nodded and turned my back towards him. With his impressive height, Dominic was tall enough to wash my hair without having to raise his arms too much. I tilted my head backwards to allow the water to flow through.

When he started massaging his fingertips into my scalp, my eyes rolled back into my head. "You're so good at that." I whispered as I felt myself relax.

"Oh yeah? When is it my turn?" He asked and my lips tilted up into the faintest smile.

"You're way too tall. You're going to have to get on your knees if you want me to wash your hair."

"I'd get on my knees for you any day." Dominic said so quietly that for a second I thought I might have heard him wrong. His proximity was a hairs width away and I could feel the warmth emitting from him. It took every single ounce of self-control to not turn around and kiss him.

"Dominic..." I muttered softly.

"Yes, angel?"

I took a deep breath in. "Thank you for being here."

His movements halted before he removed his hands from my hair. With a swift grab of my arm, he spun me around to face him and my heart trembled when I caught sight of his beautiful face.

"I'll always be here for you. You know that, right? I'm not going to leave just when things get a little rocky. That's not how this works." Dominic cupped my cheeks with his foam covered hands and bent down the slightest bit.

The volume of relief that bubbled through my entire being resulted in a small smile of thanks forming on my lips. I didn't expect it to affect me that way but Dominic speaking words of assurance was needed and appreciated.

"Tha-"

"Sshh, baby. You say thank you way too much." He said softly and kissed the tip of my nose.

Our current position felt more intimate than any sexual experience we've had together and I suddenly felt vulnerability in his presence. My cheeks warmed with an untameable blush as Dominic held firm eye contact with me not wavering for a split second.

I was the first one to look away.

"No," he grabbed my chin and carefully tilted my head to face him. "Don't do that. You're not someone who backs away and you're not about to start now."

There I was completely naked with suds in my hair underneath the calculating inspection of a man who held such adoration and respect in his eyes when he looked at me. It was enough to have anyone melting but I plastered a genuine smile on my face and stood on the tip of my toes to kiss him.

It was gentle in every sense of the word. The soft velvety touch of his lips against mine caused a burst of emotions to scurry through me unlike anything I've felt before. I leaned back down onto my heels but Dominic didn't separate from me. His mouth followed mine until he was bent over with his hands still firmly on my cheeks.

"I love kissing you." He whispered against my lips.

"Let's finish up here and go to bed?" I asked and he smiled before pulling away.

"Okay," he nodded. "Turn around."

"Dominic...what are we going to do about my dad?" I asked looking down at him. The fact that my own father and the man I was seeing were rivals played at the back of my mind constantly.

"We'll figure something out. Stop worrying about it." He said and dragged the sock up my foot. He finally stood up and placed a chaste kiss on my forehead.

"Okay," I sighed deciding to just let it go and enjoy the time I had with Dominic. "I'll leave it."

I still had to find out if Micah knew or not.

I stretched out onto the mattress. The feel of my bare legs against the freshly changed sheets was nearly orgasmic and I let out a throaty groan. My body was exhausted and I wanted nothing more than to lay in bed and cuddle.

"I have nothing to wear." Dominic suddenly spoke and I opened my eyes to gaze down at where he sat on the edge of the bed. His lower half was covered in one of my pink towels and it definitely a sight to behold.

"Stay naked."

It was becoming a regular thing for Dominic to stay the night. The spare toothbrush was opened and officially became his own to use whenever he just so happen to stay over. My array of toiletries were suddenly divided between two people and I didn't mind at all.

Dominic loved them and gave me the task of restocking his bathroom. He seemed to have an awakening when he realised just how trash his own products were and it made me unbelievably happy.

"I don't know what I did before you. My skin feels amazing." Dominic commented in awe.

"You smell good too." I said with a slight smirk.

"I know, right? We need to go shopping together. Soon."

"You are literally the cutest person ever. I forget sometimes that you're a mafia boss with the world at your feet." I said and sat up to lean my palms behind me.

"You let me forget that that side even exists. I like it but it's also very dangerous." He said and removed the towel from his waist. He neatly folded it and placed it over the chair at my desk.

"Dangerous?"

"You're a liability. A weakness of mine. It's dangerous because there are people who will take advantage of that." Dominic said and got underneath the covers with me. We laid on our sides and he grabbed my waist to pull me closer to him.

I knew the minute I found out who and what Dominic was that I would be taking a step into risky territory. It was my decision and I continued to stand with it regardless of what might happen.

"Then why do you continue to see me?" I asked gently and reached up to stroke my thumb against his full lower lip.

"Because..." he paused. "I wouldn't be able to stay away. Despite already knowing that having you in my life would put you in danger, I couldn't help but fall for you. I'm still falling and I can't stop. I won't stop until your heart is mine and even then..." He placed his fingertips underneath my chin and tilted my head up to lay the softest kiss on my lips.

My heart shuddered in my chest and an unfamiliar wave of emotion caused my body to warm up.

Dominic is definitely worth it.

CHAPTER 21

C AITLIN

I woke up horny as fuck.

It didn't help that Dominic's arm was protectively wrapped around my stomach and his bare bulge was flushed against my ass. The sunlight peeked through my sheer curtains aiding in pulling me out of my slumber but all I could think about was the dick pressed against me.

I wiggled my hips and proceeded to shove myself closer to him. Wake the fuck up.

"If you wanted to fuck..." Dominic's hoarse morning voice halted my movements and he gripped my hip tightly. "You could've just told me."

"Shut up." I croaked. The feeling of need spread through me like wildfire and I could feel my pussy throbbing desperately for his touch. I didn't want foreplay - I didn't want the unnecessary trimmings. I just needed a quick morning fuck to get my bearings straight.

Dominic wordlessly looped his fingers into the hem of my underwear and dragged it down my thighs.

The excitement I felt in that moment took control of every part of me as I waited to be filled by him. He scooted closer to me until our heads were resting on the same pillow and the space between us was non-existent. I kicked the thin white cover off exposing our nakedness and allowing the sunshine to highlight our bodies.

His tattooed thigh against mine turned me on notably and my patience was wearing thin. He kissed my shoulder before his hand found its way between my legs. Dominic clasped my inner thigh and lifted it to allow easier access. I could already feel how hard he was - it was pressed against me in the most daunting way.

"Come on." I demanded softly and wiggled my ass closer to him. I sounded like a desperate mess but I had no time to ponder on it before the tip of his dick was slowly inching into me. I couldn't see his face but I could picture his expression vividly.

"Oh." My body jerked when his tip passed through the tight opening and he gradually started stroking my inner muscles.

It hurt in the most pleasurable way and I grabbed the sheets in my fist in an attempt to compose myself. He waited for me to get used to his size before moving again.

"I've always wanted to do this." Dominic whispered and wrapped his hand around my neck. The satisfaction of having him fully inside me with my ass squashed against his pelvis was borderline orgasmic.

He moved and my lips parted with a throaty moan. He moved again and my eyes rolled back into my head. His hand tightened but not to the point of suffocation as he kept it firmly on my neck acting as a guidance to his unbelievably deep strokes.

"Fuck, angel." Dominic breathed out. Even on our sides he managed to fuck me so good that I could barely let out coherent words.

He rolled us over pressing my stomach flat against the mattress with his large body covering mine completely. I let out a loud groan as he went deeper than before but it got muffled by the palm of his hand. Dominic silenced my cries of pleasure into inaudible murmuring.

I pressed my palms on the bed with the intentions of getting on all fours but he roughly pushed me back down and I had no choice but to succumb to his quiet demand of telling me to be still.

My body hitched uncontrollably with each hard thrust as he laid his full weight on me ensuring that I wouldn't move. With one hand still on my mouth and the other gripping my waist, I felt enclosed within his space.

"Shh, my good girl."

He pulled out fully, letting his tip linger at my entrance for a few seconds before slamming down so hard that my eyes widened in shock.

"So fucking good." He grunted and finally removed his hand to let me take in much needed gulps of air. My hair fell over my face sticking to my flushed cheeks and rising with each exhale. Dominic was consistent with his long and hard pounding never faltering for a second causing me to clench around him repeatedly

He gasped. "Don't do that."

"I can't-" I quivered underneath him and clenched again involuntarily.

"Stop doing that! For fucks sake, you're going to make me cum." Dominic hissed and clutched the back of my neck to turn my head to the side. He tilted his upper half to gaze down at me and the sight of his face and messy hair had me at the edge of an orgasm.

"Stop that- oh fuck." Dominic groaned and dropped his head into the side of my neck. The feel of his weight on me and the dick inside me had shudders of pleasure travelling through my spine and down my legs.

I couldn't fathom how fucking good it felt.

Dominic removed his top half from me and the sudden lack of skin on skin had me looking up at him quizzically. He answered my soundless question by placing both palms besides my head to hold himself up and that's when I knew.

"Shit." I whispered and turned to face the headboard bracing myself for the blows he was about to lay on me. Dominic chuckled.

I grabbed the pillow and clutched it within my arms. For a man who just woke up, his stamina was through the roof and I wasn't sure my pussy could take it anymore.

I had woken him with the purpose of just a quick fuck but that thought got thrown out the door and now I had endure his pleasurable torment on my body head-on.

Dominic began to pound so aggressively and roughly that my headboard slammed into the wall with thunderous claps. The sound of his pelvis meeting my ass echoed through the room and I had to take hold of the sheets to stop myself from moving up the bed.

"Fuck!" I hissed through my teeth and furrowed my brows. My hand reached out behind me, blindly tapping his stomach as a sign to slow down. Dominic grabbed my forearm and placed it firmly down onto my lower back. I groaned and wiggled trying to escape the restraint he had on me.

"Safeword. Use it if you really want me to stop." He instructed and I nodded clumsily. He held himself up with one hand and grabbed my ass with the other. He slapped it hard sending waves of rippling pain though the flesh and emitting a gasp of surprise from my throat. I tried to get up again but it was futile.

"Look at you trying to run away when you were the one who started this." Dominic laughed at me and my cheeks flamed embarrassingly. I opened my mouth to retort something cheeky but I changed my mind at the last second - I was already being punished enough.

"You're so wet around me, angel. You hear that?" Dominic mumbled and slowed his thrusts to deep rolling. I sighed in relief at the change of pace.

"Tell me," he stroked my hair away from my face. "That you're mine."

In my state of pure bliss, I said without hesitation, "No. You first."

I wanted to be his so badly but I wasn't going to let things be one-sided.

"Of course I'm yours. I've been yours." Dominic said without a hint of reluctance. I smiled into the sheets. His words were enough to send me over the edge and I squeezed around him so hard that he stilled completely.

The orgasm sent shivers of sensual ecstasy throughout my entire body and I couldn't stop convulsing even when Dominic pulled out and released himself onto my ass. He fell down beside me with his chest heaving slightly and a ghost of a smile on his lips.

I raised my fist to him and routinely, he raised his own to gently collide with mine. "Yours." I breathed out and the smile on his face widened.

"Best gift ever." He said in a daze.

"Gift?" I chuckled. "What is it? Your birthday?"

"Yes." He replied and my mouth dropped. I went to push myself off the bed but the cum began leaking down my thighs instantly stopping me.

"Why didn't you tell me?! I didn't get you anything or plan anything." I said feeling slightly disappointed. Birthdays were meant to be celebrated even if it was the bare minimum.

"You gave me the best present I could have asked for, angel. That was..." He exhaled deeply and rested his hands onto his stomach. "Amazing."

"Yeah, yeah, whatever. But I didn't physically get you anything." I explained. "Wipe your children off me so I can go make you breakfast."

"Nope." He crossed his arms underneath his head and stared at the ceiling ignoring me.

"Dominic, I swear..."

He didn't say anything.

"Fine, I'll just throw it at you." I said and cupped my hand to imitate a bowl. Dominic sprung up from the bed at the speed of lightning and returned with tissues to wipe me clean. I smiled in victory and finally stood up.

I immediately wobbled feeling unbalanced and the ache between my legs increased significantly. I held the underside of my stomach and groaned out loud. Dominic fucked me so hard that I could barely walk straight.

"I'm going to run us a bath. Just rest, baby. It's fine." He kissed my forehead and guided me back down onto the bed. I sighed but made no move to argue.

"Thank you for breakfast." Dominic said appreciatively and leaned over the table to place a kiss on my lips. He was wearing yesterday's clothes fresh out of the dryer and his hair was still slightly damp.

"You're welcome. Do you have any plans for the day? Can we do something?" I asked a little too excitedly and gripped the mug in both hands.

"I wish I could spend the day with you but I have a few things to attend to this afternoon and tonight I have supper with my parents. Do you want to come?" Dominic's question caught me off guard and I choked on my coffee. Parents?

"Is that a good idea? I mean...considering everything with my dad right now and-"

"Let me rephrase that. You're coming." Dominic stated bluntly. My shoulders slumped and I bit my bottom lip. The idea of meeting Dominic's parents had my mind whirling with all sorts of scenarios.

"Okay. Wait, how old are you?" I asked curiously.

"Twenty-six."

"Young." I mumbled and took a sip of my coffee.

"I'm four years older than you, how am I young?" Dominic looked at me incredulously as if I had just offended him.

"I just meant for your position. You're a bratva leader at twenty-six. That's...impressive." Is that the right word to use for a mafia boss?

"Impressive?" He smirked and leaned forward to cross his arms on the table. "I knew it! You're into criminals, aren't you?" Dominic laughed and shook his head.

"Shut up." I muttered and relaxed into the chair. Why was I attracted to who and what Dominic was? It felt wrong on some many levels but the thrill that he offered into my life was unquestionably the most exciting thing to ever happen to me.

"You're so perfect." He complimented and shook his head before getting up to walk over to me.

This man told me I'm perfect after I told him to shut up.

"I'll see you later. Kuzma will be here at 7 to pick you up. Enjoy your day, my angel." Dominic said and placed a kiss on top my head. I grinned at him feeling my heart about to combust with happiness.

"Bye, angel." I replied and the glare he sent my way had me stifling my laughter.

I've never been to a house that had its own street.

"Thank you, Kuzma." I said to the driver. He nodded his head once and offered a warm smile in response. Sweet man.

The first thing I noticed when I stepped out of the car was the fountain in the middle of the circular driveway with a constant flow of running water. The next thing was the luxury triple story mansion with the best architectural design I've ever seen. It was surrounded by guards carrying large guns and illuminated by ground lights glaring upwards.

My mouth dropped and I looked down at my simple camisole dress. The entire atmosphere of the area screamed money.

By the amount of cars parked around me, I could tell that this was not just a supper.

CHAPTER 22

C AITLIN

"Caitlin, sweetheart!" Yurik opened the door and out-stretched his arms for a hug. As much as I hated to admit it - I missed him. He reminded me of the cousins I would hang out with at family gatherings. I flung myself into his hold and proceeded to wrap my arms around his neck.

His previously lengthy hair was now cropped into a short buzz cut. An all-black suit adorned his body but the tie was left out and the silver chain around his neck glistened underneath the bright lights. An earring dangled from his left ear and when he smiled at me, the tongue ring immediately caught my attention.

I see why Micah likes him so much.

"Yurik. It's so good to see you again." I gushed and pulled away once he set me back onto my feet. Only then did I have the chance to finally look around the spacious area and I frowned when I saw all the curious eyes on us.

"Why are they-" I started but Yurik nudged my shoulder cutting me off.

"You're beautiful, do I have to tell you that all the time?" He laughed and wrapped an arm around my shoulder guiding me to an unknown location. Yurik grabbed a glass of champagne from a passing waitress and handed it to me.

"Thank you," I responded taking it from him. "Your brother said this was going to be just a dinner with your parents." My tone faltered along with my strides as I took in the breathtakingly stunning home.

It was occupied by some of the wealthiest looking people I've ever seen. Dominic was nowhere to be found.

"It was supposed to be just a simple dinner but my mother insisted on whatever the fuck this is. They're not even here yet." Yurik said disapprovingly and circled his hand around. I took a sip of the champagne and grimaced at the bitter taste.

Yurik noticed my facial expression. "Too dry? Man, I hate rich people." He took the glass from me and set it down on the counter. The champagne tasted expensive and left a dry feeling in my mouth.

"But aren't you-"

"Yes but let's not talk about that." Yurik waved it off. With his arm still lazily hanging around my shoulders, he greeted an unfamiliar face with a firm handshake while conversing in a language I couldn't understand. The conversation barely lasted a few seconds before Yurik was guiding us somewhere else.

"Is Micah here?" I asked. I hadn't had the chance to talk to him.

Yurik's face twisted into a scowl. "Your brother gets on my last fucking nerve, I swear to God. He didn't want to come. Something about 'feeling out of place' I don't get that - I really don't. I always try to make him feel comfortable."

"Mmm." I hummed in thought. "I'm sure he has his reasons."

"Yeah well, as my boyfriend he should be here with me right now." Yurik sighed and I could tell that he was disappointed.

I wrapped my arm around his waist and offered a comforting squeeze. He looked down at me and a small smile tilted his lips.

"I understand how he feels. Did you forget who your family is? I can see why he would feel out of place." I commented.

"So what you're saying is that I should go over to his place afterwards?" Yurik asked and I looked at him in confusion but nevertheless decided to humour him.

"Yes."

"Okay," He grinned. "There's Domo. Go ahead." Giving me a slight push to where Dominic stood, he quickly turned on his heels and disappeared within the crowd.

Dominic had his back to me, talking to two men and a short black haired woman. I took a deep breath in and approached the group. I announced myself by wrapping my arm around his waist and he immediately looked down at me with the small smile that quickly faltered into a look of awe.

His black shirt somehow accentuated his tattoos. The only colour on his body was the silver gun peeking through his waistband. Even at his own party, Dominic was armed.

His eyes unashamedly travelled down my body before he leaned down.

"You look so good." Dominic whispered in my ear and pulled away clearing his throat. "Let me introduce you. This is Caitlin." My name sounded strange coming from his lips.

"Aria." The woman introduced herself first and I offered my palm to her. She was beautiful. Her cheeks were littered with freckles and her head was covered in shiny natural curls. Aria surprised me by pushing my hand away and walking forward for a hug.

"Finally, I'm getting sick of these men." She said just so I could hear and I laughed out loud. I knew exactly how she felt. She let go and my eyes flicked to the tall man next to her.

"Alessandro." His name brought out the Italian accent he held. Unlike Aria, he accepted my hand for a quick shake. I smiled at him, noticing how green his eyes were.

"Carlo. It's so nice to finally meet you." The last man stepped forward and placed his hands on my shoulders to lay a kiss on both cheeks. Dominic narrowed his eyes at him before protectively pulling me into his chest.

"Nice to meet you too." I replied ignoring how Dominic squeezed my waist possessively. I pressed myself closer to him as reassurance.

"Remember that restaurant I took you to? Alessandro here used to own it before moving back to Italy." Dominic said circling his thumb over the thin material of my dress. My eyebrows shot up in realisation.

"Oh. I love that place - it's definitely my favourite."

"I'm happy to know Dominic didn't completely ruin it." Alessandro said and Aria slapped him on the bicep playfully. They were one of the hottest couples I've ever seen.

"I feel so fucking single, this is not fair." Carlo scowled and downed the remnants of his clear drink. He had an accent as well with the bluest eyes I've ever seen.

"Not our fault, Carlo." Aria said. He side-glared at her and pinched his lips into a tight line.

"Where are your parents?" I asked looking at Dominic. I was nervous - beyond nervous but I swallowed it down and put a brave face on. What's the worst thing that could happen?

"They'll be here in about an hour and that's when we eat."

"Okay, good." I turned to Aria. "Do you want to go get a drink with me?" I asked and her eyes lit up excitedly before nodding. She grabbed my hand and started leading us away from the group of men and I had an idea that she was grateful for the interference.

"Bellissima, don't go far." Alessandro warned sending Aria a pointed look to which she just rolled her eyes.

"Angel, stay close." Dominic said to me with the same warning tone as Alessandro. Aria and I burst out laughing at our overly-protective men.

"Fuck this. I hate it here." Carlo grumbled and twisted his face into a frown. "I want a person too." He said under his breath and Dominic offered a sympathetic pat on the back.

"Vodka Redbull for me, please." Aria requested to the bartender and he nodded before looking at me, drying a glass with a cloth. The home was big enough to have its own personal bar in the very corner and it shouldn't have surprised me the way it did.

"Double whiskey with ice, please." I sat down on the stool and Aria followed suite, sitting down alongside me and getting comfortable.

"Thank you for that. Sandro was never going to let me go alone." She muttered and crossed her arms on the counter.

"They're looking over here as if we're going to run away or someone is going to attack us." I said and waved my hand at Dominic in a dismissive manner while he kept his eyes trained on me. His chest sighed before he turned away and continued the conversation.

"That's what happens when you're with a-" Aria cut herself off and turned her head to look at me.

"I know." I replied and took a sip of the whiskey the bartender had set down in front of me. The strong alcohol brought a sense of relief through my veins and managed to calm my nerves to a certain extent.

"Even though Sandro isn't in the business anymore I still have to wear this every time I leave the house." Aria whispered before glancing around to make sure nobody was watching.

When she was satisfied with the clearance, she lifted the hem of her dress to reveal a sharp blade attached to her thigh.

"Oh my God, look." I said and did the same to show her a similar blade secured to my outer thigh. Dominic insisted on me wearing it - even if I was going to be within in his presence I always had to have some form of protection on me.

Aria's mouth dropped. "It's so nice talking to someone I can relate to."

"I know, right? But that's why you guys moved to Italy, to get away from all of this." I said and wrapped my hand around the broad glass enjoying the coolness. The music was now lowered to a soft tune in the background and as much as I wanted to down my entire drink, my self-control had to be maintained.

"Yes but every now and then Sandro has to come back just to make sure things are running smoothly. Our flights actually leaving in a few hours so we thought why not show-face for his friend's birthday." Aria said and I nodded in understanding. She took a big gulp of her own drink and grimaced once she set the glass down.

That reminds me. Did I even wish Dominic a happy birthday?

"And you? How did you and Dominic meet?" Aria asked facing her body to me and I smiled down at rich brown liquid swirling around clear blocks of ice. I could already sense that Aria and I were somewhat the same - falling for men we had no business falling for in the first place.

"Honestly," I leaned closer to her and she did the same wide-eyed and eager to hear what I have to say. "He was just supposed to be a random fuck I found in the middle of a bar but here I am. I'm going to meet his parents and he doesn't know how nervous I actually am." I said looking at where Dominic stood.

His height was the same of the men in front of him but he stood out the most and I kept my eyes on him for a few seconds longer.

Handsome man.

"A random fuck, huh?" She smirked cheekily. "Must've been fucking good because look where you are now."

"Who would've thought?" I uttered pinching my eyebrows together in wonder. The conversation with Aria had me pondering on the past few weeks.

"My whole life is a 'who would've thought'" Aria mumbled and toyed with the tiny straw in her glass.

"How did you and Alessandro meet?"

Aria smiled sheepishly and glanced at me. "I was walking home from work one night..."

As soon as she was done with the story-telling of how they met, our drinks were done and the house suddenly seemed to have gained a few more guests.

"These mafia men, I swear..." She said softly with a gentle shake of her head. Alessandro was...protective, that's for sure. I nodded slowly, pursing my lips.

"They're...intense."

"Who's intense?" Dominic asked coming up from behind me and swinging his arm over my shoulders. My gaze met his and I frowned when I caught that familiar look on his face - the one that had me sitting up straight and clenching my thighs together.

He looked like he wanted to rip my clothes off right there.

"Nobody." I murmured.

"Okay, fine! I'm coming, jeez." Aria blurted out and jumped down from her stool. She was scowling into the direction of where

Alessandro stood with outstretched arms making grabby hands at her. I laughed - he seemed to be suffering from withdrawals.

As soon as she was gone, Dominic leaned down and brushed my hair away to whisper in my ear, "Come with me."

"What-"

"No questions, angel. Come with me. Now."

CHAPTER 23

D OMINIC

I hated how clingy I was.

I hated that Caitlin stood a few feet away from me looking as beautiful as ever in her small black dress and I was unable to touch her.

With my hand firmly clasped around hers, I started leading her to an empty office with the objective of letting her know exactly how I felt. I had no reason to be pissed but I couldn't help the emotions clouding all form of logical thinking.

We passed by guests, some I knew, some I didn't, I didn't pay enough attention to find out. The only thing that ran through my mind was flashbacks of Caitlin's soft skin hidden by a thin material that was practically screaming at me to tear apart like the feral wild animal I was starting to feel like.

"Dominic." She called out behind me as her much shorter legs struggled to keep up with my pace. Once we rounded the corner into a secluded hallway, I let go of her hand.

"Dominic!" Caitlin yelped when I bent down to fling her body over my shoulder. I grabbed the back of her thighs securing her in place.

Her dress had hiked up a few inches above her ass revealing the plump flesh and unadulterated lust begin to pump straight to my dick. I squeezed her ass hard and relished in how fucking full it felt in my hand. God, I wanted her so badly.

My bottom lip got pulled between my teeth when I saw the blade against her thigh. My good girl.

"What-"

"Shut the fuck up." I muttered through gritted teeth. She let out a loud frustrated groan and relaxed her body against mine with her arms gently flopping against my back.

"You-"

I slapped her ass hard earning a yap of surprise. "Be quiet or I'll drag you out there and fuck you in front of everyone." I threatened meaning every single word of it. It wasn't her fault that men struggled to keep their eyes off her and I was in the right mind to shoot all of them in the fucking head.

I was usually good with maintaining my jealousy but heaven knew how badly I wanted to show everyone she's all mine.

Mine to touch, mine to fuck, mine to take care of, mine to tend to.

Her body stilled and her hands held onto my lower back as we continued walking. Her intoxicating scent wafted through my nostrils and I took a deep breath. Pull yourself together, she must be so confused.

I kicked open the partially ajar door and set Caitlin down before turning and locking it. The office was neat and vacant, long forgotten at the back of my parents' home while they spent their time travelling the world. It provided the privacy I needed to stake my claim.

My mouth watered as I thought about how desperately I wanted to taste her and stick my face in her wet pussy to try and quench the unquenchable thirst I had for her.

I whirled around and she was glaring at me with her arms crossed, pressing her breasts further up her chest. Any other day and that specific look would have had me begging on my knees for her but I was so far past the point of rationality that I paid no attention to it.

In a blur, I was striding towards her with long purposeful steps until my hands were on her waist lifting her and planting her ass on the edge of the empty table. She opened her mouth to speak but my hand around her throat gave off the silent warning I wanted it to. Caitlins eyes widened and she grabbed my wrist.

"You are so fucking beautiful that it pisses me off." I grumbled bringing my face closer to hers.

I rarely got angry. I rarely let my temper get the best of me. But seeing Caitlin tonight broke the gates that held my frustrations at bay and I wanted nothing more than to shove my tongue in her pussy.

Her eyes dropped low, a sultry smirk forming on her face. Her expression changed so quickly that it could have been missed by a blink of an eye. It reminded me about who she was - a woman who appreciated a good rough fuck just as much as I did.

"Oh?" I murmured bending down to stroke my nose against her jawline.

Let's test her boundaries.

Without warning, I put enough force into the hand I had around her neck to push her back down onto the table. "Open these legs." I instructed. Caitlin let out a strangled gasp and she obediently spread her legs for me.

The sight of her barely covered pussy had my dick throbbing nearly painfully. I gripped her lacy thong and quickly dragged it down her thighs.

"Dominic, please." Caitlin whined impatiently.

I got on my knees and took a few seconds to visually appreciate the sight of her. Her slit was slick with wetness, her hole already drenched with a clear substance. I smirked - she was already soaking and I was only just getting started.

"So fucking pretty." I groaned and bit her inner thigh, hard enough for her hands to fly to my hair in an attempt to push my head away. I wanted to devour her, cover her with my mouth and pleasure her with my best efforts.

She was going to have to do better than that.

I grabbed her thick thighs, hoisting it over my shoulders and leaned forward to flick my tongue against her clit. It tasted like sinful heaven and when she moaned loudly, my dick throbbed even harder. Fuck.

She lifted herself off the table into a sitting position and looked down at me, her hands still clasped into my hair. I gave her another long, teasingly slow lick and her lips parted accompanied by a look of pure lust on her features. I opened my mouth wide, my top lip covered her clit and my tongue began to delve into her.

"What if someone-"

"Do you want me to gag you?" I asked a bit harsher than I intended. I removed myself from her and my departure left a long string of her wetness still linked to my lips.

"Oh, fuck it." Caitlin moaned and grabbed my head to attach myself to her once again. This time she didn't hold back, controlling my head as I moved however she wanted me to. I flattened my tongue against her clit and looked up at her, letting her witness how much I was enjoying it. The look on her face could have made me cum right there.

I should have been out there with the guests entertaining the tedious conversations and sipping the champagne but my main priority at that moment was Caitlin. My angel with the long brown hair and golden skin.

"That feels so good." She groaned and started grinding against my face. I used my fingers to separate her even further sending my tongue deep inside until I had nothing more left to give.

Her moans were soft, her grip on my hair firm and her thighs around my head silky and warm. It was an honour I didn't know I needed.

Cherishing every moment of it, I lost myself within her legs and my eyes began to flutter close. I got off my knees, not separating from her hole and laid her back down on the table making sure to do it gentle enough to not hurt her.

With her knees to her shoulders and my hands holding the back of her thighs, it was best fucking view ever.

I moved my head side to side and the sound of her juices and my saliva mixed together made me groan out loud. The vibrations resulted in her inhaling a sharp breath and her chest started to heave.

"Fuck, yes. Just like that, don't stop." She mewled.

I looped my fingers over the top of her dress pulling it down to expose one of her full breasts. My hands never left her, grabbing wherever I could and squeezing hard.

"So fucking gorgeous." I whispered and continued thrusting my tongue in and out of her.

"Dominic, wait. I-" Ignoring her, I carried on with my meal.

If I could unhinge my jaw like a snake...

"It's...your bir- oh fuck I'm going to-" She slapped her fists against the hard wood as her legs stiffened. With a long moan that sounded like the opening to paradise, she shakily came inside my mouth.

Even when she was done riding out her orgasm, I couldn't bring myself to pull away. I swallowed every last drop of her essence like a water-deprived man. Only when her body went limp, I disconnected from her with a smile of complete awe. I straightened up and gazed down at her sprawled body unable to take my eyes off her redden pussy.

"I was supposed to do that to you." Caitlin said breathlessly looking up at the ceiling. I leaned down and kissed her, letting her taste herself. When I tried pulling away, her hand clasped around the back of my neck and kept me in place. Her tongue dove into my mouth and I graciously accepted it.

"Mmm." I moaned against her lips. Caitlin - she had me wrapped around her finger, a blessing in my life that I valued to the greatest extents.

The vulnerability frightened me and the thought of losing her because of a decade long feud between her father and the Romanovs was enough to have uncanny chills running through my body.

It wasn't going to happen.

"You tasted so good, angel." I whispered and she gently tugged my bottom lip between her teeth before letting go. Her hand reached down to my crotch but I grabbed her wrist stopping her - it wasn't necessary, I was more than satisfied knowing that I satisfied her.

"Let's get ourselves cleaned up, okay?" I said and pressed a kiss to her forehead. She sighed before nodding in agreement. Just as I was about to pick up her underwear, her voice stopped me.

"Wait," I looked at her and her tiny fist was reaching out to me. "Happy birthday, Dominic."

I smiled like the pussy-whipped idiot I was. "Thank you, baby." I replied before meeting my own fist with hers. The tattoos and rings on my fingers contrasted against her own clear skin and I took her hand to place my lips on her knuckles for a brief peck.

I am so fucked.

"Mama." I bent down to hug the person who I haven't seen in months. A short silver-haired woman with grey eyes and a formal appearance. Their flight was delayed because of a storm - hence the reason for their lateness and I had no idea how my mother managed to pull a party together with an absent presence.

"I missed you so much." My mother cooed and I grinned before letting go. While Yurik hugged her, I moved on to my father who stood there with the widest smile and open arms.

My upbringing was one of rules and regulations, albeit within an environment of illicit activities and deadly training, my father remained the most level-headed man I've ever met.

"□□□ □□□." He said and gave me a hug. When he let go, I turned to Caitlin who stood there with a small smile on her face as she watched the interactions. [translation; my son]

"I want you to meet Caitlin." I put my hand around her waist pulling her closer to me. My mother's eyes lit up and she practically threw herself into the arms of Caitlin who grinned widely and hugged her tightly back with the same liveliness.

"□□□□□□□." Mama gushed. "I'm Yelena. Urvan, come meet our sons girlfriend." [translation; beautiful]

The sound of that made me bite back a smile. I was hers but I still needed to make it official. The term didn't seem to bother Caitlin as she stood on the tip of her toes and embraced my father.

I forgot to let her know that my family were huggers.

As they communicated, I noticed Yurik staring at them with a longing expression on his face. I tightened my lips together placing a hand on his shoulder. He was hurt that Micah wasn't there to share the experience with us.

He smiled and waved his hand. "It's fine. I'm fine."

I nodded even though I was already planning the death of Micah in my head. He needed to get his shit together.

"No, get that look off your face, Domo. You're not touching him." Yurik threatened pointing a finger at me. I faked a launch at him and he squealed before jumping back and behind my mother who was currently glaring at me.

"Stop this nonsense. I'm hungry, let's go eat."

Seated at a dinner table with the majority of guests being unfamiliar was not how I wanted to spend my birthday. I wanted to be with Caitlin, on her couch underneath a cosy blanket getting high and watching trash movies. She sat beside me with my hand on her bare thigh as she chatted to my parents about whatever.

The server set her appetizer plate in front of her and I frowned looking down at the food. I grabbed the waiters forearm and clenched my jaw.

"I thought I told the kitchen not to put mushrooms on our plates." I said irritably. Caitlin being deathly allergic to the food item and still receiving it when I had mentioned not to angered me to the point where I wanted to snap the entire staffs neck.

"Oh, my apologies." The server, Timothy, said with wide eyes and I let go of him trying to calm myself. He quickly grabbed the plate and scurried away before I had a chance to lash out on him.

"I could've eaten around it." Caitlin said and I looked her in disbelief. Absolutely not.

"No." I stated.

"Damn Domo, you nearly sent the guy into cardiac arrest." Yurik commented and my parents just watched us in amusement.

"No he just cares for her." My mother said gently and my father nodded sending me a look that meant we were going to talk later. I already knew what the conversation was going to be about and I mentally prepared myself for it.

The night went smoothly, the food was delicious and Caitlin seemed to be enjoying it. Wishes upon wishes, I was starting to get annoyed at my own birthday. I had a hunch that my mother had invited all the guests for herself to catch up with and not for the sake of celebrating my birth.

There was a point when Caitlin, Aria and my mother were so deep in conversation that they paid no mind to us. That's when my father got up from his seat. I excused myself and started following him to the balcony.

I closed the sliding door behind us and saw him standing at the railing overlooking the dark golf course. Although my parents were never home, their house was one of the biggest in the city - I lived there for a while until I realised that the space was too much.

It felt cold, lifeless and empty.

"Valencia's kid, huh?" He muttered and cut off the end of a Cuban cigar with a mini guillotine.

"Yes." I replied and rested my hands on the cold white railing. My father lit the cigar away from him before handing it to me. I wasn't a nicotine smoker - I hated the taste but I took it from him anyway.

"You knew?" He asked and started focusing on his own cigar. The smell of tobacco lingered in the air along with the scent of freshly cut grass.

"No I didn't." I said truthfully toying with the brown stick between my fingers. He was analysing the situation, the same way he always did when we would run into any conflict.

"I'm guessing Yurik didn't either." He sighed.

"If I'm going to do this for you, you have to be one hundred percent sure that you want this. I don't know how both my sons ended up with the opposition but it is what it is." My father said before taking a deep thoughtful inhale of the cigar. It lit up the end and the paper begin to vanish. When he exhaled, the thin cloud of smoke vanished into the cold air within seconds.

"What if I want to talk to him? He needs to know how much I care for his daughter." I said and brought the cigar up to my lips. The smoke cascaded down my throat and I held it there for a brief moment before exhaling.

"And I'll make sure he gets the message. It started with me and it's going to end with me." He said determinedly and I nodded not bothering to disagree. He always cleaned up his own messes without seeking help from others and I knew an argument would be in vain.

My grandfather was the foundation to our empire, passed down to my father and eventually passed down to me. A hundred years of the Romanovs and a shitload of commemorations with an even bigger load of rising competitors, a few wars were bound to occur.

"Ultimately, it all comes down to Alarico and his decision. The stubborn bastard." My father said with a disapproving shake of his head. In the long run, our side was willing to establish peace and if Caitlin's father wasn't up for it then there was nothing we could do.

"Despite all of that, I have to admit that he's very family orientated and loyal. That's why he's behind bars while his men are roaming free." He said and held a certain respect in his eyes.

Loyalty was one of the most important principles we carried. Love, respect, awe, it all meant nothing without a full-hearted devotion.

"One more thing," He said and turned to me. "I'm only going to ask him once. If he says no then that's that."

"I know."

CHAPTER 24

C AITLIN

"I've had enough social interaction to last a life-time." I said exasperatedly and fell down onto my couch face first. Dominic groaned out loud and shrugged his jacket off before setting his gun down and unbuttoning his shirt.

After having a mind-blowing orgasm on a table then proceeding to act normally in front of his parents was beyond draining.

"Me too. I don't want to talk to another human, besides you, for like a month." He said exhaustedly and walked to my fridge to grab a bottle of wine and two glasses. I smiled as I watched him, loving how he made himself at home.

"I love your parents." I said. Dominic had the hottest dad I've ever seen but I clamped my mouth shut to prevent myself from blurting it out impulsively. The resemblance was uncanny.

His mother - absolutely gorgeous. So beautiful that it stunned me but her soft personality stunned me even more. I could see where Dominic got certain characteristics, the way he carried himself and the way he longed to take care of those around him was evidence that he grew up with a loving family.

"They love you." He replied while focusing on pouring the red liquid into a tilted wine glass. He handed it to me and I took it appreciatively sitting up.

"I wish you could have met my extended family, my grandparents, cousins, but they're in Russia. One day I'll take you there." He muttered and took a seat next to me. My eyes widened down to my glass and I avoided looking at him. Things were moving so fast - I was only just crossing the invisible line into unwandered territory but it felt like I was about to walk off a cliff.

"Or not...why do you look so frightened? Hey, stop. We don't have to, it was just a thought." Dominic said quickly and squeezed my bare shoulder. I took a deep breath in and nodded.

"Don't stress me out like that. I'm still recovering from conversing the entire night." I muttered and took a small sip. My bubble was one that consisted of very few people. I liked to keep to myself, stay at home and lately it felt like my bubble was being broadened to accompany more and more.

"I know." Dominic replied and stretched his arm out on the back of the couch. I set my glass down onto the table and stood up, grinning down at him.

"What is it?" He asked smiling slightly.

"I know you said you didn't want anything," I said excitedly and raised my hand when he opened his mouth to speak. "What's done is done, don't argue with me."

"I didn't know what to get so I asked Yurik but he could only give me answers like 'a mouthful of tits' or 'a face full of ass' which didn't help at all because that's a daily occurrence." I muttered and walked to my kitchen.

Dominic chuckled holding the wineglass to his lips. "He's not wrong."

I furrowed my brows at him. "Later, not now. First," I retrieved the box from the counter along with a lighter from the cutlery drawer. "Cake!"

"Cake?" Dominic laughed and his eyes sparkled with pure joy. "I love cake."

"A special choco-cara-nilla cake that I spent all afternoon on." I said proudly and set the box down in front of him. I lifted the lid and the four sides fell to reveal the three-layered cake covered in chocolate frosting and topped with just one white candle.

I wasn't about to place twenty six candles on a cake.

Dominic's grin widened and his face radiated pure happiness. "You baked me a cake?"

"I did indeed bake you a cake." I nodded feeling self-satisfied with my little experiment.

"And you remembered my favourite flavours." Dominic said softly and scooted to the edge of his seat, gazing down at the circular cake.

On our first date Dominic ordered a sundae with those flavours and I remembered thinking to myself how the fuck does he eat that?

"Duh," I rolled my eyes. "You're the only person I know who'll order this." I said and lit the candle sparking a small orange flame. The frosting was a bit messy but it didn't look too bad and I was proud of my hard-work.

"Go on. Make a wish." I gestured with my hand. Dominic gave me a glance before leaning forward and blowing out the candle with a quick huff. The flame died, leaving nothing but blackened thread and a small swirl of smoke. A satisfied grin crossed both our faces.

"Thank you." Dominic said genuinely and I stepped forward to give him a peck on the forehead. He deserved it and so much more.

"It's the least I can do." I mumbled and kissed him across his face, down his nose and onto his lips. "I have to warn you thoug h..."

"Mmm?" He hummed and I pulled away but kept my hand on his cheek while softly stroking my thumb. Towering over him as he stayed seated, he had to crane his neck to keep eye-contact.

"I made cannabutter and used it in the chocolate sponge. I figured putting it in the entire cake would be a bit much." I said and watched his eyes widened, almost eagerly.

"We getting high?" He asked with an excited smile and clasped my hand in his own.

"We getting high." I replied with a nod.

"This is perfect. This is how I wanted to spend my birthday. Thank-"

"Ssh, baby. You say thank you way too much." I repeated his own words and witnessed his expression soften. Dominic stood up and hugged me, just a regular platonic hug that accelerated my pulse and caused a sigh of content to escape me.

Dominic sighed. "What are we doing right now?" He asked solemnly and I frowned at his sudden change of tone. I went to pull away but he held me tightly against him. "No, don't let go."

"Okay," I circled my arms around him again and applied the tiniest bit of pressure. "I won't."

"I mean...okay, fuck that..." Dominic gripped my cheeks in one hand, squeezing it and stared at me with a look of seriousness. "You are my girlfriend, yes?" He stated more than questioned, eyes filled with a strong intensity.

I gazed at him for a while before a slow smile spread across my face.

"What?" He asked looking taken aback.

"I thought we already established that this morning when you said you're mine." I replied softly and put my hands underneath his shirt to feel the bare skin on his back.

"Yeah?" Dominic grinned biting his lower lip. The dimple on his cheek was emphasised and his eyes shone with a glee that almost knocked me off my feet. Why wouldn't I want to be this handsome as fuck mans girlfriend?

"Yeah." I said with a nod and he let out a small chuckle before leaning down and kissing me. The taste of red wine lingered on his lips and I moaned against him.

Dominic's growing bulge against my stomach ruined the moment.

"Really?" I questioned cocking an eyebrow down at his crotch.

"Oh don't look at me like that. I can't help it. Let's have some cake." He waved it off and walked to my kitchen to collect plates and forks.

As I kept my eyes on him, a strange feeling swept through me, one I couldn't quite understand. It was nearing midnight, almost the end of Dominic's birthday and instead of accepting the offer of staying at his parents' house, he was there with me in my small apartment.

I sat down and twiddled my thumbs together, deep in thought. Dominic helped me overcome my own personal issues without even trying, he did it with his mere presence and proceeded to alleviate the protective barrier I had built.

It was just supposed to be sex.

"Angel, your fridge is empty. We need to go do that shopping." Dominic muttered and plopped down next to me. I couldn't help the twitch of my lips and the euphoric heat pumping through my chest.

It stopped being just sex a long time ago.

The next morning I woke up unbelievably confused. The sound of something buzzing resonated through the back of my mind, gradually getting louder and louder. I shifted and my leg brushed against a large body scaring the literal fuck out of me.

"Fuck!"

I completely forgot that I was lying next to Dominic.

My heart thumped repeatedly against my ribcage as I clutched my chest trying to calm myself down. Dominic didn't move, he continued sleeping on his side holding a pillow in his arms oblivious to outburst. The buzzing continued and I groaned rubbing my eyes and sitting up.

The clock besides my bed read 15:23. At first I ignored it, not paying much attention before it finally sunk in and I gasped.

We had slept for over fourteen hours.

"Dominic, wake up." I croaked and climbed out of bed trying to find the fucking vibration noise that wouldn't stop. I glanced around, not finding anything.

My hair was a messy, my t-shirt wrinkly and my face felt swollen. I realised in that moment that we ate way too much cake but that was one of the best sleeps I've ever had.

"Where the fuck are you?" I muttered to myself. Dominic was still in a deep sleep, looking like he was dreaming of the most amazing scenario ever. I felt like smacking him in the face.

I picked up Dominic's suit jacket and felt around until my hand wrapped around his phone. As soon as my eyes focused on the screen, the buzzing stopped and a dozen messages popped up followed by even more missed calls.

All from someone called Natalia.

"Hey, wake up." I shook his shoulder gently but he remained unmoving.

I paused and took a step back, frowning down at him. He was unusually still and I attentively watched his chest for the faintest breathing, sighing in relief when I saw the tiniest movement.

After trying to be gentle with him, I realised that it wasn't working. I took a pillow and hit him on the head with it as hard as I possibly could. Finally his eyes shot open and as expected, Dominic grabbed me and threw me on the bed wrapping his hand around my neck tightly.

"Mmm, kinky." I rasped out, unable to breathe. Dominic had a puzzled look on his face, looking as confused as I felt when I just woke up.

"Shit, I'm sorry." Dominic murmured hastily and quickly removed himself. I sat up and coughed, soothing my neck with my hand.

"It's fine." I wheezed and stretched my arm out to him giving him his phone "Natalia is looking for you."

Dominic didn't take it from me but his face recognition unlocked the messages, showcasing every single one of them. One of them was an image, the tiny block a light brown with a distinct pink. Another one popped up but this time it was very clearly a girls cleavage covered in a pink lacy bra.

'Happy belated birthday Nick! I'm sorry for not wishing you yesterday, I was so caught up in work. I was wondering if you're free today? We could get something to eat and you could come to my place afterwards. Let me know xx'

The blood drained from Dominic's face and I bit my lip dropping the phone on his lap when he wouldn't take it. It started to vibrate again and her name flashed on her screen.

"Angel..." Dominic said softly and turned to me, ignoring the incoming call. I stared at him with a blank face, a nauseous feeling washing over me. The amount of rage that begin to pump through my veins had me clenching my fists. Eventually I stood up and walked away - Dominic caught me immediately by circling his hand around my wrist.

"Stop. I don't know why she's sending me that. I told her to leave me alone." He explained and I swallowed down the tight feeling in my throat. Why do you have her number? I ripped my arm out his hold and carried on walking to my bathroom.

"Angel."

"Caitlin." Dominic's voice hardened, immediately freezing my steps.

He wouldn't...you know that.

I turned around and sighed, slumping my shoulders. The phone rang again, but this time Dominic answered and switched it to loud speaker.

"Oh my gosh, finally! You hungover or what?" A feminine voice nearly screeched and my face turned cold.

"Why are you irritating me, Natalia? Didn't I tell you to stop bothering me?" Dominic asking glaring down at the screen with a murderous expression.

"Did you get my pictures? Sexy, right? Come help me take it off." The girl whined and I scoffed crossing my arms.

"No. Call me one more time and I'll have someone drive to your house to slit your fucking throat." Dominic growled and my eyes widened - my first time ever hearing him speak that way. He put the phone off and threw it on the bed before pinching the bridge of his nose.

"Dominic..." I said softly and when he finally looked at me, I couldn't help but take a step back at the icy expression on his face.

"You have such little faith in me." He muttered and picked up his pants, rushing to put it on. My jaw dropped - Dominic looked hurt.

"No...don't do that, please. I just-"

"You just what? After everything we spoke about, been through, you were so quick to assume the worst of me." He said frowning. He zipped up his pants and fastened his belt before collecting his shirt.

"Where are you going?" I asked watching him pick up all his things. I felt terrible - Dominic never gave me a reason to not trust him.

"I have missed calls from Yurik and my parents. I have to go." He replied not looking at me. I grabbed his hand stopping him from leaving.

"Don't be mad at me, please." I said quietly, intertwining our fingers together. Dominic sighed and brought my hand up to his lips for a kiss.

"I'm not mad at you. We kind of slept the day away and I have people looking for me." He mumbled and let go of me. I nodded giving him some space even though my mind was screaming at me not to.

With a kiss on the forehead, Dominic left my room and a moment later the front door opened and closed. I groaned out loud and covered my hands with my face, falling down onto my bed.

I didn't know who Natalia was but I wanted to beat her face in.

CHAPTER 25

C AITLIN

"Caitlin, can you open the door please? I need to talk to you." Micah's voice emitted from the front door followed by the soft banging of his fist. I groaned out loud setting my wine glass and book down on the table. I was having the most peaceful relaxing evening and the disturbance rattled me.

I tied my silk gown covering up my bra clad breasts and underwear. Being semi-nude in the comfort of my own home all alone was magnificent even though I'd much rather have the company of Dominic.

"Hey." I opened the door and he wasted no time in stepping inside.

Micah wrapped his arms around me for a brief hug and let out a heavy sigh. "I'm sorry for being the worst brother ever." He apologised tightening his hold nearly to the point of suffocation. A small smile graced my lips when he pulled away and looked at me with a sullen expression.

"Yurik got to you?" I asked laughing slightly.

Micah shook his head. "No. Dominic did. He threatened to break my knees if I don't sort out my shit but please don't tell Yurik. I kind of needed to hear it."

My eyes widened. "He said that?"

"Yes. He made me realise what a trash person I've been lately, caught up in my own bullshit and failing to see who I'm hurting." Micah muttered and we both took a seat at the kitchen table. I poured him a glass of wine and he took it appreciatively.

"Micah, it's really not-"

"No, let me take responsibility." He interrupted giving me a look and I had a feeling Dominic did a lot more than just threaten him.

"You're my sister, mi hermana and I'm barely in your life. I wasn't even at your graduation and I am so sorry. The...chat with Dominic opened my eyes and made me understand how selfish I've been. With you and Yurik." Micah mumbled the last sentence and took a sip of the deep red wine. I had to admit that Micah not showing up for my graduation hurt me more than I'd like to admit.

"Yurik really likes you. You need to stop pushing him away." I said and clasped my hands together.

"I know I do. It's just so hard when Papa and the Romanovs-"

"Wait, you knew?" I asked and perked up in the seat.

"Shit," He whispered and looked to the side. "I was going to tell you but Mama told him it's best if you didn't know." Micah said. Why was my mother so dead-set on me not finding out?

"Wow," I breathed out. "How long have you known?"

"Only a few months. Once I found out about the rivalry, I stopped visiting him because I didn't want him to find out I'm with the enemy. It's so fucked up and I don't know what to do anymore." Micah said solemnly and I nodded. It was a shitty situation to be in and I understood fully.

"Yurik says he doesn't care and I'm sure Dominic doesn't care too but I'm still scared. That's why I'm trying to stay away from Yurik but it's hard. He's so persistent." Micah said and a small smile brightened up his face. I could see that he cared deeply, even though he struggled to show it sometimes.

I leaned back into my seat taking it the information I had just found out. Perhaps I was making it a bigger deal than what it was - perhaps I was looking too deep into it.

"Look, I promise I'm going to be better, okay?" Micah said. "Dominic made sure of that." He mumbled so lowly that I barely heard him.

"What did he do? Did he hurt you?" I asked frowning.

"My feelings, yes." Micah laughed. "That one has no filter but he's just looking out for you and his brother."

I glanced at the clock on the wall. It was 8pm and I haven't heard from Dominic since he left which was only a few hours ago. Usually he would text throughout the day. Maybe he's just busy

Micah and I continued talking for the next hour, catching up and talking about life in general when he reminded me why we couldn't hang out for too long.

"You fucking little shit. I will fucking kill you." I sneered when he hit me over the head with a sofa pillow. I was trying to steady my hand to remove a block without causing the entire stack to fall over but Micah kept trying to distract me.

"Just remove it." Micah taunted and threw another cushion at me. It hit me in the face and caused the entire rack of blocks to fall over. I grit my teeth and glared at him - he was so fucking annoying.

"Oh, you want to make me angry." I stood up immediately but Micah was already sprinting to the front door, dodging all the objects on the floor and nearly tripping.

"Love you, bye!" Micah said quickly and waved at me before exiting my apartment hastily. The door slammed shut instantly. I sighed out loud and started fixing my living room until the place was back to its prior tidy state.

I picked up my phone, contemplating whether or not to call Dominic until eventually deciding to just go ahead and click his name. The phone rang and rang and just as I was about to accept defeat, he answered.

"Hi, angel." Dominic greeted breathlessly. He was panting heavily and I resisted the urge to assume the worst.

"You busy?" I asked gingerly, feeling as if I had just disturbed him.

"No," he breathed out. "I'm never too busy for you." Dominic murmured before he grunted and someone in the background gave out a loud cry. My face twisted into confusion.

"What are you doing?" I asked, my curiosity heightened.

"Just...wait, hang on." He said and a second later a loud gunshot startled me. "Oh wow, this fucker was getting on my last nerve. Yurik, request a clean-up." Dominic demanded and the sound of metal clanking against metal could be heard. He sighed heavily.

Okay...he just killed someone.

"I was going to call you and apologise for how I left," Dominic said and a door slammed shut and a chair scraped against a wood. "I'm sorry. I was the one who overreacted and did the dramatic-ass exit. Who the fuck do I think I am?" He said and I kept in my laughter.

"It's only because I care about you so much and the slightest indication that I'm going to lose you gets me so unreasonably mad. Insecure? Probably but just know that if you leave me, I will fight whoever ends up with you." Dominic said and a chuckle left my lips.

"I don't doubt that you will. I should've known that you weren't doing anything wrong, it just happened and I'm sorry too." I apologised and laid down on the sofa. My body was hot from the wine so I undid the tie around my robe.

"I should've taken care of it a long time ago when I realised she was going to be a problem but don't worry, Yurik is going to sort it out. I was going to but he insisted."

"What is he going to do?"

"Don't worry about it, angel. You know how he is." Dominic reassured dismissively.

"Okay...I won't. Micah just left, he said you-"

"He's lying." He interrupted me.

"But-"

"Whatever he said, he's lying. I didn't do anything of the sort." Dominic said quickly and I grinned.

This man...

"Alright. I'm going to pretend I believe you. I'm bored, can we do something?" I asked and turned over to lay on my stomach, crossing my ankles.

"It's almost 10..." Dominic said and I tightened my lips in slight disappointed. "Of course we can do something. Pack and I'll be there in about half an hour. We're going to a hotel. I need to get away from all of this shit."

"A hotel?" I repeated excitedly. "That sounds so nice right now."

"There's a Jacuzzi...just saying." Dominic mumbled but I could hear the suggestiveness.

"Right." I nodded despite the fact that he couldn't see me.

"See you soon, angel."

As soon as he put the phone off, I was jumping up and heading straight to my bathroom to freshen up. Dominic had a habit of showing up sooner than he said he would, so I had to be quick.

When I was done, I started packing all necessary items feeling all giddy inside.

It didn't take long before Dominic was at my door greeting me with a kiss on the lips. "You don't have to walk to my door every time you pick me up." I said as he took the bag from my hands.

"That's disgusting. Don't ever say that to me again." Dominic scowled.

My eyes travelled down his body noticing the gun holsters strapped to his suspenders. His white shirt was tight, emphasising every crevice of muscle. Dominic was carrying two firearms out in the open, with no attempt to hide it

I loved how he literally didn't give a fuck if anyone saw it or not.

"Dominic, you're bleeding." I stated looking down at his knuckles. The skin was torn open, bruised and a crimson colour. It looked like it hurt...a lot.

"I know," he clenched his fist and brought his hand up to his face examining it. "Another rapist."

My skin began to crawl when Dominic said that and my expression twisted into one of disgust. He noticed and wrapped a comforting arm around my shoulders.

The things Dominic did in his daily life was something that I thought about often. I wondered if it would one day take its toll on him and as I paid close attention, I realised that perhaps I was Dominic's escape from the reality he had to face every day. I smiled at him and leaned up to kiss his jawline.

"I hope he suffered. Next time, can I watch?" I asked hopefully. Dominic looked at me quizzically and his brows furrowed.

"What do you want me to do? Call you and say 'I'm going to kill someone, do you want to come over' because I'll do it...I just don't think you'll be able to handle it." He shrugged and my mouth fell open.

"We both know that I'll be able to handle it. In fact, we both know how hot I'll find it." I muttered.

Dominic looked pleasantly surprised. "Alright, but don't say I didn't warn you. It can get pretty ugly."

"Woah." I gawked when I stepped out of the elevator. The hotel room was far from what I expected. It was open, spacious and resembled a lavish penthouse. Fine marble flooring, dark walls, ceiling to floor glass and a king sized bed just calling my name. It was beautiful.

Upon arriving, we didn't need to book in and Dominic revealed that he owned the hotel. It didn't surprise me - the amount of buildings that he owned was countless and I knew not to question it.

I nearly squealed in delight when I saw the cart of canapés and fruit salad waiting us. There were also two bottles of bubbly resting on a bed of ice.

"How the...this is so pretty." I said in awe and walked to the glass sliding door, stepping out onto the large patio balcony. Just like Dominic said, there was a Jacuzzi as well as a brightly lit pool. The night was dark, strewn with twinkling stars and lit by orange streetlights. I breathed in the crisp air and sighed out loud.

Strong arms wrapped around my chest from behind and a chin rested on my head. Dominic hummed in content and I kissed his forearm. The amount of versatility that Dominic had was unmatched, ranging from hot as fuck to cute as fuck. As much as I enjoyed both sides of him, in that moment I was craving control and aching for his submission.

He needed to know that he had nothing to worry about.

I turned around in his hold and grabbed the collar of his shirt, bringing him down to my height. A look of surprised flickered through his features but I ignored it, pressing my lips against his with enough force to have him gasping into my mouth.

"Bed," I said. "Now." I demanded, gazing at him with enough intensity to convey how serious I was.

CHAPTER 26

D OMINIC

"Now, be still. Don't fucking move." Caitlin whispered, her attitude making me want to grab her by the neck and fuck the breath out of her.

I was laid in the centre of the bed, her thighs straddling my waist and her clothing covered pussy pressed against my dick with enough force to have shivers travelling through me.

I grit my teeth in annoyance and clenched my fists in an attempt to stop myself from flipping us over and ripping her underwear off. Caitlin wanted to be in charge, she wanted to control the pace and it took every sliver of my resistance to grant her her wish.

I was two seconds away from doing the exact opposite of what she so greatly sought.

She leaned down and patted my cheek, a condescending smirk on her face. "Good job."

Those two words made me kiss my teeth and I yanked my chin away from her touch. Good job? The woman on top of me had all sorts of emotions running through me, ones that were venturing to a place that I was afraid I would struggle to return from.

"You are always fucking me." Caitlin leaned down and brushed her soft lips against my neck. A sigh of content escaped my lungs and when she flicked her tongue out, I grinded upwards desperate for any form of friction.

"Tonight, I'm going to fuck you." She whispered before I was hit with cool air as she scurried off me. Her weight on me disappeared, her warmth vanishing and I looked at her puzzled, wanting her back immediately. She began rummaging through her suitcase, pulling out a black cloth.

"Come back." I demanded, sounding like a love-struck fool as I propped myself onto my elbows. I wanted her close to me and she was way too fucking far.

"A loss of one sense enhances the others." She said sultrily, fiddling with the cloth dangling off her fingertips. For a moment, I thought she was talking about herself until her gaze flicked to me and I saw her agenda in high definition.

I shook my head. "No way."

I wanted to see her, every part of her. I wanted to see the look on her face, the way her lips tainted red each time we fucked and the way her skin would glow with perspiration. Blindfolding me would be...a robbery of my visual pleasure.

"I'm sorry, what did you say?" Yet again, her thighs were around my waist and she sunk down on me. Even with the separation of our clothes, I found myself groaning nearly forgetting the item she had in her hand.

"I said..." I tried to utter the words but she moved her hips and pleasure sparked through me. It melted down any objection I had building up and I caught myself saying, "fine."

At that point if she wanted to empty my bank accounts, I'd let her. Caitlin was powerful in a way that rendered me hopeless against my own inhibitions and when she smiled at me, I lost it entirely.

Her hands went to place the blindfold around my eyes but I stopped her, gesturing down to the guns still on my suspenders. "Wait. Let me take these off."

Caitlin smirked. "I'll do it." Then my head was lifted and my vision was darkened as the cloth covered my eyes. Immediately, the feel of her body on mine heightened significantly and my breathing automatically quickened.

I gulped, feeling her hands trail down my stomach until it rested on my crotch, right above the zipper. I was hard - painfully hard.

A moment later her lips were teasingly grazing mine and as soon as I strained my neck to deepen the kiss, she pulled away producing a growl of frustration from me. Her mischievousness was going to earn her a hard fucking but I relaxed against the mattress, much to my own dismay.

"Give me a fucking kiss." I demanded scowling into her direction. I heard her chuckle at me and it only powered my infuriation. My hand raised to grab her hip but she was quick to grasp it, pinning it above my head against the bed. The force of it had my mouth parting in surprise and I was impressed by the amount of strength she had.

Damn.

"Keep your hands to yourself, Dominic." She warned and I nodded, feeling her slowly let go of me. My hands returned to my sides, holding the sheets in my fists in an effort to stop myself from reaching out to her again.

Caitlin unclipped my suspenders, letting it fall besides me and she started unbuttoning my shirt, torturously slow. With each button, her fingers caressed my skin and that's when the excitement began to lay its foundation. Eventually my shirt was flung open and I felt her move slightly, my brows furrowed in scepticism.

The cold tip of something hard and metallic stroked my bare stomach and I gasped. "Is that my gun?"

"Maybe it is, maybe it isn't." She teased and the familiar sound of the safety getting clicked off reached my ears. She cocked it like a pro and the noise was loud enough to have my heart accelerating. I quickly grabbed the barrel of the gun pointing it away from me while mentally glaring at her.

"What are you doing?" I frowned knowing that I always kept it fully loaded and a slight flick of her finger would have my guts decorating the sheets.

"Just relax," Caitlin rubbed my knuckles with her thumb and I gradually let go of it, feeling like I was putting my life at risk. The adrenaline of it had my erection aching with need, need for her and only her. "What's your safeword?" She asked, managing to surprise me again.

"Red." I chose the same one as her. "Don't fucking shoot me."

She knew how to handle a gun, I've seen it firsthand but anything could've gone wrong.

Caitlin wasted no time in placing the gun against my stomach again, pressing it until it hurt but the pain was welcomed along with the tingles jolting through my nerves. I inhaled sharply, hissing through my teeth.

She dragged it lower and lower until the muzzle reached my dick and I swallowed hard, my senses being overloaded by an unfamiliar feeling of ecstasy.

I couldn't believe what I was allowing.

"Shit." I whispered, my chest heaving as if I had just ran a marathon. Caitlin pushed further, holding the gun steady against the length of my dick and a tremble reverberated through my bones.

The danger...the darkness...the heat of her body...it all grouped together to form a mind-blowing euphoric pleasure that I didn't expect to enjoy.

She swirled the tip over my dick and I heard her intake a quick breath. Caitlin was enjoying it, seeing me quiver beneath her as I bent to her will. A storm began brewing inside me, riddled with impatience and anticipation.

With her free hand, she unbuttoned my pants and pulled my zipper down. Is this what falling for someone entails? Wanting to make them so happy you're willing to step out of your comfort zone for them? The thought seemed surreal but I stopped thinking about it the second my pants and boxers were dragged down.

Caitlin rested the gun on my stomach, the cool metal soothing my hot skin and I breathed out a shaky sigh of relief. "Put the safety back on, angel." I told her.

"No."

My gun was heavy, sensitive to touch and a bullet awaited in the chamber ready to be released at any given time.

"Put the- Oh shit." Her warm, wet mouth was wrapped around my dick and I threw my head back onto the bed. It hit the back of her throat when she started fucking her own face with me, reaching the base and holding me there until she pulled away gasping for air.

My mouth was open in disbelief at how good it felt and my hands were itching to reach for her head.

She wrapped her hand around it, twisting while simultaneously moving her head. Her mouth left me and I felt her spit onto my dick before placing me right inside of her throat again. If I wasn't laying, I would have collapsed.

Caitlin moaned around me, the vibration of her vocal chords nearly enough to send me over the edge.

"You fucking whore." I breathed out as she sucked me off passionately and hastily. Just when I thought it couldn't get any better, my words seemed to be the encouragement that she needed. She tightened her lips and pulled her cheeks in, vacuuming me into her mouth.

An array of cuss words spewed from me, English and Russian mixing together to produce incoherent sentences and mumbled gibberish.

The gun on my stomach began to feel like a figment of my imagination, even though I knew it was there. It was no longer cold, the heat of my body soaked into it but the weight was hard to ignore.

Her fist moved up and down my dick, lubricated by her saliva and her mouth went down to my balls. My hips jerked upwards, semi caught off guard but fuck, it felt amazing. I wanted to see her...I wanted to see her watery eyes and flushed face.

"Let me-"

"No. Shut the fuck up." She snapped, her hand compressing around me tightly.

I groaned and squeezed my eyes shut behind the cloth. Caitlin was right. Being blindfolded intensified the feeling of her mouth around me and it increased the pleasure in a way I didn't know was possible. She suddenly stopped, shocking me by grabbing my hands and placing them on her head.

"Fuck!" I hissed, fisting her hair and guiding her. She was putting her everything into making me feel good - but I could sense that she loved doing it.

"I'm going to cum." It came out like a whimper, my voice betraying me. Balls-deep inside of Caitlin's mouth without vision seemed like a fever dream, an erotic fever dream that I never wanted to wake up from.

Caitlin wiggled myself further into her throat and for the first time ever, I felt her gag. She didn't let up, holding me there until my orgasm spurted against her insides.

By the time I was done, I was breathless and high from one of the best orgasms I've ever had.

I heard her swallow, gulping it down until it was finished and she was panting for air. Caitlin crawled up my body and pressed her lips against mine, kissing me hard and I moaned unto her mouth. I grabbed her cheeks and shoved my tongue passed her lips, meeting her own and sucking it.

She pulled away and I felt her discard her clothes, a moment later she was straddling me again and her clit brushed the tip of my still-hard dick. Caitlin sunk down onto me, sliding me into her pussy until her ass was planted on the top of my thighs.

Fuck. She's so wet.

"You feel so good." Caitlin whispered and I grunted when she started to move. Her hands were on my chest and mine were on her hips, ignoring the fact that she told me to keep my hands to myself. I don't even think she cared anymore so I squeezed her flesh hard underneath my palms.

"Can I take this off, angel?" I asked, my words escaping shakily.

"Say please." Caitlin said softly, still moving at an intricately slow pace.

"Please, can I take this off?" I begged, desperate to see her.

"Yes."

Mistake. It's my turn now.

I pulled the blindfold off my eyes and blinked a few times, trying to adjust to the dull light of the room. Eventually, the blurriness faded away and I focused on Caitlin, nearly getting a heart-attack by how beautiful she looked.

Our pelvises were adjoined, the silver object still resting on my stomach and I stared at it for a while until my hard gaze met hers and her eyes widened. I grabbed the handle of the gun leaving the safety off and quickly flipped us over, letting her back hit the mattress. She let out a small scream, immediately getting muffled by the palm of my hand.

"You want to play with guns? Let's play." I sneered, pointing it at her head.

The look on her face should've been one of terror or horror...it was anything but. She moaned, her eyes droopy and lust-filled. I thrust into her hard, her body hitching with the force of it. With my hand still clamped on her mouth, I pinched her nostrils shut with my thumb and index finger, suffocating her.

"A loss of one sense enhances the others, right? Right?!" I growled, pounding her into the mattress. Her response was a long moan, but she made no attempt to push me away.

"Cum if you want to breathe." I said and like the obedient slut she was, she nodded.

Not long I felt her clenching around me and I decided to relieve her. Immediately gasping for air, she choked on her own breath. I pressed the gun against her temple, wanting her and needing her to feel the danger of it.

Was the thought of death such an appetising idea that she wanted to be fucked with a gun to her head? Or did she simply enjoy the adrenaline that pumped through her veins knowing that a simple push of my finger would be enough to end her life?

Not only was she being physically stimulated, but mentally as well.

One orgasm wasn't enough and I knew she could give me more. I pushed myself up on one hand and dragged the gun down her neck and to her breasts, deciding to take an extra step...or two.

"Dominic-"

"No, it's your turn to shut up now." I cut her off, pushing it into her side and lower until it reached between her legs.

We both stilled, looking at each other and that's when I pressed the tip of my gun against her clit. Caitlin gasped, her head falling back onto the bed exposing her neck and her fists frantically grasped the sheets.

What we were doing was stupid, dangerous...but also mind-numbingly fucking good.

"This is what you want?"

"Yes." She whimpered, grabbing the barrel and pushing it further into her skin. I continued to brutally fuck her into the sheets.

I was astounded by her. We unlocked several levels to our relationship and it felt like I had made Caitlin in a lab, custom-built just for me. I moved the gun away from her clit, back to her neck and persistently pulled myself in and out of her at a rapid pace.

"Fuck. I- you're so fucking amazing." I whispered, moving her sweaty hair out of her face to kiss her forehead. I flicked the safety back on and dropped the metal object on the floor besides us, picking her up and pushing her against her wall next to the bed.

Her legs spread wide, wrapping around me and I repeatedly slammed into her. The angle was deeper, her hole meeting the brim of my dick and I watched it disappear into her.

"Yes, yes, yes. Fuck. Don't stop." She bounced on me, circling her arms around my neck and locking me in place. I sucked her taut nipple into my mouth and twirled my tongue around it. Caitlin grabbed my hair, radiating pain through my scalp but I didn't mind at all.

"I'm going to cum." I said, speeding up and she tightened around me signalling that she was on the brink of another orgasm too.

"I-in me," she croaked. "It's been a week." She said, referring to the birth control shot she had taken. That was all I needed to coat her walls with my cum. I released into her and groaned out loud feeling the world around me vanishing. Caitlin followed suite, freeing her juices all over me and our essences mixed together.

That was the best sex I've ever had.

Our lips formed into grins as we stared at other each other, our heavy breathing mingling together. I pulled out and the liquid begin to trail down her legs. She shivered and I set her down onto her feet, holding her so she doesn't fall.

"That was so fucking good." We said simultaneously, chuckling when we realised. Again, at the same time our fists reached out to each other and our smiles turned into laughter as we bumped them together.

CHapTer 27

C AITLIN

Two words; fucked up.

The cum leaked out of me, covering my inner thighs and creating a ticklish sensation. My knees were bent awkwardly, trying to stop it from dripping onto the floor. Dominic watched me amused.

"Help me!" I whined reaching out to him. My throat was raw and aching, a reminder of how I had completely lost myself onto him. My legs felt weak and tingly, a tell-tale of the hard fucking I had just received. The gun on the floor, abandoned after serving its unsaid purpose.

He laughed and walked to the bathroom, returning with wet-wipes and dry towels. Dominic crouched down and wiped me clean, paying close attention to his actions. Eventually, I could sit on the bed and I blew out a relieved breath. I grimaced and laid down, holding my hands to my forehead.

"You okay?" Dominic asked and I looked at him with a blank face. The nerve of him to ask if I'm okay after he fucked me into outer space.

He smiled sheepishly before grabbing a block of ice from the champagne bucket, placing it into his mouth. I cringed - my teeth were too sensitive for that but Dominic didn't seem to be bothered by it.

He grabbed my ankles, positioning my feet flat on the bed and exposing me to him. I observed him with inquisitive eyes, wondering what he's up to.

My silent question was answered when he bent down to latch his cool mouth onto my throbbing clit. I moaned out loud, closing my eyes as he dragged the ice all over my raw pussy and relieving the heat.

"Oh, that's nice." I groaned out enjoying every second of it. When the ice was fully melted, his cold mouth remained on me until I placed my hands on his cheeks pulling him towards me for a kiss.

"Thank you." I said gratefully and pecked his lips. Dominic grinned and it was the most beautiful sight ever - his messy hair, his sparkling eyes and the fucking dimples. I hated how he managed to look good all the time.

"Let's get into the hot tub, angel."

Ten minutes later I had my white bikini on treading out into the cold early morning, late night air. It was around 2am but the streets below were still buzzing with cars and people stumbling out of clubs. We were high enough for them to appear minuscule, dark tiny spots littering the streets and illuminated by bright lights.

"Do not look at me like that." I warned Dominic when he formed that familiar lusty look on his face as his eyes wandered down my body. He was already in the tub, resting both tattooed arms on the ridge and examining me as I joined him.

"Why not? You're fucking beautiful." He complimented me with a shrug. I stepped into the hot water feeling it tingle my skin and soothing my tense muscles. I sighed once my body was emerged until just above my breasts.

Dominic glared at me when I sat opposite him.

"What?" I asked.

"You're too far. Come here." He said, reaching his arms out to me and frowning. The water bubbled and splashed as I scooted towards him, turning around and resting my back against his front. It felt amazing, being within his arms as he held me tightly.

"I'm driving to my mother on Monday." I said after a few moments of contented silence.

"Alone? How long is the drive?" He asked stroking my hair.

"Yes. It's about an hour and a half away and I'll only be there for the day." I informed him, already knowing that he wouldn't want me to go alone but it's something I've been thinking about. Dominic's hands stilled before he reached underneath the water to rest them on my belly, softly stroking the skin.

"Do you want me to...?" Dominic asked and I cuddled further into his body.

"Thank you, but I'll be fine." I assured, letting my head fall back on to his chest. I could have fallen asleep right there.

"But you'll call me if you need me, right?" He tilted his head to look down at me, a serious expression on his face. "I don't care how small the reason is, you'll call me?" Dominic placed his hand on my cheek and caressed the skin with his thumb.

"I'll call you." I said nodding my head. Dominic was attached to me in the same way I was to him. I turned around in his hold and straddled his waist, letting my core drop down on his crotch. Resting the side of my head against his chest, my arms wrapped around his back and I held on firmly.

I sighed, snuggling into him and enjoying the hot water. The position was comforting and needed after being stimulated to the point of nearly passing out.

"You're so beautiful...and you're all mine." Dominic said softly and gave me a kiss on my forehead. I closed my eyes and a gentle smile tilted on my lips.

He fucked me like he loathed my existence and then tended to me afterwards as if he cared more than he could explain. He adapted to the situation we were in easily and right then Dominic held me as if he was scared I would wither away and disappear.

"Yes I'm all yours." I whispered, feeling like I was floating on a cloud.

"You have no idea how happy that makes me, angel." Dominic responded, still caressing my hair. I could feel his heartbeat, a slow rhythmic pace that soothed my soul.

"Me too."

"What does this mean?" I asked pointing to the Russian dialect on the inside of his bicep. I wish I could read it but it looked far too complicated.

"You'll laugh at me." He said dismissively and I frowned.

"Come on, I won't."

"Promise?"

"I promise."

"Okay," he breathed and gazed down at it. "▯▯▯▯▯ ▯▯▯▯▯ ▯▯▯▯▯▯ ▯▯▯▯▯▯, ▯▯▯ ▯▯▯ ▯▯▯▯▯▯▯▯▯▯▯▯▯▯ which translates to 'life is only precious because it ends'"

My face softened when Dominic looked away from me. "I love it."

His head snapped to me. "You do? Thank you. A lot of the tattoos on my body have no real meaning but I like this quote. Every time I look at it I'm reminded about the most precious things in my life. Family...you. Angel, if I lose you, I don't think I'll be able to handle that sort of heartbreak." Dominic muttered and his grip on me tightened.

"Hey, you have no reason to be thinking about that. I might die tonight, tomorrow or fifty years from now. We're all dying so we might as well make the best of it and stop worrying about the little things." I said and craned my neck to kiss just below his ear.

Dominic smiled. "You are amazing. Do you want to go to bed?" He asked and I nodded. My eyes started to feel drowsy a while ago but I didn't want to ruin the relaxing ambiance we had created.

He stood up with me still clinging onto him. I shivered, feeling the cool breeze hit my wet skin. "Shower first and then feed me. I'm starving." I said and rested my head on his shoulder.

"Of course."

Before heading to my mother's house, I decided to stop by the prison.

It was a cold, wet Monday morning. The sky was covered with grey clouds and a light mist dampened the roads. I loved dark and dreary weather...when I was at home. I wanted to crawl back into the warm hotel bed and snuggle with Dominic's big tattooed body as he peppered kisses on my face.

I sat in my car for a while, staring at the bleak parking lot while contemplating the words I would use on my father. He cared for me, he loved me and that alone lightened the stress beginning to form. If my father were to choose a different road from what I had in mind, his verdict would go unheard. I wouldn't stop seeing Dominic.

I couldn't.

My phone rang, Dominic's name popping up and I quickly answered. "Hey."

"Hi, angel. Are you okay? I miss you."

"I left an hour ago." I said, a smiling softly. I took the knife out of my pocket and flipped it open. Dominic had 'angel' engraved on it and I examined it, my heart heavy.

If I were to enter the prison with that, surely I would be gunned down immediately so I pushed it underneath my seat.

"Doesn't matter." He said matter-of-factly.

"I miss you too but I'm about to head inside. I'll speak to you later." I muttered and leaned my forehead against the steering wheel. I was nervous.

"Okay, be safe. Bye, angel."

"Bye." I put off and inhaled deeply, preparing myself for a conversation I wasn't ready for.

Finally stepping out of my car, the soft mist fell onto me and I quickly put the hood over my head. My clothing consisted of a stolen hoodie that belonged to Dominic, loose mom jeans and sneakers. Not exactly the warmest attire for the icy weather but it made do.

I peered up to the guards standing on the tall building and holding large guns. Just as I was about to enter through the double doors, it automatically opened and a tall man walked out.

"Mr Romanov?" I said in confusion and my steps slowed down until eventually coming to a halt in front of Dominic's father. A brief shocked expression flashed on his face before it was masked by a smile. I could see where Dominic got those dimples from.

"Hello, Caitlin." He greeted, his accent thick and deep. He strode forward to give me a hug and I wrapped my arms around him, still feeling slightly perplexed. The Romanovs were definitely huggers.

"Visiting someone?" I asked when he let go.

"Yes, darling. Dominic didn't tell you?" Mr Romanov frowned, shoving his hands into his pants pockets. Everything about his three-piece suit screamed authority along with the tattoos on his neck and knuckles.

His dark hair was slightly greying but his face still looked youthful for a man who was in his late forties.

"Tell me what?" I questioned and dragged the hoodie over my hands, feeling the cold begin to seep in.

"It's best if you speak to your father. He has some good news for you." He said looking around to make sure nobody was listening. It was quiet, unusually quiet and the guards seemed to purposely have their backs to us.

Dominic must have not told me so I wouldn't get my hopes up.

"Wait," I raised a hand and paused, trying to stop myself from getting too excited at the thought of not having to deal with mafia related drama. "Please tell me that he's okay with me and Dominic, that's all."

Mr Romanov nodded, looking pleased with himself. "Yes. You're welcome."

"Oh my God," A grin formed on my face, my worries melting and vanishing into thin air. "How? It's that easy?" It sounded way too good to be true.

"Your father will explain everything to you, darling. Welcome to the family." With that, he smiled and walked to an all-black Rolls Royce where a chauffeur awaited.

CHAPTER 28

C AITLIN

"Baby girl. You're here." Papa stood up from his seat, a wide grin on his face and he stepped forward for a hug. Usually no touching was allowed but that day, the prison guards turned a blind eye and overlooked the close contact. They left us alone, closing the door behind them.

"Hi, papa." I said softly and uncharacteristically timid. My father pulled away and held me at arm's length, examining me before his face turned stern.

"You should've come to me, mija. I'm disappointed that you thought I wouldn't be okay with you following your heart." Papa spoke, gazing down at me with a slight purse of his lips. I was temporarily stunned and for a moment the air got caught in my lungs.

"Are you serious?" I mumbled and threw my head back, looking at the ceiling. "Are you actually serious?"

"Wait," He took a step back, scrunching his brows together with a confused look etched his face. "You're not happy? You're supposed to be happy. I thought this is what you want, for us to make peace so you could be with Dominic." He paused. "Wait a damn minute, did I just get played?"

"Papa, I am happy. I'm really happy." I said but the confusion remained on his features.

"You don't look happy." He mumbled, frowning.

"I spent the whole ride anxious and stressed out thinking that my own father was going to disown me when really I should have known better than that." I sighed and sat down on the metal chair, ignoring the coldness soaking through my jeans.

"I love you, okay? I just want you to be happy and if that means putting my pride aside, then so be it." He said sincerely, placing his hand on top of mine as he sat opposite me.

"I love you, too." I replied and his smile reached his eyes, glinting with happiness. It had been a while since I told him that.

"I have a proposition for you, Caitlin." He said seriously, shifting in his seat and giving me his full attention. He let go of my hand and I pulled them back into my lap.

"Yes?" I muttered warily, eyeing him suspiciously

"Don't give me that look. We both know how strong and diligent you are, you can do anything you set your mind to even if the consequences might be...hazardous. You have the potential, the will-power and the intelligence to be a great leader." He said and stilled, looking for any reaction from me but all I could do was listen intently.

"With Dominic at your side and enough training, you can have the most powerful cartel slash mafia this world has ever known." He continued and the intensity in his eyes was enough to get his point across.

My mouth dropped. "The Colombians and the Russians merging together? That's..." I shuddered. "That doesn't sound right."

"It doesn't sound right but you can make it work. I'm supposed to pass it down to Micah but I believe in you, mija."

I dragged a hand over my face, taking a deep breath in. I hated that I loved that idea.

"You have to understand that years of rivalry doesn't get forgotten so easily. You have to work for it, form an alliance and see what you can gain from establishing peace. It's a 'You scratch my back, I scratch yours' circumstance. There's no one I trust more than you to make this happen." He said leaning forward and resting his forearms on the steel table.

I chewed on my bottom lip and looked down at my hands. "Papa, your men aren't going to accept a woman as their leader. That's how this world works, unfortunately."

"You have cousins, second cousins and close family friends working for me that'll fuck up anyone who dares question your authority. That's something you don't have to worry about, I can assure you. I'm also sure Dominic won't let that happen."

It seemed too easy.

"What's the catch?" I asked, narrowing my eyes at him. There had to be something.

My father stared at me for a moment before sighing, "Marriage."

I knew it was coming but I still wasn't prepared to hear it. Growing up, marriage was never something that crossed my mind. The idea of it didn't appeal to me because I was never interested in the thought of signing a piece of paper to prove my love for someone. However, this situation was very different.

"And if Dominic doesn't accept?" I asked.

"Mija, it was his idea."

I wanted to strangle Dominic but at the same a grin slowly formed on my face as I thought about him. He wanted to be with me so badly that he was willing to merge families knowing that the amount of things that could go wrong was endless.

"I hate him." I muttered, the stupid smile still on my lips as I shook my head.

"You clearly don't." My father replied, watching me with sparkling eyes.

"I know." I sighed and rested my chin into the palm of my hand. "You still haven't told me how all of this started."

"Our parents are the ones that drove this wedge between us. They convinced us that we weren't the same and we let it get to our heads. Years went by and we went our own separate ways but somehow, friendship turned into remorse. When Urvan came to me this morning and told me that both his sons are head over heels for my own kids, I knew I had to do something to make you and Micah happy."

That's when I realised I wouldn't just be doing for it for Dominic and I. I'd be doing it for Micah and Yurik as well. That alone was enough but the amount of pressure that began to settle on me laid heavy.

"I'll do it." I deadpanned, ignoring the flashing red lights in my mind signalling danger. I wanted to be with Dominic, through everything.

Papa seemed surprised. "You will?"

"Yes, I will."

For the next hour, my father and I spoke about all things business-related. From the process I'd have to go through, the training I'd have to take and even to the house I'd have to move into. Eventually, it got too much for me to handle in one sitting that I stood up and stretched my tensed muscles.

"I still have to go to mama." I said, yawning into the back of my hand.

He pushed himself off the seat. "Your mother is not going to be happy about this. She hates everything that we are."

"But she still lives in the house you bought her." I said scrunching my nose. My parents were long divorced but everything my father ever had was still in her possession. The cars, the beach house, the money. She lived a lavish lifestyle all thanks to my father but never bothered to pay him a visit.

"I know." Papa muttered and his eyes grew sad. My chest began to feel heavy and I swallowed hard reaching out to hug him.

"I'll come see you soon, okay?"

"Thank you."

As soon as I pulled up into the familiar double door garage of my mother's home, my phone rang.

"Don't yell at me. I'm just checking in on you." Dominic said before I could even open my mouth to speak.

"I wasn't going to yell at you." I mumbled and stared out the window at the white two story house. The grass was long, the paint peeling and I could see the lack of care.

"How was the talk with your father?" Dominic asked and I could sense the nervousness in his voice. Apparently, we're getting married.

"It was okay."

"Anything interesting?"

"Not really."

"No news? Anything? Are you sure?"

"Yes, I am sure."

There was a long pause of silence. "Caitlin, I know you know what I mean. Stop fucking with me!" He whined and I finally laughed out loud. I loved messing with him.

"Who the fuck is Caitlin? I don't know her." I said and rolled my eyes.

"Sorry, angel. You're just making me feel all nervy and scared. I really, really don't want to lose you. It would ruin my day." He said and I grinned, feeling all warm inside at the sound of his deep voice.

"You won't." I reassured. "We're good. My father and I had a nice chat about everything and I said yes."

"You did?!" He yelled out excitedly before he cleared his throat. "I mean, you did?" He said in a deeper, more monotonous tone and I squeezed my lips together to stop myself from chuckling.

"I did."

"That's amazing. I can't wait to see you later, angel. I'm going to let you sit on my face." Dominic whispered the last part and I groaned out letting the back of my scalp fall back onto the headrest. I needed that.

"Don't tempt me to turn this car around right now. I might just-" I stopped when my mother opened the front door and started to frantically wave her arm at me. "Never mind. I'll see you later."

"Bye, angel."

"Bye, angel." I said and before he could protest, I put the phone off.

Stepping out of my car, I plastered a smile on my face but everything about it felt forced. I don't know why I was there - I missed her but as soon as I saw her blonde hair and blue eyes I was reminded about how different we were. Not just in looks but personality and just general behaviour.

"Caitlin, my baby." She greeted, her thin arms wrapping around my neck and nearly squeezing the life out of me.

"Hey, mama. You look so beautiful." I said softly, breathing in her strong scent of No 5 Chanel.

"I know!" She said as if it was the most obvious thing in the world and pulled away, holding my shoulder with one hand and taking a lock of my hair with the other. "What's going on with your hair? Since when do you have it curly?" My mother frowned before dropping it as if it disgusted her.

"My natural hair is curly, mama." I scowled, already annoyed with her. Her nose scrunched up, visibly repulsed. I grit my teeth, feeling that familiar wave of hot anger spreading through me.

I don't know why I was hoping she'd be different.

"I know. Just leave it. Come inside, I have a surprise for you!" She beamed, grabbing my hand and pulling me into the house. It was the home I grew up in but I felt unwelcomed even after my mother invited me in. It looked the same but felt strange and cold.

"What is it? I hate surprises." I said following behind her. I didn't hate surprises but coming from my mother, I had a gut feeling that it wasn't going to be something that I particularly liked.

And I was right.

Standing by the fire pit was my high school ex-boyfriend, Ezra. Immediately turning around and deciding that I wasn't going to deal with whatever my mother was throwing at me, I started to leave.

I wanted Dominic.

"Caitlin! How rude of you! At least talk to him." She yelled, wrapping her claw around my arm and staring at me wide-eyed. I glared at her - she knew he cheated on me and she knew he was the reason why my nudes got leaked.

"Why is he here?" I asked pointing at Ezra who stood there with a grin on his face and his hands stuffed into his pockets. That cocky, conceited smirk started to boil my blood and I clenched my jaw so hard I thought my teeth would shatter.

"I was thinking that the both of you could reconcile. Ezra was so sad when you left and he misses you." She said softly and stroked my cheek with the back of her knuckles. I stared at the brunette boy, already knowing that he hadn't changed at all and he just loved making me uncomfortable.

"Come on, don't be like that." Ezra muttered and shrugged off his leather jacket, draping it over the couch. His arms were exposed, revealing the one piece of tattoo on his bicep that he knew I used to like but right then, I almost laughed.

Dominic was covered in those.

"It was a mistake coming here." I said, more to myself than the two other figures in the living room. I wanted to leave.

"No it wasn't. Stay, please. Just talk to him and-"

"I have a boyfriend, mama. I don't want to talk to Ezra and I don't want to talk to you either." I snapped, my brows scrunching together into a frown. "Waste of my fucking time." I whispered under my breath.

"Watch your language! You are going to stay and you are going to talk to him. His father left him the Laundromat company and-"

"This is what this is about? You think he's rich?" I laughed, not believing the audacity of the woman who raised me.

"Actually, I am-" Ezra started but with one glare from me, he had his mouth snapping shut.

"I'm going. Let go of me." I declared at her, her vice grip on my arm not faltering. The amount of times I've been disappointed by my own mother was outstanding but I always had the tiniest bit of hope that she'd change for the better. As always, I was wrong.

"No, you're staying. Ezra, you can leave. I'm sorry for my daughters embarrassing behaviour." She said distastefully, her lip turning up into a snarl. I'm the embarrassing one?

"Don't worry about it, Olivia. I know when I'm not wanted." He said, almost sadly and my eyes narrowed at the blatant manipulative performance. Fucking idiot.

"What do you think you're doing? Now he's never going to want you back!" She whisper-yelled at me as soon as Ezra was out of sight. I couldn't believe what I was hearing.

"Do you not understand me? I said, I do not want him. When the fuck are you planning on letting go of my arm?" My voice raised and I tried to pry her fingers off with my free hand.

Her sick mind thought I'd want to get back with Ezra after finding out that he'd inherited a company, as if I was a leech seeking for wealth. She was blinded by the fact that he broke my heart numerous times and exposed my naked body to the entire school. I was enraged, beyond pissed.

"How dare you speak to me like that." She gasped, digging her nails into me and if it wasn't for the protective layer of my clothing, the skin would've broke.

"Like how you deserve to be spoken to?" I retorted, bending her fingers back until she eventually let go.

Her hand flew up fast, a blurry sight before it went straight to my face, slapping me on the cheek so hard that my head whipped to the side. My mouth dropped, knowing that she cut me with her nails when I felt the blood dripping down to my jaw.

My first thought; Dominic is going to kill you.

"You will not talk to me like that. I am your mother." She scolded, pointing her finger at me as I were a child. My eyes welled up with unshed tears, completely in disbelief that my own mother hit me and despite how angry I was, I couldn't find it in me to retaliate.

"You are never going to see me again." I whispered, clutching my cheek to stop the bleeding. Not waiting for her response, I turned around walking out of the house and out of her life.

"Good!" I heard her shout but it sounded far away, her voice ringing at the back of my mind. The floor was fuzzy, distorted by the tears threatening to fall. My first time crying in months and an instant headache occurred.

I halted, creasing my brows and looked straight ahead. I wiped my tears away and took a deep breath in, trying to calm my racing heart. She was not worth crying over.

"You are just like your father! A low-life who has nothing going for them. You are going to die poor, in that crappy apartment with that crappy fucking car." My mother shouted from the porch, her face red with anger.

Her words pierced me like knives but I ignored them, jumping into the driver's seat and switching on the ignition.

Driving away, I vowed to become the one thing she hated, the one thing she absolutely detested. She called me a low life so I was going to show her exactly how low I could get.

After all, I am my father's daughter.

CHAPTER 29

C AITLIN

"You do understand that I have to kill her now, right?" Dominic murmured, softly dabbing my cheek with an alcohol soaked cotton pad. His eyes were hard, his jaw clenched as he cleaned my wound with the most delicate touches.

The second he saw he saw my bruised face, his hands started to shake with a rage I've never seen before. Violent orders spurted from him, demanding to find the 'suka' who touched me.

If I hadn't stopped him, my mother would have been assassinated within the next hour. The thought pleased me more than it should have.

"Dominic." I warned, seeing the murder he had planning his head. He sighed, leaned forward and kissed my open cut.

"Angel, if someone hits you, you hit them back ten times harder. I don't care that she's your mother." He muttered, staring at me with those cold brown eyes. Dipping his middle finger into a cream, he started to lather it onto my cheek.

"I know," my chest heaved with a sigh. "I wanted to, so badly but..."

"No buts. Stop trying to turn the other cheek." He said before pausing, us both realising his innuendo and our lips broke out into grins.

"What's wrong with her anyway? She doesn't sound right in the head." Dominic commented, packing all the items back into the first aid kit. I stayed on the counter, between his legs and not wanting to move.

"I don't know. Micah thinks it's jealousy but what could she possibly be jealous of? She has everything that I don't, a fancy fucking house and a fancy fucking car." I replied, leaning back onto my palms.

My cheek was burning from where her nails had cut me, scraping the flesh away but it wasn't necessary for any sutures.

What I had planned for her was going to have her crawling back to me. I was going to make sure of it.

Dominic hummed, laying his open palms on my bare thighs. "I've heard of mothers envying their daughters. She fits the description. Trying to push you into a relationship you clearly don't want so that she can live her own pathetic life through you. Commenting on the way you look and being disgusted if you go against what she thinks is perfect. Hitting you, wanting to bruise this pretty little face. You better hope I don't run into her, angel."

"Wait...envy? Living her life through me?" I muttered, deep in thought. "You remember that one secret I told you?"

Dominic looked confused so I elaborated, "that night we got high together for the first time."

He nodded, realising what I was speaking of. "You told me that you lost your virginity to the captain of a cruise ship while on vacation with your...no, don't tell me that she-"

"Yes," I nodded. "She was the one who spoke me into it. God, how could I have been so fucking stupid? I was barely seventeen, celebrating my birthday on the deck and there she was convincing me to fuck someone 13 years my senior." I whispered, disgusted with the revelation and disgusted that I didn't realise it sooner.

"Okay, now I really have to kill her." Dominic said, his fists clenching on my thighs. He was pissed but I could see him trying to keep himself from lashing out.

"No," I grabbed his hand, looking at him determined. "We're going to wipe her clean. Take everything back that my father has ever given her and leave her begging for a buck. I want to see her regret ever fucking up with the one person who would've given her the time of day."

Slowly the fire in his eyes diminished, only to be placed by an impressed smirk. "Go on." He gestured with his hand and I jumped off the table, furrowing my brows as rage started to pump through my blood the more I thought about her.

"Even after she treated me horribly my entire life, I still drove there hoping that she had changed. Just to be slapped in the fucking face! Who the fuck does she think she is?" I yelled out, breathing heavily.

Dominic leaned against the wall, crossing his arms and silently watching me vent.

"Inviting my ex, pushing me to get back together with him knowing what he did to me. She was there! She heard me sob, all alone in my room and not once did she try to comfort me." The more I spoke, the more the realisation hit me.

My mother was a horrible woman.

My locked up father was better than her.

"She bleached and damaged my hair, wanting me to look like her. She expected me to pop out with her strawberry blonde locks." I scoffed, balling up my fists and pacing around the kitchen.

"Changing my surname from Valencia, to Haynes. I'm a Valencia, I've always been a Valencia. I don't even know to speak Spanish because of her! It was practically forbidden in our household. My abuela would give me lessons but I never caught on because I couldn't practice." I was getting angry, really fucking angry.

Dominic was quiet, letting me get out all my frustrations.

"Encouraging me to fuck the captain of a fucking cruise ship and my small brain thought it would be a good idea. I just wanted to impress her, I just wanted her to be proud of me for once in her life. I'm done trying. If she thinks I'm going to keep letting this go, she has another thing coming." I grumbled still pacing in the silent kitchen.

"She hates my father but still uses his money. The fucking leech. I'm taking everything and I'm going to leave her ass on the streets." I murmured, eventually stopped pacing after my head started to pound.

I wanted to hit something, preferably her face. I shouldn't have left.

"That's my girl." Dominic muttered proudly, pushing himself off the wall and approaching me.

"Your anger is valid. You don't let anyone mess with you, family or not. You are going to show her exactly who the fuck you are." He said softly, laying his hand on my cheek and I started to feel myself calm down. I took a deep breath in, leaning into his palm.

"That's right." I replied quietly. "You and I, we're going to build an empire bigger than this world has ever seen. Nobody, and I mean nobody, will be able to fuck with us." I said, gazing at him intensely. Determination that I've never felt before began to flow through me, and I revelled in it.

"You and I." Dominic confirmed, nodding his head. He wrapped his arms around me, pulling me in for an embrace and burying his face in my neck.

"I love you, angel." He whispered, his breath fanning my collarbone faintly.

My body stilled, my heart thrumming in my chest. When I tried to pull away, he held me firmly in place and tightened his hold on me.

"I mean it. I love you. So fucking much that it consumes me and I don't know how to stop it. I don't want to stop it. You are everything to me." He said sincerely, his voice slightly muffled by my neck and I swallowed hard, draping my fingers through his hair.

"I love you. I'm in love with you. I adore you. Whatever the fuck you want to call it, I promise that I feel it." He murmured softly, sounding somewhat scared of my reaction.

"Dominic," I breathed out, gripping his hair in my fist and pulling his head back to observe the sullen look on his face. "I love you more."

It was the truth. I loved Dominic, I loved him with every inch my heart and soul had to offer.

He scoffed, looking away from me before he stilled and slowly started gazing at me again. "Wait, you love me?"

"No, I-" I started, completely ready to say something sarcastic.

"Now is not the time to be messing with me, angel. I swear you better say you fucking love me again or I'm putting another gun to your pussy." He retorted, straightening up and wrapping a hand around my throat. I smirked, leaning up to give him a kiss.

"I'd like that." I whispered, pecking him on the tip of his nose.

"Say it." He grunted as his grip on my neck tightened.

"I love you." I wheezed, clutching onto his wrist and finding it hard to breathe. Despite that, arousal ached at my core and I squeezed my legs together.

"Louder." Dominic demanded, bringing his face closer to mine. His pupils were dilated, a dark black surrounded by a rich brown. His long eyelashes shielded his eyes when he closed them as he inhaled a stuttering breath through his mouth.

"I love you, Dominic." I said, speaking through the tight grip around my neck.

A grin formed on his face but it was different from his usual playful smile. No, this one was full of desire, relief and something obscure hidden underneath. I didn't recognise it and when I was backed into the wall with Dominic dropping to his knees, I didn't question it.

When my underwear was pulled down my thighs, I let him. He was a man possessed, enchanted by the bare pussy ahead of him and he grabbed my thigh in his large hands, hoisting it over his shoulder.

I watched him carefully, wondering how a man of his status and eminence could go on his knees for a woman and look happy doing so.

Until I remembered that he did it our very first night together. He did it again, and again, all proudly as if I was the one doing him the favour.

He didn't say anything. With a quick lick of his bottom lip and a slight nudge of his head, he silently instructed me to lift up my too big t-shirt. I did it, my heart swirling with emotions as I kept my eyes fixated on him.

He treated me like a queen from the very beginning, giving me space when I wanted and caring for me when I needed.

Dominic gave it his all, without seeking anything in return. Not once was I pushed into metaphorical corner with demands thrown in my face as he expected me to fall at his feet. Dominic never expected anything, he cared for me and slowly let me fall for him at my own pace.

I only had myself to offer and that was enough.

My pussy throbbed like a heartbeat and goosebumps adorned my skin. His tongue slid into my wet hole and I forgot how to breathe. The wall behind me was cool and hard against the back of my scalp but the hands on my thighs were warm and comforting. I moaned, closing my eyes and getting lost within the pleasure he gifted me.

He was silent, lapping me up and down with closed eyes and a peaceful expression on his handsome features. No words were spoken, even when he carried me to his bed and dropped me on all fours before sliding underneath and sinking me back onto his face.

I held the headboard tightly, my knuckles turning white from the pressure I was applying. Dominic moaned against me, swirling his tongue around while holding onto my ass. I was the one receiving the pleasure but judging from Dominic's reaction, he was loving it too.

"Lower, baby." He whispered against me, grabbing my hips and pushing me further into him. I looked down, his eyes were still closed and his mouth was still attached to my clit. I spread my knees further, lowering myself. Dominic groaned in approval.

"I love this so much." He said softly, kissing my most intimate part with thoughtful licks and pecks. His arm circled around me and that's when I felt his finger at my hole. I took a deep breath in, my stomach tightening with an approaching orgasm.

There was something different about it. Dominic wasn't just giving me head, he was showing me how much he appreciated me and I felt every piece of it.

"Cum on my tongue, angel." He instructed, and I started moving my hips, grinding against his lips. Dominic didn't care that I was making a mess from how wet I was. He didn't care that my hair had grown out over the past few days. He didn't care that I wasn't returning the act. He just cared about making me feel good.

He accepted me with the small flab on my stomach refusing to disappear no matter how hard I worked out, the stretch marks on my body and the childhood scars on my legs.

All my flaws were there but acknowledged with the most wholesome compliments and kissed with the most tender kisses.

"I love you." I said softly, knowing that I was never going to stop telling him that. His eyes shot open, a grin forming on his face before he delved into my hole, releasing my orgasm.

"I love you more, angel."

"I'm driving!" I yelled, stretching and trying to grab the keys from his hand. Dominic held it above his head, one hand on his hip as he watched me struggle to reach for it. I wasn't even getting close.

"Okay, so get it then." He said casually and beyond amused. I groaned out loud and wrapped my hands around his bicep, trying to pull it down but it only resulted in me hanging from him with my feet off the ground.

"Let's all agree that I'm driving." Dominic shrugged. There we were, outside his home in the driveway, arguing about whose driving back to my apartment.

"It's my car." I narrowed my eyes. It didn't faze him, so eventually I sighed and headed to the passenger's seat. Not forgetting to glare at him while doing so.

"Thank you." Dominic muttered, rolling his eyes and rounding the car to the driver's side. Every time he drove my car, the seat was pushed so far back and all my mirrors were changed but he insisted. I had a feeling he just loved driving a manual.

The drive back to my place was quiet, except the low murmuring of my music and the soft roar of my engine. I relaxed in the seat, watching the full moon and the cloudless starry night.

We stopped at a red light and I looked over at Dominic. He opened his mouth to say something but decided against it and turned to look out the window, a sceptical frown on his forehead. But it was too late. Three gunshots, the shattering of glass and flashes so bright it lit up the entire car.

Through the newly broken window, I saw Lucas holding a pistol in his hand. He dropped it, his face turning into a look of utter horror but he wasn't looking at me, he was staring at something next to me. Lucas slapped his hands against the outside of the car door, hurriedly gesturing for his driver to speed away.

"Fuck!" He yelled, still banging his open palms. "Go, go, go, go!" With squealing tires and a gush of smoke, he was gone.

"Angel." Dominic whispered, staring down at his chest as he attempted to stop the bleeding with his own shaky hands. There was so much blood, escaping through his fingertips and running down his arms.

Three bullet wounds.

I sniffed, pulling my t-shirt over my head and bunching it up to press against his chest. I was in shock, my body on auto-pilot even when I picked up my phone and called Yurik. I don't even remember what I told him.

"Help is coming. You're going to be okay." I said shakily, clenching my jaw as tears flowed down my cheeks. I clicked my seatbelt off and scooted closer to him, applying more pressure but I couldn't see where he was bleeding from.

There was too much blood, seeping through his white shirt.

"Angel..." Dominic croaked, coughing and blood splattered out of his mouth.

"You're going to be okay." I whimpered, trying to convince myself. Dominic smiled, his face void of any colour and his eyelashes wet with tears.

"No...please, no. Please, I'm begging you." I pleaded with him, completely scared and terrified. His smile faltered, a grimace replacing it. He was losing so much blood, so fast. I held his head in my arms, cradling him and praying for him to be okay.

"Listen, you're going to continue this, okay? You're going to make me proud, you hear me?" He grunted, clenching his eyes shut. He was finding it hard to talk, his lungs whistling as he struggled to breathe.

"I can't do this without you. I won't do this without you." I sobbed, feeling more frantic than ever.

"You will." Dominic deadpanned, hissing through his bloodied teeth.

"Where the fuck is the help!" I screamed, hitting the seat. "I'm going to drive you to the hospital, okay?" I whimpered and started to climb over. His red stained hand stopped me.

"I'm going, angel. I love you." He wheezed, cringing with each breath.

I leaned forward and kissed him on the forehead, holding my sobs in but the tears were endless. "I love you more, but it's too soon. Please, Dominic."

"No..." I whispered when his head started to fall against my lips. "No!" I yelled when he finally went limp.

"Please." I cried, holding his unmoving head in my arms, too scared to look at his face.

CHAPTER 30

CAITLIN

One week later

"Are you ready?" Yurik asked, offering me a hand and I gratefully took it. I stood up and straightened out my dress, giving him a thankful smile that he half-heartedly returned.

We were both trying so hard to stay strong.

"I've never been more ready." I said, nodding my head and putting my game face on. My blood was hot with a fierce anger but my heart, my heart was completely shattered into a million remains.

It consumed me so much that I would find it hard to sleep, hard to eat...hard to exist.

"We both know Domo would want you to do this." Yurik said, a grave expression on his face but his eyes held a fury that matched mine.

"And he'd be so damn proud of me." I murmured, lifting my head to look at the ceiling when I felt tears start to spring to my eyes.

Yurik looked away, seeking comfort in Micah who stood right alongside him with a hand on his shoulder. We were all hurting.

Yurik had Micah. Mrs Romanov had Mr Romanov. Me? I was supposed to have Dominic.

"Come on, you can do this." Yurik said, his voice hard with a newfound strength. I swallowed hard, following him downstairs into the secluded basement. At the closed metal door, I squeezed my fists closed trying to stop them from shaking.

"Here." Yurik muttered, handing me one of Dominic's guns. "I'll be right behind you. Micah, go wait for us upstairs." He instructed and Micah nodded, already knowing his attempt to stop me would be useless.

Yurik effortlessly twirled his knife around his fingers, a blood-seeking vengeance taking over the both of us. When he opened the door, that feeling heightened to the greatest lengths and I grit my molars together.

Lucas was in the middle of the room, his wrists bounded by a chain hanging from the ceiling as he balanced on the tips of his toes. The sight should have had me grimacing, but a sadistic smirk made its way to my lips instead.

He lifted his head when he heard us entering, a patronising but tired smile on his chapped lips. He had been dangling like that for at least two days and it was finally time for me to settle my scores.

"Hi, babe. You don't look too good." Lucas teased, watching me as I walked to the tray in the corner of the room. Yurik was quiet behind me as I set Dominic's gun down and put the surgical gloves on.

Humming and pursing my lips in thought at the item I should use, I opted for a pair of long nose pliers.

"What? You think you some hot-shot mafia queen now? You don't have it in you, little lady." Lucas remarked, grinning when I stood right in front of him.

He was sweaty, dirty and he smelled like horse shit.

"What you going to do, huh? Come on, I'm having a bad day, gimme a kiss." He pouted his lips at me and I licked my teeth, tilting my head to the side.

"Nice piercing." I mumbled, trailing the pliers over his eyebrow where the black bar was located. When he opened his mouth to speak, I clamped the pliers over skin and metal and ripped it out, successfully shutting him the fuck up.

Lucas grunted and I know he was trying not to scream out loud even when blood started pouring over his eye and down his face.

"Is that the best you got?" He taunted, flicking his tongue out and tasting his own blood. He had energy after being fed the minimal amount of water and food to keep him going just the slightest bit.

"I thought he's supposed to be doing the dirty work?" Lucas asked, referring to Yurik. "You're too pretty to be doing this."

"How many piercings do you have, Lucas?" I asked, trailing the bloody pliers over his neck and leaving a long trail of red smears.

"That's my only one." He breathed, blinking through the blood in his eye and I could see it bothering him. I didn't believe him so with one nod of my head at Yurik, he started to cut up Lucas's clothes.

"Oohh," I said in awe, staring down at his pierced belly button. "We got a liar."

"A killer, drug dealer, thief, whatever floats your boat." He shrugged nonchalantly.

"Okay," I muttered, pressing the sharp edge of the pliers into his naval while watching his wincing face.

"You're not going to need this anymore." I said before clamping it onto the metal, twisting and effectively tearing it through the skin. Blood gushed out, a gaping wound left that had him groaning in agony.

"Fuck," He exhaled shaking his head and giving me another dark grin. "The ladies loved that, but you don't mind, right? Turn around, all this action is making me hard." He licked his lower lip and peered down my body.

I hadn't noticed that Yurik had his fingers in a brass knuckle until his fist went slamming into Lucas's cheek.

A sickening crunch was heard followed by blood leaking out of his mouth as he spit his broken teeth on the floor. His smile was now gone.

"Sorry, I couldn't help myself." Yurik apologised, taking a step backwards.

"I think you're hiding another piercing, Lucas. Tell me where it is." I instructed, leading the pliers down to his sweatpants cladded crotch. He tried to hide the slight widening of his eyes but I saw it and smiled. Lucas was scared.

"Why don't you put your mouth there and find out." He growled, darting his eyes between Yurik and I. "Or wait, I don't mind the silver haired psycho. I hear you like dicks, huh? Isn't that right? Come here, baby." Lucas gave air kisses to Yurik, laughing in the process.

Not wanting to see his disgusting dick, I clamped the pliers over the sweatpants latching onto the soft flesh underneath. Lucas's face went stoic, the brave expression faltering by the second.

"Why did you do it?" I asked, gradually increasing the pressure until his eyes were pleading me to stop but Lucas was stubborn.

"I'm not telling you shit." He hissed, his wrists starting to thrash against the chains. I shrugged, squeezing the handles until a pan- icked whimper left his lips.

"Stop." He gasped, his knees buckling from the pain. I didn't stop.

"Tell me why you did it." I demanded, unfazed by his terrified and hasty thrashes.

"Fuck you." Lucas snapped, baring his bloodied and broken teeth at me.

"Very well." I said, adjusting the handles in my hand to squeeze so tight that blood started to soak through his pants.

Lucas screamed, his actions turning up a notch to a violent level. The long tipped pliers had managed to break the thin skin underneath the cotton material.

"Stop!" Lucas yelled out, shutting his eyes and I watched with a blank face as the red liquid start to cover his entire crotch. The scent of piss begin to waft through the air and I scrunched my nose up watching the light grey turn dark down his leg.

Ew.

"You know what you have to do, Lucas. I'm not going to stop." I taunted, clenching my hand forcefully. His face was flushed red and sweat travelled down his body, mixing with the blood coming from his eyebrow and naval.

"Your dick is going to be on the floor if you don't tell me your agenda, Lucas." I yelled out, putting all my anger into it.

"Fuck, fuck! Okay, okay, okay! I'll tell you, just stop. Please." He screamed, breathing heavily with tears streaming down his dirty cheeks. Where did the tough guy act disappear so quickly to?

"Nope," I shook my head. "You tell me then I'll stop." I said, smirking when I heard a lovely crunch as the sharp metal finally snapped a ligament.

"Fuck! It was supposed to be you! It was supposed to be you!" Lucas yelled out, throwing his head back and I paused, removing the pliers and taking a step back.

"Thank you-" he whimpered and his eyes widened when I headed back to the tray. "Wait, what are you doing?"

I picked up Dominic's gun and cocked it, holding it at my side as I returned to Lucas. "You are not telling me what I want to know." I raised the gun, pointing it between his eyebrows.

"3." I started.

"Wait."

"2."

"Shit! Please don't shoot! I was jealous, okay?! I worked my ass off for your father only for him to kick me to the side and pass the entire empire down to his daughter who barely even knew about it in the first place! I swear, I didn't mean for it to be Dominic. I saw your car and I thought you were driving." Lucas screamed, his voice laced with agony.

"You would betray my father just because your ego got hurt." I pressed the muzzle into his forehead, my face hard. I wanted blood.

"It's more than that. What the fuck do you know about running a Cartel? You're going to sink his business into the ground!" Lucas snarled, his body now entirely covered in blood and the metallic scent lingered in the air.

"Why do you think that?" I asked, really wanting to know why he thought I wasn't capable and he gave me the answer I expected.

"Because you're a woman." Lucas laughed through the pain and more teeth started to fall out of his slimy red mouth.

Yurik really packed a punch. Where is Yurik? I turned around and he was standing there, watching me with an impressed look.

"You are small. You are weak." Lucas spat, gazing with disgust at me.

"Do you know what happens to women who think they own the place?" Lucas asked, sniffing and gasping. "They get put in their place by men like me." He whispered, and I tightened my grip on the handle feeling my body start to heat up with rage.

"Tough talk for someone who was begging me not to end their life a few seconds ago."

"Desperate times." Lucas shrugged and I stepped away from him, dropping the gun to my side.

"See. If you have a pussy, that makes you a pussy. Little bitch, you're not going to survive in our world." Lucas shouted from behind me and I paused. He just had to go and say something.

"I'm not going to kill you, yet." I aimed to his abdomen and pulled the trigger, shooting him in a non-fatal but sore as fuck area.

Lucas let out a blood-curling high pitched scream as the bullet lodged itself in his body. His head slumped, his eyes closed and he seemed to be slipping in and out of consciousness.

Yurik headed over to the tray and collected a mini blow-torch. Lucas watched with frightened eyes as Yurik started to scorch his open wound to stop the bleeding and preserve his life. The smell of burnt skin and hair was overpowering and I swallowed down a gag.

Lucas screamed so loud it left a ringing noise in my ear. He coughed a few times, before vomiting all over himself.

A phone tinged in the now silent room and Yurik collected it from his pocket. He smiled widely and looked at me, and that's when I knew. Tears flooded my eyes immediately and I let out a sad but relieved chuckle.

"He's awake." Yurik confirmed with a nod.

Dominic was finally awake.

Another ting and Yurik read off the screen. "Dominic wants Caitlin to bring her fat ass over here, right now."

That man...

I laughed, feeling the weight of the world miraculously lift itself off my shoulders. "Who's that from?"

"My mother."

"You know, I'm impressed." Lucas said weakly, his head down casted to the floor. "I've never been tortured by a woman before." He's still talking? I observed him as I snapped the bloody latex gloves off my hands, turning them inside out and discarding it in the bin.

I wanted to play some more but Dominic was waiting for me.

"Now that you know your boyfriend is alive, you can let me go and I swear you'll never see me again." Lucas was now struggling to talk, the same way Dominic struggled when he shot him in the chest three times.

I glared at him, not believing that he thought for a second I'd let him walk out of here alive.

"No. You're going to hang there until I feel it's time for you to go." I said, tying my hair and heading to the door, ready to see Dominic. I missed him so fucking much.

"Yurik, man, please." Lucas was begging, sending a pleading look to Yurik who couldn't care less.

Yurik shrugged. "Sorry, she's the boss."

"I thought I lost you." I said sadly, wrapping my arms around Dominic's neck gently as he sat up in the hospital bed. My heart was hammering in my chest, overflowing with relief and indescribable happiness.

He was shirtless, his chest bare except the white bandages wrapped around his back.

"Nah, you're not getting rid of me that easily." He murmured, his voice hoarse.

Dominic wasted no time in sliding his hand down my back and latching onto my ass. He groaned in my ear and I chuckled pulling away, wiping my tears with the back of my hand.

"Pervert." I muttered, glancing around the empty private hospital room. Yurik had given us privacy after greeting Dominic with a ruffle of his hair and a 'don't do that shit again' punch on the shoulder.

Dominic scowled, taking my hand and laying a kiss on my knuckles. "Angel, I'm so sorry for putting you through that. If the roles were reversed, heaven knows how I would have completely lost it."

"Stop," I gave him a kiss on his tattooed fingers too. "What matters is that you're okay. Doctor says if one of those bullets were a millimetre closer to your heart..." I trailed off, feeling the lump in my throat start to grow. Guilt gnawed at me. I was the one who was supposed to be shot.

The week was horrible and I never wanted to experience that sort of pain ever again. The uncertainty was the worst part but luckily the Romanovs had the best doctors in the country at their beck and call.

Dominic shivered, reaching his hand over to the zip-up hoodie hanging near the bed.

"Can you help me put that on, please?" He asked and I jumped up with no hesitation. My heart ached when we tried putting his arms in the hoodie and his face contorted into a pained expression.

"What's that?" Dominic asked, frowning towards my arm. I looked down and there was drops of blood dried up against my forearm. I grabbed disinfectant wipes and cleaned myself before disposing it in the bin.

"Lucas. He's dangling from your ceiling getting what he deserves." I stated, sighing.

Dominic stared at me before he started grinning, a proud smile that erupted fireworks in my chest and I felt my cheeks warm up. "My angel got my back?"

My face dropped. "Dominic, of course. I know you'd do the same."

When Dominic passed out in my arms, the feeling was inconceivable. My heart was swollen with hurt, my mind a hazy mess and I barely slept for the seven days he was laid up in a hospital bed.

I wanted revenge, I wanted Lucas to feel the pain that I felt and I contemplated finding the ones he loved the most. That's how angry I was but with a quick talk from my father, he explained that that wasn't the way to go.

"Worse."

I looked down at my lap, playing with my fingers. I had imagined myself in his position more than I thought about anything else.

I imagined myself in the driver's seat with three bullet wounds in my chest. I hated that Dominic got hurt because of me. I fucking hated it.

"Angel, stop thinking. You didn't do this, Lucas did. You have nothing to feel guilty about, okay? Stop it." Dominic murmured, burying his face in my neck and laying a kiss on my collarbone.

"I know but..."

"No. Lucas was very clearly aiming at your head and if that was you in the driver's seat, you would've died. I'm thankful that it was me. Please, don't argue." Dominic said and despite his injuries, he still managed to sound demanding.

"Fine," I huffed, averting my gaze from my hands. "When can you go home?" I asked, ignoring the ringing coming from my phone. I wasn't interested in answering whoever the fuck that was.

"They still need to run some tests. Angel, answer that. It might be important."

I sighed, picking my phone and answering the unfamiliar number.

"Caitlin! Can you explain to me why the fuck- hey, put that back down! Can you explain to me why there are people carrying out my belongings. They're taking my fucking car too - don't touch me!- They said you sent them so you tell them to put everything back where they found it right this instant!"

"No." I said bluntly, ignoring the tantrum my mother was throwing.

"Caitlin!" She gasped. "I raised you better than this-"

"Oh my God, shut the fuck up! You're so fucking annoying." I said exasperatedly and put the phone off. When she phoned back, I switched it off and threw it onto the bed.

I took a deep breath in, feeling the lack of sleep starting to catch up on me.

"You need to sleep, baby. Come lay here by me." Dominic patted the empty space besides him.

"I don't want to hurt you." I mumbled, rolling my shoulders. Dominic didn't say anything, he just gave me that look that had me scooting closer to him.

"For someone who just woke up from a coma, you have a lot of energy to be ordering me around." I muttered. Dominic was sat up straight leaning against the pillows so I laid down next to him on my side, resting my head on his lap. My eyes shut closed and I felt my entire body relax.

He stroked my hair. "I'll be here when you wake up, angel. I'll always be here for you. I'm not going anywhere."

"I love you so much, Dominic." I whispered, holding him and cherishing the moment we had together.

"I love you so much more. So much more." He said softly, caressing his knuckles over my cheek.

After a few minutes, with my heart finally at peace, I fell asleep.

CHAPTER 31

C AITLIN

Three days later and Lucas's barely breathing body was still in the basement.

Yurik had his fun. I had my fun. Mr Romanov had his fun. Dominic just sat back and watched as the people he loved slowly take the life of the man who almost killed him.

Lucas begged, he pleaded and at one point he asked to be killed. We didn't grant him his wish, no, we wanted him to suffer. A quick death was too easy. A quick death was mercy.

We were making an example of Lucas, a warning for any future adversaries.

"Please." Lucas gasped, reaching out to me with his broken fingers and missing nails.

He was no longer chained up and even with all the free will, he couldn't move. His knees were hammered in, separated from the bone and leaving him incapable of standing up from the concrete floor.

I towered over him in my heels, holding a gun to my side and watched blankly as he pathetically tried using his palms to stand up.

This man almost made me lose Dominic.

That thought played repeatedly, a broken record torturing me and haunting me. It riled me up whenever I laid my eyes on him. Gazing down at Lucas, all I could see was the look of horror on his face after he fired those three shots into Dominic's chest. He knew he fucked up.

The sound of my own cries kept me up at night. The blood was a vivid image every time I closed my eyes. The way Yurik held his brother and begged him not to leave us tore my heart open.

"Just let me go." Lucas begged, his eyes teary and crusty. The gunshot wound on his stomach was infected, a sickening stench emitting from it. He didn't have much longer to live.

"You are small. You are weak." I repeated his words, leaning my head to the side as I scrutinised him.

"Does your father know you're doing this?" Lucas sobbed desperately, hitting the floor in frustration.

"Yes. He approves." I replied, observing how his eyes widened in response.

"Please, I'm begging you!" Lucas yelled, clasping his shaky hands into a prayer.

I raised my gun. "What am I?"

"I-I don't- please just-"

"What am I?" I asked again, more firmly.

Lucas stopped wailing and took a deep breath in. "You're a woman."

"That's right." I said and pulled the trigger. The shot was loud and the kickback almost knocked me over. Lucas's eyes rolled back and blood started to leak from the hole in his forehead. His lifeless body finally sagged to the floor.

My first kill...and I never felt more alive.

"You okay?" Dominic asked, looking at me in the mirror when I walked up behind him. I nodded my head and wrapped my arms around him, resting my cheek on his back. Dominic was concerned and hesitant about letting me into room alone with Lucas but he also trusted me.

He wasn't afraid to let me explore. He didn't treat me as if I was fragile. He let me do whatever I wanted and if it didn't work out, he was there to comfort me.

"I don't know what I did to deserve you." I murmured, letting my hand slide down his bare stomach as I laid a kiss on his shoulder blade.

"I should be telling you that, angel." He whispered, staring down at something in his hand. Dominic sounded nervous and his body seemed to be trembling under my touch. The last time he acted that way was when he asked me out on our first date.

I frowned. "What's wrong?"

His chest raised as he took in a deep breath, his face cringing. Dominic was still sore, although he was healing up nicely but I could tell he was trying to hide the pain.

"Do you need me to get anything for you? Have you taken your pills?" I asked, interlacing my fingers with his and tilting my head to peer up at him.

"I just took them, I'll be fine." Dominic assured, kissing me on the forehead and returning his gaze to the item in his hand. I looked down but Dominic was quick to hide it in his fist.

"Okay..." I whispered, letting go of him.

He turned around. "I'm scared because the last thing I want is you thinking I'm doing this because it was your father's condition. I swear I'm not. You know I love you so much so please don't-"

"Hey, I believe you." I cut him off, laying a hand on his cheek. He looked so worried and his eyebrows were stuck in a concerned frown. Dominic's hands were shaking with nerves and he looked like he was about to explode.

"Relax." I said softly, taking his hand and kissing his knuckles. He visibly calmed down, smiling gently.

"I don't know if there's a right or wrong way to do this but fuck it." Dominic said, opening his hand and revealing a bright diamond on top of a white gold band. A ring.

"Shit." I breathed out, staring down at it.

Dominic stepped forward, wrapping his hand around the back of my neck and making me look up at him. "I was thinking long and hard about what to say. I know you're not one for all that fancy speeches so I thought about just putting it on your finger while you're sleeping and telling you in the morning 'We're getting married, deal with it.'"

I laughed. "I don't think I'd mind that, to be honest."

"I know that, so here." Dominic took my left hand, sliding the ring up my finger while looking at me. "We're getting married. Deal with it."

"Fuck, yes!" I gushed, wrapping my arms around his neck and hugging him. My heart threatened to combust with happiness and Dominic's joyful laugh was the final straw.

"I love you. I love you. I love you." I chanted, planting kisses all over his laughing face and holding his cheeks.

"You have no fucking clue how happy you make me." Dominic whispered, his forehead against mine. My face softened when I saw the tears brimming in his eyes.

"I'm so grateful for that little nod you give me in that bar." He murmured, kissing the tip of my nose.

"You remember?" I asked, playing with the hair at the nape of his neck.

"Of course I remember. I remember everything. The black dress you had on, the red colour on your nails, the heels on your feet. Everything, angel." He said, staring at me with a strong focus while circling his thumb on my hip.

"I remember asking you if there would be anyone upset that you complimented me and you said 'Why? You can't fight?'" I chuckled. That night was the start of our lives together, we just didn't know it.

"Your response was 'Over a man? I'd rather eat glass' but look at you now, killing for me." Dominic teased, grinning cheekily.

"That's different." I argued.

"I know, baby. There's a lot of things I'd changed but that night would never be one of them, because I got to meet you." Dominic muttered, leaning down and placing a firm kiss on my lips.

Our first kiss as an officially engaged couple and I couldn't help but smile into it.

A pure physical attraction between us morphed into something deeper than both of us expected it to and I would be lying if I said I didn't absolutely love it.

I went to that bar with the intentions of just finding someone for the night, but I ended up finding the person I was going to spend the rest of my life with.

Just thinking about all the adventures we were going to face together as a couple excited me and feeling his warm body against mine, I knew I made the right decision. I wasn't going to let the opportunity to be his slip through my fingertips.

"Me neither." I responded, snuggling into him.

"I have something else for you." Dominic said, stroking my hair.

"You do?"

"Yes," He said, letting go of me. Picking up a piece of paper from the desk, he handed it to me. "Here."

I took it, flipped it over and my eyes started to scan the words. It was a proof of payment and by the time I was done reading, my jaw was practically on the floor.

"Dominic...you paid my school fees?" I whispered in astonishment. He had paid the full 30K into my student account.

My mother refused to give me a cent after high school and I tried my best to get myself through university. But eventually the bills started piling up and I had no choice but to take out a student loan. My eyes started to sting and I blinked, trying to get rid of the tears.

"I'm here for you, angel. You don't have to struggle." Dominic said reassuringly, taking a sliver of my hair and pushing it behind my ear. His hand lingered on my jawline a few seconds longer as I tried to find the appropriate words to say.

"I- this is...thank you." I breathed, wiping my tears with the bottom of my palm.

"You deserve the world, and I'm going to give it to you." Dominic said, those brown eyes that I fell in love with sparkling with a simmering vigour.

Dominic had my heart and I had his. With the piece of paper clutched to my chest, I stood on the tips of my toes and kissed him hard, pouring every ounce of my love into it.

"Yours." I murmured, looking up at him.

"Yours." He replied and gave me the softest kiss on my forehead.

I couldn't wait to start our lives together.

CHAPTER 32

D OMINIC

       6 months later

I've never felt so fucking nervous in my entire life.

Yurik stood beside me on the altar, laughing at my nerve-stricken face. My hands were sweaty, my heart pounding in my chest, my throat felt tight and my tuxedo suddenly seemed a size too small.

Why is this air so hot?

Fuck.

I took a deep breath in, clasping my hands together at my zipper and fiddling with my thumbs. I never felt that amount of edginess before, not even in the face of death and it seemed like time was moving in slow motion.

I glanced to the small crowd, hoping that the familiar faces of my family would calm me down but no, it only fuelled my peaking anxiety.

Why was I so scared? I had no reason to be so scared. It wasn't like I was marrying a stranger. I was marrying my angel with the beautiful face and beautiful personality and beautiful...everything. Shit.

What if she changed her mind? What if she took one look at me standing there waiting for her and went, 'nope, i don't want you anymore' What if she realised that I wasn't worthy of her love?

I never used to be an over thinker so why the fuck was I starting now?

"Domo, you need to calm down. You look ready to shoot the entire place down." Yurik said and I glared at him.

"You would be an absolute wreck if this was you standing here. Let me be nervous in peace." I retorted, returning my gaze to the long aisle. At least we were outside and not in an enclosed space, it would've made my uneasiness so much worse.

"Yes but you're supposed to look happy and not as if you're marrying someone you don't want to marry." He said and my eyes widened.

"I am happy! Does it look like I'm not happy? Shit, she's probably going to think I don't want to do this." I said hastily, wiping my palms on my jacket. I tried to smile but it turned into a grimace and Yurik burst out laughing.

"Don't do that ever again. Just breathe, it's just Caitlin. She's not a stranger." Yurik said, giving me a comforting pat on the shoulder. My breath shuddered and I wiped a hand over my face. Why is this taking so long?

"I know but fuck-" The priest cleared his throat, interrupting me and my head snapped towards him. I completely forgot he was there.

"Swearing in front of the priest, Domo. You should be ashamed of yourself." Yurik taunted, shaking his head and pursing his lips in disapproval.

"Shut up." I grumbled, looking down the aisle. My heart literally trembled when the familiar red sports car belonging to my father stopped at the end.

Yurik nudged the priest on his arm. "Look at how nervous he is. Isn't that adorable?"

I couldn't pay attention to them and the casual conversation they were having while I was nearly about to collapse on the altar. My father stepped out of the car and rounded the hood, stopping at the passenger's side. I watched nervously as he opened the door and took Caitlin's hand to help her step out.

My mouth dropped.

"Holy..." I breathed, suddenly remembering the priest in my presence. "Fudge." I finished.

"Whoa." I gawked. She looked so perfect, so beautiful and my chest swelled with pride. She was all mine.

She wasn't carrying a flower bouquet or wearing a veil. Her dress was a simple white silk, spaghetti strapped, long and tight around the hips with a slit up her tanned leg. In her own words 'I'm not wearing a fucking ball gown'

I love her so much.

Her long hair was loose, parted down the middle and down her back, leaving her cleavage and collarbones bare. When she locked arms with my father, her lips pulled up into a breath-taking smile and I gazed at her in awe. Nobody else existed in that moment besides her.

The most beautiful woman ever.

I waited way too fucking long for this moment.

Even when the music started playing and heads were turning to look at her, her eyes were locked with mine. Our smiles matched each other's, full blown grins despite the thumping of my heartbeat in my ears. The blood rushed to my face, warming my cheeks.

My mother sat in the front row, wiping her tears away with a handkerchief and Micah had the biggest smile on his face. Caitlin was the star of the moment, a silent force that turned heads and ignited positive emotions from every single guest.

When she finally stopped in front of me and my father shook my hand, I was still in complete disbelief. Don't fucking cry. Don't fucking cry.

"Beautiful." I mouthed, taking her hand and helping her up the altar. She smiled and licked her lower lip, eyes travelling down my body.

When the priest started speaking, his words went through one ear and out the other. Caitlin stifled her laughter, witnessing my face turn into one of annoyance. I just wanted to be married to her already.

My expression softened as I kept my eyes on her, unable to peel them away from the stunning sight. I thought I had the waterworks under control but when I saw her eyes tearing up, my own lip started to quiver.

"Stop it." I mouthed at her, frowning.

"I can't." She mouthed back and her lips tightened as more tears pooled in her eyes. Fuck, she's going to make me cry.

"Stop crying." I formed with my lips, scrunching my eyebrows as my own tears started to fall down my cheeks. I grit my teeth.

"You stop crying." She retorted back silently and I took a deep breath in.

"I can't."

I looked at Yurik and he was starting to cry too. We were having one big crying fest.

The ceremony continued until it was time for us to say our vows. We repeated the words the priest said and then the moment to present the rings came. Our ring bearer was a light brown female pitbull wearing a pink flower crown. It was Yurik's idea.

I smiled and bent down to collect the rings from the basket in her mouth. Her trainer gave her a treat and her tail wagged excitedly.

"I want one." Caitlin whispered, staring at the dog with loving eyes.

"We'll adopt one." I said.

"Do you, Dominic Sasha-" Caitlin snorted, her cheeks puffing up as she tried to hold in her laughter. "-Romanov take Caitlin Essie-" I laughed out loud. "Valencia to be your lawfully wedded wife?"

"Answer the question, idiot." She grumbled, glaring at me as I bit my bottom lip.

"I do." I said cheekily. I can't wait to fuck my wife later.

"Do you, Caitlin Essie-" I looked down at my shoes, clenching my jaw so I wouldn't make a sound as a chuckle started to form in my chest.

"Dominic, shut up." Caitlin said, her tone oozing frustration. "Father, continue please."

"Do you, Caitlin Essie-" I can't do this. "Valencia take Dominic Sasha-" Caitlin snorted again. "Romanov to be your lawfully wedded husband?"

"I do." She said and together we placed the rings on each other's fingers. I smiled widely, feeling my heart about to implode with joy.

"I now pronounce you husband and wife, you may kiss- okay then." My lips were already on hers, holding her waist as I dipped her down giving her a long, deep kiss. The guests cheered and Yurik was the loudest.

I was finally married.

My wife.

My angel.

My Queen.

I kicked the door of the hotel room shut, breathing heavily. I rested my forehead against the cool wood and flattened my palms, trying to compose myself.

When I finally looked at Caitlin standing there, her chest heaving and her breasts threatening to spill out of her dress, my restraint diminished into thin air.

I wanted her so fucking badly. Needed her so fucking badly.

"Fuck, baby, come here." I breathed, reaching out and clasping both my hands underneath her ears, pressing my lips against hers. She was sweet, tasting of chocolate vodka from the shot we just took and I wanted no time in delving my tongue into her mouth.

"Oh my God, I want you inside me. Now, please." Caitlin whimpered, her trembling fingers going to unfasten my belt. I groaned, her words making my dick throb harder than ever. I was aching for her.

The entire night was pure fucking torture not being able to touch her and I had enough.

I wrapped my arm around her, quickly pulling the zip down at the small of her back. The straps of her dress fell down her arms, exposing her full breasts and I leaned down to take her nipple into my mouth.

Her skin tasted so good and fuck, she smelled so fucking delicious. Shea and vanilla but underneath all that was her, my favourite.

"Tell me how you want to be fucked, angel. Tell me." I practically begged, grasping her ass in my palms. I was desperate.

"Rough, hard. Dominic, I can't take it." She groaned before dropping to her knees, her fingers pulled my pants and boxers down to my knees and off my body. My eyes rolled when her warm mouth and pink plump lips wrapped around my dick.

"Shit, what are you doing to me? Fuck, angel." I hissed, fisting her hair and moving my hips. The tip hit the back of her throat and her mouth started to produce more sticky saliva from the sudden intrusion.

I gasped when her hand started to play with my balls. I couldn't even think straight. I shrugged my jacket off and unbuttoned my shirt, letting it fall wherever.

She looked up at me, and her eyes bright and beautiful. I don't want to cum already. Caitlin moaned around me, working both hands on my dick and twisting it while she sucked her cheeks in. A mewl escaped me. A fucking mewl.

"Goddammit, are you trying to kill me?" I gasped, my words jumbled and I could barely understand myself. I let go of her hair and pressed my palms against my lower back, thrusting into her mouth.

Her spit was all over my dick, all over her hands and dripping onto the floor. Her dress was so elegant, her make up done to perfection and the beautiful diamond on her finger shone underneath the light. But there she was on her knees giving me the nastiest, sloppiest head ever.

I'm so fucking lucky.

"Fuck, angel, just like that. Yes, baby, you're doing so fucking good." I croaked, panting as her lips tightened around me. She stuck her tongue out, licking the underside of my dick before shoving me back into her mouth.

"I'm going to cum." I let her know, giving her a chance to pull away but she continued.

I paused. "Oh you want me to cum down your throat, huh? You would like that, wouldn't you?" I growled, grabbing her hair and pulling her head back. Damn, I wanted to do some horrible things to her.

"Get up." I demanded.

"But-"

"Get the fuck up." I said again, more harshly and she quickly scurried to her feet. My good girl.

I grabbed the inside of her elbow and led her to the bed, throwing her on it. She landed with a yelp, bouncing a few times on the mattress and I flipped her around onto her back. Her head hung off the bed, her neck exposed and I wasted no time in shoving myself back into her mouth. She let out a muffled groan.

With that angle, I could see the bulge in her throat every time I pulled myself in and out.

I grabbed beneath her chin, watching with lustful eyes as she took all of me, every single inch. "That feels so fucking good." I grunted and her response was a moan.

She reached down and spread her legs, her feet flat on the mattress and her dress bunched up around her waist. She started circling her clit over her lace underwear. Such a beautiful fucking sight.

Rough fucking was our love language. We never took it slow. We never took it easy. Since the beginning, we always did it hard and it wasn't about to change just because we got married.

I loved it that way.

Holding her head still, I started fucking her face. I kept myself there, leaving her no room to breathe until she started fighting to be released. The thrill of it had my orgasm approaching quicker.

I threw my head back as my balls pulled up and with a groan, I started to cum inside her mouth. I gulped hard, a sheen of sweat decorating my forehead as I watched her swallow every bit of it.

"My turn." I whispered, turning her around and pulling her towards me by her hips. My mouth watered, seeing how fucking wet she was through her underwear. She was driving me absolutely insane.

I closed my eyes, my lips parted as I dragged my nose along her inner thigh.

"Dominic, please." She whimpered, pulling her own underwear down. Caitlin wanted me just as bad as I wanted her.

"I know, baby. Let's just take your dress off, okay?" I said and started to help her remove the silk. I hung it up in the large built in cupboard and closed the door, revealing the giant mirror facing the bed. She smirked, her pink tongue flicking out to give her bottom lip a quick lick.

Even though I just came, my dick was still fucking hard.

With her dress finally gone and her ring, earrings and heels the only items on her body, I nearly lost my mind at how gorgeous she looked.

"You are so fucking beautiful." I whispered, getting on my knees and giving her a clit a peck. The touch was delicate and tender, a contradiction against the tight fist currently holding my hair.

She wanted more, and I was going to give it to her.

I used my finger to spread her juices around her hole, groaning when I felt exactly how soaked and ready she was for me. Her arousal was leaking out of her.

I couldn't hold back any more so I dove forward, my tongue finding the tight ring of muscle at the brim of pussy. Fuck. She tasted so good, like a summer fruit that I couldn't get enough of.

"That's so hot." She breathed and I looked up at her, finding her eyes on me as she watched my tongue thrust in and out of her.

I moved to her clit, making out with her pussy with soft groans. My hand stretched up and my middle finger and ring finger nudged at her lips until she opened her mouth and started to suck. I scowled - it had no reason feeling so good.

"That's right, angel." I whispered, feeling my fingertips hit the back of her throat until it was well lubricated. I pulled out and shoved it into her hole, keeping my mouth on her swollen clit.

"Shit, Dominic, that feels so good. God, that feels so good." She panted, her body starting to shake with the force of my hand. Her breath hitched, her moans getting louder by the second and my dick threatened to combust with the sound of it.

I needed to be inside of her.

She needed to orgasm on my tongue first.

"Cum for me, baby, please cum for me." I begged, closing my eyes and putting my everything into it. I wanted to make her feel so good. She deserved it. She deserved it so fucking much.

"I'm going to- fuck, do that again." She yelled and I gently scraped my teeth against her clit again, just how she wanted.

"Tell me what else you want me to do, angel. I'll do it." I said, still moving my fingers in and out of her.

"Fuck me, please. Now. I want it so badly." She was gasping as I guided her through her orgasm until she stopped clenching and her essence was in my mouth. I moaned against her and stood up - happy with her first climax. I was planning on giving her a lot more.

I climbed on top of her, feeling her breasts squashed against my chest and then...I was finally inside her, enveloped by her warm pussy.

Her naked skin, her flushed face, her legs around my waist. Fuck, it couldn't get any better than that. She moaned loudly, softly biting my earlobe as I buried my face in her neck.

"Harder." She whined and I granted her wish, holding myself up as I pounded into her. Our first fuck as a married couple. No gimmicks, no prolonging, just two people who couldn't keep their hands off each other and everything about it felt right.

I slammed into her and little breathy sounds fell from her lips as her fingers entangle themselves in my hair. Her back arched and her head fell onto the soft mattress, showing me her neck and I bent down to give it a lick. I wanted to lick every part of her, kiss every part.

I switched our positions until she was on top of me with my dick still inside her. "Ride me, baby." I said softly, resting my hands behind my head.

With her palms on my chest, she started to roll her stomach, fast and hard.

I tilted my head to peer past her body and gaze at the mirror facing the bed, smirking when I saw her ass and the tattoo on her spine. So fucking sexy. It was her first ink and she took it without flinching.

Noticing my staring, Caitlin stopped moving and turned around before sliding me into her pussy again. Reverse cowgirl. I groaned, my hands reaching out to grab her ass as I watched the tattoo and her gorgeous lower back dimples.

"What...the...fuck..." I grunted. What a stunning fucking view. My fingertips trailed down her back as she rolled her hips on me. I was getting close.

Sitting up, I clasped my fingers together around her neck, arching her back. "Don't stop. Don't stop." Caitlin whimpered as she came again, clenching around me so tightly that I couldn't help but cum inside of her. My release spewed into her until it started to drip down her thighs.

We both shivered but we weren't finished.

An hour and a half later, we collapsed on the bed, utterly drained. My balls were empty, and Caitlin was full. She laid besides me, her chest heaving as she rested her hand on her lower belly.

We grinned and as if reading each other's mind, our fists reached out simultaneously and we bumped them together.

"I love you so much, Dominic." Caitlin said sincerely. Her skin was glowing, her hair messy and with my cum all over her and inside her, she looked like the most beautiful piece of art.

"I love you more, angel." I replied, rolling over to lay a soft kiss on her lips.

4 years later

"A beretta is a fucking cop gun. I don't want that shit. Tell them I want my 38's and 9's. Add some butterfly knives in there too and we have a deal." I said into the phone, ignoring how Ruby, our pitbull, was nudging at my leg.

"You got it, boss." The man said before switching the call off. I looked down at Ruby, frowning when I saw how in distress she was.

She started barking as she bounced on her front paws. She moved behind me and started pushing her snout against the back of my legs.

"Okay, okay, what is it? Where are you taking me?" I said and shoved my phone into pants pocket.

I followed behind her. Ruby kept running and stopping, waiting for me to catch up before running again. I scowled - something was wrong.

"Is it mama?" I asked as if she could understand. It was then that I realised I hadn't heard a sound from my wife in a while. Panic started to arise and I rushed up the stairs, following behind Ruby as she led me to the bedroom.

"Baby?" I called out and that's when I heard it. Soft groans and heavy breathing coming from the en-suite.

I pushed the door open, my eyes widening when I saw Caitlin holding her rounded belly as water dripped down her legs. It stunned me. She wasn't due for another month or so.

"Don't just fucking stand there!" She snapped, pulling me out of my frozen stated. Her face was red and sweaty, contorted into an expression of agony.

Ruby barked again, urging me to help her mama. "I know, I know. Good job, Ruby."

I walked over to her, wrapping an around her lower back to steady her as I pulled my phone out of my pocket. Quickly dialling our doctor, I let her know of the situation.

"They're going to be here in ten minutes, angel. I'm sorry I wasn't here, shit - let's go lay you down." I said hastily, guiding her to the room we had prepared for her to give birth in. My heart was pounding, scared for my wife and my unborn child.

"For fucks sake." She grunted, buckling over from the pain. "You did this to me, you little shit." Caitlin growled, wincing and whining.

I shouldn't have chuckled - it was my biggest mistake. Her hand balled into a fist and hit me so fucking hard in the chest that it knocked my wind out.

"Don't laugh at me!"

"Okay, I'm sorry." I breathed, rubbing the sore area. "Lay here, angel. Hold my hand." I informed her, settling her down on the bed. She was in so much pain and it pulled at my heart that I couldn't take it away.

But I couldn't deny how excited I was.

Please, please, let them both be okay. Please.

Caitlin squeezed my hand tightly, my fingertips turning blue from being compressed but I let her. If it provided the tiniest bit of comfort, I'd let her do anything.

I kneeled on the floor besides her bed, stroking her hair out of her face and whispering sweet words of encouragement. It didn't take long for the doctor and her nurses to arrive. I stepped away to give them space as I paced around the room, my head filled with chaotic thoughts.

"Hey, Doc, isn't it too soon?" I asked dumbly, feeling nervous and panicky.

"Babies born at 32 weeks have a 95% survival rate." The doctor assured and I couldn't help but let out a sigh of relief. The odds seemed good.

"Dominic, stop pacing around." Caitlin said, glaring at me as the nurses set her up to the machines. It was her idea to give birth in the privacy of our own home and after consulting many healthcare providers, we finally found a method that would work best.

"Sorry, angel." I apologised and sat my ass down in the corner of the room.

I wasn't sure how long it took. She was in labour for hours and when it was finally time for her to push, I could tell that she was already exhausted.

Caitlin was always strong. She led our mafia with her head held high and an iron fist. Seeing her crying and trembling from the pain damn near tore my heart out of my chest. I swallowed hard, shaking my head as I watched and waited.

Ruby was whining and crying outside the door. She wasn't allowed into the room so I called Yurik over to try and console her. They were basically best friends.

I also called Alarico, Caitlins father, and let him know that his daughter was giving birth. Living somewhere on an island after being released from prison, he said he'll get on a plane immediately.

"Come on, Mrs Romanov. Push." The doctor encouraged. Caitlin grunted, huffing short quick breaths before she squeezed my hand so tightly that my fingers went numb. She screamed, her body tensing as she clenched her eyes shut. She went limp, still breathing heavily.

"Again."

This went on for thirty minutes and finally, the sound of a baby crying filled the room.

Our daughter.

My head fell down, an enormous amount of relief washing over me as tears filled my eyes. "Thank you. Thank you." I whispered. She was tired and lethargic, but she still managed to put a smile on her face as she watched the nurse clean our baby.

So beautiful.

"I'm so proud of you, angel. I love you so much." I said softly, kissing her hand and showing her that I was there for her. She couldn't respond but it didn't matter.

"Have you decided on a name?" The nurse carefully handed our baby wrapped in a yellow blanket to Caitlin's naked chest. I peered down, gazing at my daughter with teary eyes. She was so small and I couldn't wait to hold her.

"Anzhela." Caitlin muttered, her voice raspy. Her name meant angel in Russian. I sniffed, stroking her hair as I watched them already form that motherly-daughter bond.

She was going to be such a good mother.

Caitlin's eyes began to flutter close as she finally succumbed to her exhaustion. Before her head fell, the nurse took Anzhela and handed her to me. I almost started sobbing. She already had my whole entire heart.

"Hi, baby." I whispered, holding her in my arms as I blinked my tears away. Her nose wiggled and her glove covered tiny hands started to squirm aimlessly in the air. The small hat on her head was the cutest fucking thing I've ever seen in my life.

I vowed to protect her with every fibre of my being.

"I'm so proud of your mama and I'm so happy you're finally here with us." I said softly and gave her a kiss on the forehead.

"I love you both so much and I can't wait to spend the rest my life showing you." I bent down and gave her sleeping mother a peck on her cheek.

Our little family was finally growing.

And I've never been happier.

CHAPTER 33

C AITLIN

"Shit," I gasped, breathing hard as Dominic fucked me from behind.

"I know, baby. I know," he grunted, holding onto my hips as he thrust into me. He was rough, slamming into me with no remorse and all I could do was lay there and take it. I whimpered, clutching the sheets in my fists while he fucked me into the mattress.

Dominic's strokes were deep, consistent- sliding in and out of me at a pace I couldn't keep up with. With one hand on my hip and the other gripping my ass cheek, his touch was anything but gentle.

I groaned, reaching under me to clutch my lower stomach while I struggled to contain my never-ending moans. So deep.

He grunted, laying an open mouth kiss on the back of my neck and grazing his teeth over my skin. It was painful, but the good kind of pain that had tingles travelling down my spine. My pussy throbbed around him, and my clit ached for another source of friction.

"You feel so fucking good," his voice was a near whimper, and his lips never left me as he spoke.

He grinded into me, rolling his hips in a way that he knew I loved. No matter how many times Dominic showed me what a good fuck he was, every time felt the first fucking time. I was unable to hold myself up anymore and my front met the mattress. Dominic didn't falter, changing the angle of his strokes to meet that spot in me that had my body hitching uncontrollably.

"Fuck," I grunted through gritted teeth, clenching my eyes shut.

My pussy twitched, and I heard Dominic inhale a sharp breath.

"You okay, baby?" Dominic breathed, stroking my hair away from my face.

I nodded, but Dominic was one for verbal responses. Even knowing that, I couldn't bring myself to utter a word. He was making me feel so good I wasn't sure I could let out a cohesive sentence.

"Let me hear you," he slammed down, harder and more aggressive than before and it was a warning he didn't hesitate to give me.

I swallowed hard, "Yes. Dammit- I-"

I wasn't sure how that sounded but he seemed satisfied with my answer. Dominic trailed his fingers down my back, sliding it over my stomach to engulf my hand in his own.

With his guidance, he let my own fingertips meet my clit. He circled, making my eyes roll into the back of my head in pure and heavy ecstasy. He knew exactly where to caress and stroke. It didn't matter that he couldn't see - Dominic knew my body the way he knew the tattoos on his hands.

"Such a good girl, aren't you?" he whispered, never changing the pace of his thrusts. Consistency was key and Dominic knew that.

The feeling was intense. Borderline overwhelming. I felt it in every part of me, giving me a high that was no match for anything that wasn't him.

"Take it for me," he murmured, peppering kisses on my jawline while the side of my face pressed into our silk sheets.

My pussy clenched around him, drawing another groan from his chest and I found myself wanting to see him. And it was like he read my mind.

Dominic pulled out of me, grabbing my hips to turn me around and lay my back onto the mattress. He grabbed my thighs, wrapping my legs around his waist and wasted no time in sliding into me again.

My husband was the most gorgeous man I had ever seen.

He held himself up, trapping me between his arms while he gazed down at me through lust filled eyes. His palms next to my head, the silver ring on his finger a reminder that he was mine. Only mine. His lips parted, eyes darting from mine to my lips and he bent down to kiss me.

"You're so beautiful," he murmured, his breath mingling with my own. His mouth met mine and his tongue stroked my bottom lip until I was giving him the access he wanted. I sucked it softly, enjoying the taste of him while my nails trailed down his back.

He gasped into my mouth, and I had come to known that Dominic liked a little bit of pain too. He especially enjoyed it when I dragged my nails over his flesh. His mouth stayed on mine as he clasped one hand underneath my ear, and the other hand ventured down to cup one of my breast.

"All mine," he said, pressing his forehead against mine. "yeah?"

"Of course," I breathed, tightening my legs around to him to pull him impossibly closer.

The pleasure of it all almost had on the brink of tears. Then, Dominic bent down, latching his mouth onto my nipple and I was convinced that if I wasn't laying down, I would have collapsed right there. He sucked, moaning around my skin and the vibrations travelled through me.

"I love you so fucking much, angel," he said, and my heart swelled at the same time my pussy twitched around him.

I grabbed his hair in my fist, forcing him to look at me. "I love you. So much more."

He grinned, and it was the most beautiful sight. His messy hair, his glowing cheeks and his redden lips. There was not a day that went by where Dominic didn't make me feel like the luckiest woman in the world.

Dominic gave my nipple one last kiss, not forgetting to show some love to the other while at the same filling me up with him completely.

He pulled out, reaching between us to slide his dick through my wet pussy lips. He circled the tip over my clit, applying enough pressure to have my head falling back onto the mattress. My chest heaved, a thin layer of sweat forming on my skin while I let him do whatever the fuck he wanted to.

It was unexpected, but fuck, it felt so fucking good. He entered me again, reaching up to grip my throat. I loved it when he left his mark on my skin, and he had no problem doing so as he tightened his hold.

"Pretty girl," he murmured, giving me a kiss on my forehead.

I loved it when he showered me with compliments and the praise had my belly tensing up with an impending orgasm. Dominic's eyes were low and sensual and he looked at me as if I was the most beautiful woman in the world. God, I love him more than words can articulate.

"I'm going to cum in you," he breathed, and his jaw clenched. Dominic held himself up, and his head nestled into my neck.

Those strong shoulders. Those strong arms. His tanned and tattooed skin. I never wanted to lose him.

I gasped, wrapping my arms around his neck while Dominic fucked me into a state of delirium. Our orgasm came together. My entire body convulsed underneath him while he grunted into my neck. It didn't take long before something warm spurted inside me and our moans were in sync. Dominic's moans were the second best part of fucking him.

So fucking good.

A smile of awe formed on my lips as Dominic rolled over, slumping down on the mattress. We laid there, breathing heavily as we stared at the ceiling of our bedroom.

I'm pretty sure that was how our baby was made but there was no way to really tell.

Dominic's smile matched mine, and like clockwork, he reached his fist out to me and my grin broadened. I touched knuckles with him, and it immediately turned into a memory I would cherish forever.

"Happy Valentine's Day, angel," he whispered, turning onto his side to clear my hair from my face.

"Happy Valentine's Day, handsome," I murmured, grabbing his hand to give his fingers the gentlest kiss.

There was no place in the world where I'd rather be than right there with my husband.

EPILOGUE

C AITLIN

"Angel?"

"In here," I answered, dragging my hand over the material of my dress. His favourite. My heart raced in my chest, nearly drowning out the sound of Dominic entering the room.

I was pregnant with his baby. Our baby. And he didn't know it yet.

I felt him approach me from behind, his presence only managing to send another surge of nerves through me. There was no reason for me to be nervous, as I knew how Dominic would love a baby of his own but I was still terrified of his reaction.

With no protection and a long overdue birth control shot, it was to be expected but seeing the positive test for the first time almost gave me a fucking heart attack.

Dominic circled his arms around me, laying a warm kiss on the side of my neck and I smiled as I rested my hands on his forearms. "I miss you," he murmured.

"I'm right here," I chuckled, leaning my head to the side to grant him better access to give me all the kisses his heart desired.

I hoped he couldn't feel how fast my pulse was beating, but Dominic was observant and he paused when he reached the tender spot on the side of my neck. Shit.

I could never hide anything from him, always failing to conceal how I felt-especially because we had been married for a while and nothing went past him. It was so incredible annoying, but at the same time I was happy I found someone who knew me the way he did.

The only downside was the inability to have a poker face around him.

"I know," he whispered, pressing his chest against my back and I sighed at the warmth he always seemed to have. "Still miss you. What's wrong?"

I turned around in his arms, meeting those soft brown eyes. "Nothing. It's almost your birthday," I said, glancing at the clock on the wall.

It read eleven fifty five, and I had made the decision to hand him his gift as soon as the clock struck twelve. We had a dinner earlier that evening-just the two of us as it always was on birthdays.

We didn't have parties, always choosing to have a night consisting of getting high and eating as much junk as possible while watching the shittiest movie on the planet.

This year, it was a little different.

"I'm old as fuck, angel." Dominic frowned, pulling me closer to him.

"The big thirty. You're right," I teased, and he gave the dirtiest glare. Dominic only seemed to get more handsome with age, and there wasn't a moment that passed where I didn't appreciate every part of him.

God, how anyone could be that perfect didn't make sense at all.

"You're supposed to make me feel better," he grumbled. "What sort of wife are you?"

"Yours," I stated. "Now sit your ass down on the bed and wait for your gift."

"Gift?" he murmured cheekily, tugging at the strap of my dress. There was suggestive smirk on his face, and I rolled my eyes as I gave him a soft push with both hands.

He sat down, spread his knees and leaned back on his palms. I chuckled, shaking my head at my horny husband.

After all these years, Dominic still couldn't keep his hands off me. I might have acted as if it annoyed me, but I loved every moment of it.

If I wasn't about to break the news to him, I would have probably been giving him the sloppiest head ever.

Another thing I loved about our relationship, our sex life did not change. In fact, it became a lot better-which I didn't even know was possible.

"Okay, okay," he said, grinning as he sat up straight. "I'm sitting."

"You didn't have to get me anything," he said, watching me as I rummaged through the cupboard for the matte black gift box.

Dominic was a sucker for gifts, but he liked pretending that it wasn't necessary. It was always necessary, and the childlike excitement radiating off him proved that.

When his eyes landed on the large box, they widened for the faintest second. I grinned, holding the box as I walked over to him. His first gift was a regular gift-one that held all his favourite things in the world.

"You say the same thing every year," I said, setting it down on his lap. Dominic had a smile on his face as he examined the box. I waved my hand, gesturing for him to open it up.

He dragged his tattooed fingers over the black ribbon, pulling it loose and placing it down next to him. When he pulled the lid off, his eyes were on the contents immediately and my grin widened when his mouth dropped.

There was mini three layered cake inside, right in the centre. Choco-cara-nilla, he's favourite flavours. I would have made a bigger one but I couldn't stomach anything sweet. I had spent the afternoon preparing it, without the cannabutter-of course.

Surrounding the cake was all the snacks Dominic liked, including an imported Ecuadorian chocolate that he couldn't get enough of. He pushed the items to the side, his brown eyes glowing as he inspected everything I got for him.

I was always nervous whenever he opened his gifts, secretly terrified that he wouldn't like it but the happiness on his face was reassurance. It wasn't just food items in the box. Inside was a tie, cufflinks, his favourite vodka and a watch that left quite the dent in my bank account. It was well worth it.

Dominic looked up at me, and I was reminded of the first time I gave him a present. He still looked at me the same, so full of love and awe. Except this time, we were married.

"Angel," he murmured, and I was about to cry on the fucking spot at the sound of his tender voice.

My emotions were getting the best of me and I almost choked on the uncomfortable feeling in my throat. I gazed away from him, heading over to the bedside drawer for a lighter and candle before I really started sobbing.

I walked back over to him and grabbed the cake, holding onto the mini platter it rested on. I pushed the candle in, quickly lighting the cotton string and the flame glowed against Dominic's face. His smile was kind and his eyes gentle, a massive relief to see after the stressful week we had.

"Go on," I encouraged him. "Make a wish."

He looked at me once, leaned forward and blew the flame with a short huff. "Done."

I grinned, holding the cake in the palm of my hand when I circled the other around the back of his neck. I leaned down, giving him a kiss on his forehead. Dominic stood up, and pulled me to his chest-hugging me to his body as he placed a kiss on the top of my head.

"You're amazing, baby," he whispered. "Thank you so much."

I smiled, and I felt my cheeks warm up as it always did when Dominic loved something I did for him. "Now, for your next gift."

Dominic pulled away, looking at me with a slightly surprised expression. "Another one?"

The one I was most nervous about.

Setting the cake down, my heart has never felt that heavy before. Despite the numerous times Dominic had expressed he wanted a kid, the timing was never quite right and I wasn't sure if it was. If it wasn't, it didn't matter.

Even with the nerves rushing through me, I was excited to finally have my own baby.

As I approached the bedside drawer one more time, I felt Dominic's eyes on me. He was curious, no doubt, as I had never given him a second gift before. I grabbed the small rectangle shaped gift box, lifting it out of the drawer before shutting it again.

At first glance, one would assume that it held a watch but instead it was the third pregnancy test I took. Just for extra clarification.

I swear I saw his eyes lit up.

"Angel," he murmured slowly, eyeing me sceptically. "Don't make jokes. Please."

"You don't even know what it is," I said cheekily, nearly rolling my eyes at my husband.

"I swear-" he started, shaking his head. "If you're about to play with me right now, I'm taking you out of my will."

I laughed, handing him the box. "Just open it."

Dominic sighed, taking the item from me. He didn't open it. He stared down at it with a stoic expression, holding it at arms lengths as if he was scared of what he might find. Or what he might not find.

I was patient, although it took much doing so but I gave him the time he wanted.

With one last breath, he tentatively lifted the side of the lid and took the smallest peak. I witnessed the exact moment when he saw what was inside.

His shoulders dropped and his hands fell, the utter look of relief on his face hard to miss.

Dominic's head fell back and his eyes closed, his chest heaving as his breathing quickened. When he turned to me, his lips stretched into the most beautiful smile and he rushed to me, wrapping his arms around me as he lifted me.

I chuckled, hugging him back when he buried his face in the crook of my neck.

"Oh my God, angel," he whispered, squeezing me to his body. When he set me back down on my feet, he held my shoulders and pulled away.

He looked at me, his eyes happy and hopeful. All I had to do was nod for his eyes to instantly water.

"Really?" he asked again, holding my cheeks as he wiped away my tears with his thumbs.

"Yes," my voice cracked and I sniffed. Dominic laughed through his teary eyes, giving me kisses all of my face and all I could do was smile until it hurt.

Dominic slid his palms down my arms until he found my hands, peppering soft kisses all over my knuckles but his smile never wavered.

"Fuck," he said quietly, returning to his normal height. He clasped his hand around the back of my neck, lowering his forehead against mine as he stared at me with those brown eyes I adored. "I love you so fucking much. You have no idea how happy this makes me."

"I love you more," I murmured, my eyes brimming with tears for the millionth time that evening.

"Wow," he breathed. "You're so beautiful. You're going to be the best mama."

I don't think he knew what a wonderful father he would be.

"Our baby, angel," he whispered, smiling softly as he gave me one last peck on my lips. "Ours."

Our little angel.